THE JACOBITE MURDERS

By the same author

Oliver Twist Investigates
Wuthering Heights Revisited

THE JACOBITE MURDERS

G.M. BEST

ROBERT HALE · LONDON

First published in Great Britain 2013

ISBN 978-0-7198-0877-7

Robert Hale Limited
Clerkenwell House
Clerkenwell Green
London EC1R 0HT

www.halebooks.com

2 4 6 8 10 9 7 5 3 1

Typeset in 10/13 Palatino
Printed by MPG Printgroup, UK

CONTENTS

PROLOGUE

I remember as if it was yesterday those brave men in whose destruction I played a significant part. I see again their independent and martial bearing and the resolute look of their eyes and their rugged but unfounded confidence. I hear again their guttural voices speaking of their battles and travels, extolling the valour of many and joking occasionally about the mishaps of a few. I feel again the hands that wrongly grasped mine in gratitude for the news I brought, not realizing how false it was. Forty years ago they seemed to me a weird and barbarous people, with their strangely chequered plaids and their bright bonnets and their foreign tongue. Now I have learned to respect their courage and, although I still recognize that they were my country's enemies, I recollect with sadness how in their misguided loyalty they worshipped their prince and sacrificed their lives to his cause. And sometimes I weep that they accepted my words as if they were a gift from Heaven, not realizing I was dooming them all to the cruellest destruction.

(From the memoirs of Tom Jones, written in 1785)

1

THE HOUSE IN QUEEN SQUARE

As Lady Phyllis Overbury stepped out of the sedan chair it was obvious to even the most casual of observers that this latest visitor to Bath would be a welcome arrival. She was elegantly dressed in the latest fashion and striking to look at. Her aquiline nose and firm chin gave her a natural air of authority whilst her dark brown eyes sparkled with a natural vivacity and her graciously winning smile exuded good-humour and intelligence. Only the more discerning could see that her powdered wig and rouged cheeks indicated she had long lost the bloom of youth. The house before which she stood was one of eight on the south side of Queen Square that together formed one immense building with an elegant Palladian façade. As she gazed at its simple grandeur, Lady Overbury was grateful that Sir Robert Benson had offered her the house's use for the duration of her first stay in the city.

She looked with equal admiration at the houses on either side of the square. To her right were two attractive villa-like buildings and between them a beautiful house, while to her left were six more substantial homes, each with its own elaborate doorway and unique decoration. Turning around she viewed the square's central garden, which was enclosed by espaliered limes and elms and dominated by an immense seventy-foot obelisk that arose from a circular pool. Beyond this she could see the north side of the square, which contained seven even grander houses. These gave the appearance of being a single magnificent palace because their façades contained impressive Roman-style columns that supported a richly decorated entabulature. She thought that she had not seen a grander sight even in London.

Her maid, who had followed the sedan chair on foot, lacked all her mistress's glamour, but she was much younger and equally attractive in her own way. The simple clothes that protected her from the bitterly cold weather disguised her slender form but she had an undoubtedly pretty face. She had ruby-red lips, beautiful teeth, a small and slightly upturned nose and, most striking of all, engaging blue eyes that flashed beneath unusually long eyelashes. Her complexion was not of the milk-white kind but this did not matter because her glowing cheeks were surrounded by a mass of golden curls. From the animated expression on her face she was obviously as delighted as Lady Overbury to have finally arrived in Bath.

Before the maid even got near the door to knock for admittance, it opened. A middle-aged woman, who was tall and somewhat heavy in build, stepped out. She was dressed in an unfashionable but serviceable black gown. Some of the prettiness of her younger years was still evident in her features, particularly in the slope of her nose and in the line of her lips, but her heavily wrinkled forehead and face and greying hair spoke of a life that had seen more than its fair share of trouble. Ignoring the maid, she gave a subservient nod of her head to her mistress.

'Please come in, Lady Overbury,' she said. 'I hope that you have not had too difficult a journey from London. November is not at all a good month for travel. Permit me to introduce myself. My name is Agnes Grey and I am Sir Robert's housekeeper. I welcome you to Bath. It will be my pleasure to ensure that you have all you require while you stay here.'

'Thank you, Miss Grey,' replied Lady Overbury. Sir Robert had told her how indispensable this woman was to the running of his house and, looking at her, she thought she could see why. There was a firmness in her eyes and a steeliness in her manner that exuded efficiency and authority. This was clearly a woman who had not yet let life wear her down. 'I confess that it has been a long and tiring journey over the past two days,' she continued, 'not helped by the fact that unfortunately my companions in the coach were an exceptionally dull lot. Their only topic of conversation appeared to be about the likelihood of our being robbed by highwaymen and I have to say that was not conducive to a peaceful state of mind. As a consequence I slept little last night in Newbury. Today's journey was even worse. At times we made such slow progress that at one stage it must have taken a couple of hours to travel five miles. I never knew roads could be so uneven. You would think that a volcano had thrown up some sections.'

Lady Overbury and her maid followed the housekeeper inside. They found themselves standing in a large and gracious hallway with a grand oak staircase. Although both women were sorry to lose their view of the square they were more than glad to get out of the cold. The maid began to help divest her mistress of the protective clothing that she had worn throughout the coach ride while Lady Overbury continued her tale of the horrors of the journey.

'I can tell you, Miss Grey, there were times when I thought the coach was going to fly to pieces because we were so jolted about. Not surprisingly, I now ache in every bone, especially as the weather has been depressingly damp.'

'I trust, your ladyship, that the city's greeting has compensated in a small way for what you have endured in getting here,' responded the housekeeper solicitously. 'I heard the abbey bells ringing on your arrival.'

'Yes, I confess that I was impressed by that mode of welcoming us – and by the flutes and violins that serenaded us once the coach had come to a stop.'

Miss Grey smiled. 'And doubtless Mr Nash, our Master of Ceremonies, welcomed you personally?'

'I chose not to wait for his arrival. I preferred to leave my luggage at the coaching inn and come straight here in a sedan before it got too dark. He can see me tomorrow when I am feeling more refreshed.'

Lady Overbury permitted herself to be led into the house's spacious drawing room. She looked around her with pleasure at the oak floor, the brocatelle-covered walls, the fine marble fireplace, decorated ceiling, and the large window with its fashionable silk curtains decorated with motifs that depicted garlands of flowers, knots of ribbons, and fronds of leaves. A delightful couple of watercolours had replaced the unfashionable tapestries that so often darkened the rooms in other houses. She equally admired the comfortable curved sofa and matching fully upholstered wingback chairs and the graceful walnut cabriole-legged furniture. 'This is a most delightful room,' she declared.

Miss Grey acknowledged this compliment with a smile. 'I am pleased that you like it, your ladyship. I have prepared some refreshment for you and I will send Joseph Graves, our manservant, to fetch your luggage so that your maid can unpack it whilst you are eating. Unfortunately there are no other servants to assist because they are all in London with Sir Robert. I have his instructions to hire others once your ladyship decides what will be required during your stay here.'

'That is most kind of him. I should explain perhaps that my maid is new to my service and may require more guidance than would otherwise be the case. She is called Sarah Darr.'

The housekeeper cast the maid a sideways glance but in such a cool way as to establish her superior authority. 'Would you like me to show you both the rest of the house, your ladyship?' she asked.

'Yes, I think that would be most helpful.'

Miss Grey directed the guests back into the main hallway. 'On this entrance level there are two more reception rooms,' she explained. 'One is a library that doubles as a card room, and the other is a small dining room. They are spacious enough to enable you to entertain a number of guests once you have entered into the society currently here in Bath. You will find that both rooms are very cold at present, but I can light a fire in either of them whenever you wish to use one. I can assure you that they are both very snug even on the most wintry of nights.'

They entered the library first. It had one wall entirely covered by books and the others were richly lined with oak panelling, bar for the space taken up by a large stone fireplace. Against one wall was a large mahogany desk with a sloping front, whilst in the centre of the room there was a small walnut table with a hinged top and four oval saucers positioned to be at each player's left. Round this stood four walnut chairs, each bearing a distinctive scallop shell across their top. The dining room next to it was also wood-panelled but its elegant fireplace was made from a slightly rose-tinted marble and above it was a beautiful rococo mirror surrounded by gold stucco. Lady Overbury particularly liked the room's silk curtains, but the main feature of the room was its impressive walnut table and accompanying chairs with their unbroken curved lines.

'Where does that lead?' asked Lady Overbury, pointing to another door as they returned back into the hallway.

'That leads to a spiral staircase for use by the servants, your ladyship. It goes the full length of the house unlike this main staircase, which only links this floor to the two floors above. The spiral staircase descends from here down into the kitchen and all the other working rooms in the basement and it ascends upstairs not only to the main rooms on the next two levels but also to my and the other servants' living quarters at the top of the house. Any servants can thus pass up and down the building without having to be seen by you or any of your guests. You will find in every room a cord that, if pulled, will summon me, or, when she knows her way around, your maid.'

Lady Overbury approved of this fashionable feature of the house's design and then she and her maid followed Miss Grey up the main staircase. On the first floor they entered the room at the front of the house that was above the drawing room. It bore all the signs of a woman's touch – every item of furniture and every decorative object had been chosen to harmonize with each other and the crackling log fire provided a welcome warmth. Lady Overbury swept around the room, touching the fabrics, looking at the paintings, opening the mahogany wardrobe, admiring the dressing mirror that sat at the toilet table, and examining the fine four-poster bed, which had rich velvet hangings.

'This room was used by Sir Robert's wife until her untimely death,' explained the housekeeper.

Lady Overbury knew that Sir Robert had largely ceased visiting the house since that tragic event. As far as she knew, his son, Lord Kearsley, now used it. 'It's a very charming room,' she acknowledged.

'Through this door, your ladyship, there is a dressing room also for your use. It is furnished with some comfortable chairs and a walnut writing desk on which you will find writing paper and pens and ink. I assumed that you would bring a maid and, as you are the sole guest using the house, I have prepared a temporary bed in the other bedroom on this level so that she may sleep near you rather than providing her with a room in the servant's quarters. However, if you would prefer her to sleep upstairs I can easily arrange that.'

'Remain here, Darr, whilst I view what is proposed for you.' Lady Overbury entered the other bedroom. A small mattress and some sheets and blankets had been placed on the floor at one end so that the maidservant should not have to use the grand silk-covered bed that dominated the room. 'This room is unsuitable,' muttered Lady Overbury disapprovingly. 'I fear having such lavish accommodation will serve only to make any future place my maid sleeps seem like a prison cell!'

'You are the only person in residence and I think she will be much better placed to attend to your needs from here than if I provide her with a room in the servants' quarters.'

'You are most thoughtful, Miss Grey, but is there not a less elegant room for her on the next level?'

'The rooms on the floor above are similarly well furnished and Sir Robert instructed me to keep them all locked because he knew they would be surplus to your requirements.'

'Very well,' conceded Lady Overbury with a slight shrug of her shoulders, 'I suppose it will be helpful to have Darr near to me.'

Miss Grey gave her a dutiful smile. 'I am glad you see it that way, your ladyship. If you would like to return downstairs, I will prepare tea to accompany the refreshments that I have laid out for you, whilst your maid goes with Graves back to the coaching inn and identifies what luggage to bring back here.'

Shortly afterwards Lady Overbury found herself enjoying a delicious light supper cut from freshly baked pies and tartlets. The experience of Sarah Darr was not so happy. Joseph Graves undertook the task he had been given with little grace and made it obvious to the maid that he viewed her mistress's arrival as a nuisance. She was not sure how to respond, not least because she was rather disconcerted by the man's strange appearance. His large hairy hands, round shoulders and stocky build gave him an almost troll-like quality and this illusion was strengthened by a mouth that was unusually wide, a nose that was unattractively pointed, and jug-like ears that stuck out from his ruddy face. His eyes appeared sunken under eyebrows that were still jet black in sharp contrast to his hair, which was streaked with grey. Sarah was very glad indeed when, after fetching the luggage, he left her alone to unpack it.

By that stage Lady Overbury had finished eating and was sitting enjoying the comfortable warmth of the drawing room, which, now that evening had fallen, was lit with candles. Using the bell-rope, she summoned the housekeeper and was surprised at how speedily she responded. 'I have not been to Bath before, Miss Grey, and so I would be grateful if, before I go to bed, you would outline what is likely to be my daily routine while I am in residence here. I have heard much about the city from my friends and I gather that there are many activities open to visitors.'

'If your ladyship has come to improve her health by bathing in the spa waters, I would recommend that you begin your day early and go between six and seven in the morning. Many gentry choose the Cross Bath because it tends to be more socially exclusive but others still prefer to go the larger King's Bath, which is near the south-west side of the abbey. I would not recommend the Queen's Bath because it is a trifle cooler and, whilst that is all right in the summer months, it is less satisfactory at this time of year.'

'Why should I go so early?'

'Because the water is then at its cleanest, the pools having been emptied overnight and refilled. After eight o'clock the King's Bath in particular becomes much more crowded and, I regret to say, that not all who enter the water are very clean. As a consequence the water becomes murkier and less wholesome.'

'You do not make this bathing sound a very tempting experience,' Lady Overbury said drily.

The housekeeper smiled very slightly. 'Maybe not, your ladyship, but there are many who profess to the healing and beneficial qualities of the water.'

'So I have heard. They say the waters can cure anything from colic and gout to paralysis and palsy,' replied Lady Overbury in a tone that clearly indicated her disbelief. 'Perhaps I should say at once that I am not in need of the restorative powers of any of these baths. I would not wish to use them even if my health was poor. I am not convinced of their curative powers and I do not approve of mixed bathing. What therefore may I do instead?'

'Most people, your ladyship, would go to the Pump Room next to the King's Bath. There they can drink whatever number of glasses of the spa water their doctors have prescribed.'

'And I have heard that, like all good medicines, this water is foul to the taste?'

'I fear so, your ladyship,' acknowledged the housekeeper. 'It is like water that has been used to boil eggs. To take away the taste gentlemen retreat into their coffee houses where they can also read their newspapers and discuss business.'

Lady Overbury laughed and a mischievous twinkle lit up her eyes. 'It is my experience that men love to gather together in such places whether or not they have been drinking any spa waters! Where do the women go?'

'There are rooms set aside for women to converse with each other.'

'Well, I hope the talk is not simply about disorders and illnesses, or else their conversation will be duller then the men's.'

A flicker of surprise passed almost imperceptibly across Miss Grey's face at such outspoken words but she responded demurely. 'I cannot comment from experience, your ladyship, but I am sure that the conversations must sparkle with wit.'

In Lady Overbury's experience such social occasions were marked more by senseless gossip than by intelligent conversation, but she chose not to disillusion the housekeeper. Instead she asked, 'And what next?'

'Then it is time for breakfast. When they first arrive visitors often eat in their lodgings – and I will certainly prepare a breakfast for you here tomorrow morning – but anyone of quality, like your ladyship, is soon invited to one or more of the public breakfasts organized by the wealthy and more fashionable.'

'I hope they are not too extravagant?'

'The breakfasts are simple – tea, cream, milk, bread and butter. Once your presence is known here, your ladyship will also receive invitations to the private musical entertainments that some gentlemen choose to organize.'

'That, Miss Grey, sounds more to my taste because I love good music.' Lady Overbury sank deeper into her chair, enjoying its comfort after the rigours of having sat for so long in a coach. 'Tell me more about what the city offers.'

'After breakfast is over many choose to attend a service in the abbey. I can arrange for you to rent an appropriate pew, one that will match your social standing.'

'The attendance then is more of a social than a religious nature?' cut in Lady Overbury cynically.

'Yes, your ladyship. I regret to say that the attention of the worshippers is often more on each other than on God. Indeed some of the pews have had to be raised in order to deter ogling between the sexes.'

Lady Overbury looked shocked. 'Then I might forego the abbey. I have no wish to see mothers using God's house as a cattle market to find husbands for their daughters.'

'You could go to the Chapel of St Mary in Chapel Row instead. It has been built specially for the residents of Queen Square.'

'What else may I do?' countered Lady Overbury.

'The afternoon can be spent enjoying what Bath has to offer – the shopping here is particularly fine but, if you prefer, and the weather is dry, you can promenade along one of the many public walks that adorn this city. There are particularly fine views from the sections of the old city wall. Alternatively you can attend a puppet show or a play or a concert. In the evenings you can gather with the best of society in the Pump Room or go to various places that offer card playing and dances.

'All that sounds much more inviting. I suspect that I will enjoy my afternoons here.'

'You will enjoy the evenings even more,' said Miss Grey, warming to her theme. 'You can gather with the best of society in the Pump Room or go to various places that offer card playing and dances. I am sure that Mr Nash will call here tomorrow and explain more fully than I what events are taking place over the coming days.'

At this juncture in their conversation Lady Overbury happened to glance up at the window and was surprised to see a face staring into the room. Before she could focus on the person's features, he or she (for she could not be sure which it was) had gone. She got out of her chair and moved rapidly to look outside but the darkness meant she could see nothing of the stranger that had so startled her.

'Is it customary for people here to stare into someone's house?' she remonstrated, her eyes flashing in a mixture of resentment and disapproval.

For once her assured manner seemed to desert the housekeeper. There was a hint of real fear in her eyes. However, she quickly regained control of herself. 'No it is not customary, your ladyship. I apologize that this has happened.'

This statement failed to dissipate Lady Overbury's anger and she commented acidly, 'I assure you that I have no desire to be on public display, Miss Grey. Please will you immediately close both the shutters and the curtains and in future ensure that this happens every evening as soon as it gets dark so as to deter any future peeping Tom.'

Miss Grey's cheeks slightly coloured at the reprimand. 'As you wish, your ladyship. I will attend to the matter now.' She moved over to the window and carried out what she had been instructed to do.

Even this did not mollify Lady Overbury. For reasons that she could not understand the incident had alarmed her more than she would have expected. It was almost as if she had a premonition of some impending disaster. 'What are the security arrangements in the house?' she asked.

'Graves ensures that the house is locked before he goes off duty and returns to his home for the night.'

'Do you mean to say that he is not here overnight and that only we three women will be in this house?' exclaimed Lady Overbury, deeply shocked at such an unsuitable arrangement.

'When Sir Robert is here there are other servants in the house, but I can assure you that you need not be concerned at Graves's absence. The authorities organize patrols to ensure that Bath is a very safe place at night.'

'That is all very well, Miss Grey,' interrupted Lady Overbury acidly, 'but I think I would prefer to have a male presence in this house tonight. Fetch this manservant so that I can instruct him to stay. Presumably he can sleep in one of the servants' rooms or, better still, downstairs in the kitchen?'

'There is no problem in accommodating him, but I know he will insist on returning to his home,' replied the housekeeper. 'He is a stubborn old man and used to his routines.'

'Do I need to remind you that it is not for a servant to dictate what he should or should not do? I am sure, Miss Grey, he will not demur if I make clear that Sir Robert would want everything to be done in this house according to my wish.'

The housekeeper left the room and shortly afterwards returned with an uncomfortable-looking Graves. Lady Overbury glowered at him. 'I understand that it is your custom to return home each evening, but while I am here, you must stay in this house so that my maid and I can rest assured that we are safe. Is that clear?'

The old man shuffled his feet and hesitated before replying. 'I am sorry, your ladyship, but I cannot stay here overnight because there have been too many strange and unnatural goings-on. The house is haunted by evil spirits.'

This answer took Lady Overbury by surprise and clearly annoyed Miss Grey, who clenched her jaw and then snapped back at him, 'Graves, what nonsense you talk! You will needlessly frighten her ladyship. I suggest that you hold your tongue and just do as you are asked!'

'No, do not be silent, Graves,' countermanded Lady Overbury. 'I am intrigued. Tell me more.'

'Believe me, your ladyship, there is too much unexplained noise in this house. I have heard windows rattling and such strange knockings.'

'This is arrant nonsense!' exclaimed the housekeeper.

'Say what you like, Miss Grey,' he responded, 'but you cannot deny that I have found doors that I locked at night open in the morning.'

'What you mean is that you forgot to lock them in the first place!'

'You told me only a couple of days ago that you felt you were in some danger here.'

This comment clearly annoyed Miss Grey. Her eyes narrowed and her lips tightened. 'Whatever personal concerns I may have had are of no interest to Lady Overbury and I see no reason to worry her about them. All that matters is her ladyship's peace of mind. Stay this one night and I will find another man for tomorrow.'

'I have to say that this conversation quite alarms me!' interjected Lady Overbury, waving her hands in a gesture of impatience. 'This house appears not to be as safe as you originally would have me believe, Miss Grey.'

'Do not concern yourself over an old man's foolish fancies, your ladyship,' the housekeeper replied, trying to placate her.

'If what you say is true, Graves, surely you can see that you must stay here and protect us from any intruder, ghostly or real?'

'I am very sorry, your ladyship, but I will not stay overnight in this house, even if that decision costs me my position. However, I will doubly check to see that every door is locked for your safety overnight and I will return very early in the morning.'

Lady Overbury tried to change his mind but in vain. In the end she lost patience and angrily dismissed him from her presence, saying that she would report the whole matter of his disobedience to his master. Her indignation made her tremble.

'Please do not be afraid, your ladyship,' said Miss Grey, misinterpreting the cause. 'I assure you that we are all perfectly safe. You must forget the old man's foolish talk of this house being haunted and go to bed without worrying about your safety. I will have him bring you up some hot water before he leaves. Do not hesitate to ring me if you require anything else. I am sure that you will have a good sleep and feel refreshed in the morning.'

'But my eyes did not deceive me,' protested Lady Overbury. 'There was a person at the window this evening and Mr Graves says that you have been concerned about your safety in recent days!'

'Mere foolishness on my part.'

Lady Overbury was not convinced that Miss Grey was being truthful. The housekeeper did not strike her as a woman given to foolish fancies. However, she was too tired to make any further issue of the matter. 'We may talk more about this in the morning but for now I will retire to bed. It has been a long day and Darr must have finished unpacking by now. Tell Graves to bring up hot water in the morning rather than now. I have had enough of the man for one night.'

When Lady Overbury made her way upstairs to her bedroom she found that Sarah Darr had indeed just completed her work. As her maid moved to help her undress for bed she told her about all that had transpired in the drawing room.

'I think Mr Graves is a very strange man, madam,' responded her maid, 'but, if you wish, I will repack your bags so that we can leave at once!'

'Don't be childish, Darr. You know as well as I that we cannot leave this house at this time of night. What would Sir Robert think? I cannot turn my back on his hospitality just because a person chose to peek through a window and an old man fancies the house may be haunted. For tonight I will trust in Miss Grey's judgement. She says that the authorities have night watchmen who patrol the streets so I expect we will be perfectly safe. I suggest you check that the old fool properly locks up and then we can go to bed. If necessary, I will hire a male servant tomorrow.'

'Please, your ladyship. I am far too frightened to go round this house. Apart from the doors, there are too many windows to check and those downstairs have no bars to prevent entry by those who might be lingering outside.'

'Have some common sense, child. Those who come to Bath do not wish to see barred windows everywhere. It would make the place look like one gigantic prison!' snapped back Lady Overbury, beginning to lose her patience.

'This place might be as bad as Bedlam for all we know!' wailed her maidservant in reply.

'Enough of all this nonsense! I wish I had said nothing to you about the matter! If you are too scared to go round the house, I will put my faith in Miss Grey's ability to ensure that Graves locks up the house properly. Come and help me prepare for bed. Any more foolishness from you and I will find another maid in the morning!'

Sarah Darr opened her mouth as if to continue her protest and then, seeing from Lady Overbury's eyes that she was making no idle threat, changed her mind. 'As you wish, your ladyship, but I can assure you that I will not go to sleep. I have no desire to be murdered with my eyes closed.'

Some of Lady Overbury's tension dissipated away and she laughed, 'I cannot see how murder is made more preferable by keeping your eyes open!' she laughed.

Darr proceeded to fulfil her duties in such an exemplary manner that Lady Overbury could find no further fault with her. Indeed she wondered whether she had been sensible to ignore her maid's offer to pack and leave. She was sure that Miss Grey was hiding something from them, despite all her reassurances about the house being safe. Once Darr had left her, she decided to take the precaution of not only locking her bedroom door but also placing a chair against it in such a way as to prevent the door-handle being turned. Desperately she tried to calm her increasing sense of unease by thinking about the entertainment that Bath might hold for her in the coming days. Even when she heard the sound of a night watchman shouting out that all was well, she could not bring herself to blow out the one remaining lit candle in the room nor, despite her tiredness, fall asleep.

It was only after an hour or so had passed and all seemed quiet that Lady Overbury's natural strength of character reasserted itself and she slumbered. As a consequence she was not at all prepared for the terrible tragedy that struck later that night.

2

FIELDING AND FRIENDS

Lady Overbury was rudely awoken by a loud crashing sound and an agonizing shriek of terror that broke the night silence. Fearful that something had happened to her maid, she got out of bed, covering part of her nightgown with a shawl. She was glad that she had left one of the candles alight and so could see her way as she walked across the room. She pulled aside the chair, unlocked the door, and, after looking to see that the corridor was empty, crossed over to Darr's room. She banged heavily upon its door. At first there was no response and then she heard a voice mumbling, 'Is that you, mistress? I was fast asleep and you've woken me up.'

'Darr, I think there's somebody in the house,' replied Lady Overbury. 'Did you not hear a piercing scream?'

The door opened and Sarah's pale and frightened face appeared. 'No,' she said, 'but perhaps Mr Graves was right and we are all going to be murdered in our beds!'

'Neither of us has been murdered yet,' responded Lady Overbury firmly. 'Come with me. I think we must go and find Miss Grey. As you are all right, then something must have happened to her.'

Sarah reluctantly agreed to accompany her employer but it was obvious that her acquiescence arose solely from her fear of being left alone. 'I think it would be wise, mistress,' she urged, 'if we first armed ourselves before we set foot anywhere upstairs.' Lady Overbury picked up a poker from the fireplace and, clutching a lit candle in her other hand, slowly headed for the door that led to the spiral staircase. It was unlocked. She opened it and began to climb the stairs, though it was like entering a black void because the flickering light from her candle only partially dissipated the darkness. Sarah Darr followed behind. The staircase took them up two flights to the servants' quarters. All the rooms were empty except for one the door of which was locked.

'Miss Grey!' shouted Sarah. 'Can you hear me? Lady Overbury wishes to speak to you.'

'I should think all those in the square can hear you!' muttered her mistress, pulling her shawl around her shoulders because of the cold. 'The woman is either deaf or there is something badly wrong. Perhaps the noise I heard was her falling and she is hurt. We must go and get assistance.'

Neither woman had any desire to be left alone in the house until the mystery of what had happened was resolved and so they agreed it made sense to seek help together. They returned to their bedrooms and donned cloaks so that they could both preserve a degree of decorum and protect themselves from the bitterly cold weather outside. Then they set off down the main staircase to the hallway. They found to their relief when they opened the front door that the street outside was not entirely in darkness because the city authorities insisted on a candle-lit lantern outside every house where there were lodgers. Lady Overbury instructed Sarah Darr to knock on the door of the neighbouring house as loudly as she could. Her maid duly complied, until a servant, young in years but looking rather bleary-eyed, opened it. Given the state of their undress, the poor man would probably have denied them access, judging them to be women of the night, had not a very tall gentleman also come to the door.

'Good heavens!' exclaimed Lady Overbury, instantly recognizing him, even though they had not met for eight years. 'It's Mr Fielding!'

'Lady Overbury! What a delightful surprise!' the man declared. 'I have spent the evening here playing cards with Mr Wood and other friends. I was about to leave in order to return to my lodgings but I am more than happy to place my services at your disposal if there is a problem – and I assume that there is, given the lateness of your call and, if you pardon me saying so, the indelicate state of your attire.'

Lady Overbury and Henry Fielding had first met each other seventeen years earlier when he was a handsome youth of twenty-one. At that time his first comedy, *Love in Several Masks,* had just been performed at Drury Lane and he was seen as London's up and coming dramatist. The brilliance of his wit, the wild flow of his spirits, and the quickness of his imagination had totally charmed her. On the last occasion that they had met he had still been a handsome man but now he looked old and emaciated. It was not just that he was thin and pale and obviously badly affected by gout, his face had aged terribly and was deeply etched and lined. Here was a man who had obviously suffered much in the intervening years and she knew in part the reason for that. At the height of his success he had unwisely made the butt of one of his plays the corrupt politician, Sir Robert Walpole, who was then in charge of the government. This had proved professional suicide because Walpole had crushed Fielding's career.

As soon as he had heard what had happened, Fielding ordered the manservant to fetch a tool that could be used to break a lock and then accompany him to the housekeeper's room. The two women showed them the way upstairs. However, Lady Overbury was very surprised when Fielding turned the handle of the housekeeper's door and it swung open without any force being required. He looked over his shoulder at Darr quizzically.

'I can assure you, sir, it was locked and we could not enter.'

'Maybe in your agitated state it only seemed locked,' he said. Then, bidding both ladies stay outside in the corridor, he entered the room. Within a few seconds he reappeared looking ashen-faced. 'I fear, madam, I did you a disservice. I thought that you had led me on some wild goosechase and that I would find either the housekeeper asleep in some deep drunken stupor or missing because she was out on some illicit rendevouz with a beau. But I was wrong. I regret to inform you that Miss Grey has been most cruelly murdered. There is a considerable amount of blood and I suggest that you do not enter her room. It is far too unpleasant a sight for a lady.'

'I'm not a faint-hearted woman, sir, and Miss Grey made me most welcome here. I'll not see her body disposed of without paying my last respects. I want to see for myself what has happened to her.'

'No, my lady, do not do this,' begged Sarah Darr from behind her mistress. 'The murderer may still be in the house. Let us return to the safety of our rooms until we know for sure that he has gone.'

Lady Overbury ignored this entreaty and stepped inside the housekeeper's room. The body of Miss Grey lay face upwards on the floor in the narrow space between the bed and a small wardrobe that stood against one wall. Blood seemed to be splattered everywhere in the room but its source was obvious – the poor woman's throat had been cut almost from ear to ear and the gaping wound looked like some blackened grisly smile. Judging from the look in her eyes, death had come quickly because they seemed to stare out with shocked surprise.

'I am pretty sure that she was seized from behind – doubtless after a brief struggle,' commented Fielding. 'That would explain the noise you heard and the subsequent scream.' Lady Overbury turned her back on the gruesome sight while Fielding bent over the corpse to study it more closely. 'The wound is deep and, as far as I can judge, very clean, the product of a very sharp blade wielded by a very strong arm. If it is any comfort, I do not think she suffered much pain. She would have died almost instantaneously.'

'That does not make this crime less heinous, sir,' Lady Overbury replied, in a voice that betrayed her outrage at what had happened.

'I entirely agree and I surmise that the murderer heard the sound of you coming upstairs and locked the door, thus preventing your entrance and his disclosure.'

'And he unlocked the door and made his escape from the rear of the house while we were fetching help?'

'It would appear so, unless he has hidden in one of the other rooms.'

'But why was this man in the house and what possibly can have been his motive in coming up here to kill Miss Grey?' puzzled Lady Overbury.

'It does seem strange,' agreed Fielding. 'There is nothing of worth to steal up here and any normal intruder would have chosen to remain at the lower levels, especially as the further he entered the house the more he risked detection.'

'You are right, sir. The murderer's chance of being discovered and caught was immensely increased by coming to this attic.'

'It sounds to me as if he knew there was only the housekeeper up here and no other servants,' responded Fielding. 'I can only surmise, Lady Overbury, that Miss Grey knew the murderer and that she had invited him upstairs for reasons that I will not choose to voice in your presence.'

His reply outraged her and she snapped back, 'Although our acquaintance was short, I can assure you that Miss Grey was no strumpet, sir, but a good woman. She has been in the service of Sir Robert for many years and I know he regards her most highly. There must be another explanation than the one you so cruelly imply!'

The look in his eyes indicated that he did not entirely believe her. 'Let me notify the authorities for you while you return to your room with your maid and get dressed. Please do not move outside your room until I return and tell you it is safe to do so. I will leave a servant from next door to keep watch outside your door.'

Lady Overbury assented reluctantly. She took one last look at the unfortunate housekeeper's body and commented, 'I hope that we can bring her murderer to justice.' Then she went back downstairs. As her maid helped her dress in her room she solemnly vowed that she would not rest until the killer had been caught and she had vindicated Miss Grey's character. It was bad enough that the housekeeper's life had been so savagely squandered without the wicked world also destroying her reputation. She was sure that whoever had killed her had entered her room uninvited. The question was why? And was the murderer the same person who had stared in at the drawing-room window earlier that night? If so, what had he been seeking in the house? And how had she heard the murder take place? It would have taken a very substantial noise to wake her from her slumber and yet there had been nothing in Miss Grey's room to show that there had been a struggle of any significance. Moreover, her bedroom was sufficiently far away from that of the housekeeper to have made hearing her scream difficult. The whole thing seemed inexplicable.

By six o'clock in the morning Henry Fielding had arranged for the body of the housekeeper to be removed and for the floor to be scrubbed clean so that no trace of the brutal murder remained. He had also embarked on a closer inspection of the entire house from the kitchen to the attic rooms in the company of Joseph Graves, who had turned up for his morning duties. This had not been a happy exercise because the latter had been visibly shaken by the housekeeper's murder and he kept up a doleful monologue about how an evil spirit must have entered the house. The search had eventually proved pointless. Every room that they entered appeared to be in good order and there was nothing to indicate a break-in or to shed light on what the murderer might have been seeking. Fielding wondered whether the bedrooms that were locked on the second floor might reveal some clue, but Graves had no key to unlock them and none could be found on Miss Grey's bunch of keys. Lady Overbury refused to grant permission for them to break down the locked doors, saying that she lacked the authority to damage Sir Robert's property in such a fashion when there was no certainty that this would produce any further evidence.

Fielding did not feel strongly enough to urge her to reconsider. Instead he sent Graves to assist Sarah Darr prepare a breakfast for everyone. While they were waiting for this he and Lady Overbury talked together in the drawing room. Once again she was struck by how very old he looked for a man who was not yet forty. 'My dear Lady

Overbury, your face is like an open book,' he said. 'I can see that you think I am a shadow of my former self.'

'No, Mr Fielding, I assure you that is not the case.'

'You were never a good liar,' he chided. 'If you think I look ill now, you should have seen me when I first arrived in Bath. I could scarce eat or drink without being sick and my gouty foot prevented me venturing outside for more than a few yards at a time. Now my stomach is much restored and the only gout I have remaining is in the great toe of my right foot.'

'Are the waters then so good?'

'If used properly, for some they act like the ancient River Lethe. They wash away all pain and suffering. And I have a good doctor in Dr Oliver, who has lived in Bath many years and who is employed by the best of families. During my first week here I had the mineral water brought to my lodgings because I could neither walk nor bear the pain of being carried. However, after a week I was able to walk a few turns around my room with the help of a stick, and, a couple of days later, I began my current regime. I use the Cross Bath at seven or eight o'clock each morning and I go to the King's Bath at twelve. I am now also able to eat a good dinner again providing I drink a glass of the water two hours afterwards.'

'I am pleased to hear that the reputation of Bath is so justified,' observed Lady Overbury.

'Yes, but even in my recovered state I am not the man I once was,' he continued, 'and there is good reason for that. You see, after my career as a dramatist ended, I was forced to take up law and my wife and children lived in virtual penury whilst I scraped what living I could make. I had to watch the health and beauty of my beloved wife Charlotte decline every day.' His gaze was filled with anguish and Lady Overbury remembered the winter of 1734 when Fielding had first told her of his forthcoming marriage to Charlotte Cradock. At that time she had been renowned for her beauty and the sweetness of her smile. It must have been terrible for him to see her wither in the face of privation.

'I am sorry that I did not know of the straits into which you had fallen or I would have come to your aid,' she replied, with genuine sorrow at the poverty into which he and his wife had fallen. 'But surely your emergence in recent years as a successful novelist must have made things easier for you and your family. I was delighted when I discovered four years ago that you were the anonymous author of the novel *Shamela,* and I have read with immense pleasure both of your succeeding books, *Joseph Andrews* and *The History of the Life of the Late Mr Jonathan Wild.*' This was no idle flattery on her part. She had found them skilfully written and very entertaining, and quite unlike anything else that she had read.

'Unfortunately fate is not kind and the success of my new career as a novelist came too late to save Charlotte. Last autumn I brought her back to Bath. We had fond memories of this place because we were married in St Mary Charlcombe, a tiny church that nestles in the hills above the city. We hoped in vain that the waters might prove beneficial.' His eyes took on a haunted look as the memory of that time flooded over him. 'Her health took a sudden turn for the worse and she died in my arms almost a year ago. I had her body taken back to London.' He stared at Lady Overbury, absorbing her sympathy. 'I miss her terribly, Lady Overbury. I do not mind confessing to you that I would have long ago committed suicide had not I had the support of my sister Sarah.'

Lady Overbury expressed her deep regret at his loss and he graciously accepted her condolences. Beneath the ravages of time the evidence of his innate charm and good manners remained. 'Enough about my troubles,' he said, trying to rally his spirits. 'It is more important that I help you in your situation than dwell on my past. Do you recognize this?' He held out to her a small metal button on which was carved the symbol of a fleur-de-lis. 'It was found grasped in Miss Grey's dead hand. I think she must have snapped it off her murderer's coat in the brief struggle before she was killed. I fear it is the only clue we have.'

'Other than it is the symbol associated with the French royal family, it means nothing to me.'

'Nor yet to me. But I am making enquiries because there are few in England who would choose to wear such an emblem at a time when we are at war with France. I have a brother who is a magistrate in London and he has many useful contacts who may know about these buttons and who might wear them.'

'I appreciate your thoroughness in this matter,' she acknowledged.

'Because we have found nothing to make sense of what has happened, I think it would be prudent if you left this house and hired alternative lodgings,' continued Fielding. 'If the murderer was not known to the housekeeper, then he must have broken in with the intention of finding something very specific. He may or may not have got what he wanted. If he did not, then he might return and you or your maid could become his next victim.'

'I will not be driven out of this house by any man!' protested Lady Overbury, battling to keep her voice steady.

Fielding raised his eyebrows but did not seek to persuade her to change her mind. He could see from her face that her determination to stay was very unlikely to waiver. 'Then permit me to offer you all the assistance that I can. I will find you an alternative housekeeper and I suggest in the first instance that I also lend you two young men of my acquaintance so that there is someone in this house to protect you. Their names are Tom Jones and John Burnett. They can sleep upstairs and they can take it in turns to guard you and your maid until this murder is satisfactorily resolved.'

'Sir, I am deeply touched by your kindness and I will not say no to your generous offer.'

'Then I will send the man who has temporarily guarded you to bring Mr Jones and Mr Burnett round immediately. Foreseeing your response, Lady Overbury, I sought their agreement to protect you earlier this morning. They have already packed a few of their possessions. Both are gentlemen, but they are willing to reside temporarily in the servants' quarters.'

She smiled. 'You know me too well, Mr Fielding.'

'I know a courageous woman when I meet one, madam.' He bowed courteously.

They adjourned their meeting to eat the breakfast that had been laid out in the dining room while they were speaking. Shortly afterwards Sarah Darr brought in two young men to them. 'Permit me first,' said Fielding, 'to introduce Mr John Burnett, the nephew of Squire Woodforde, who is a wealthy landowner in this part of Somerset and a most kind-hearted and generous friend of mine. And, second, this is Mr Tom Jones, a young man who has benefitted much from the squire's patronage.'

The two young men were very different in both their looks and manner. John Burnett had little to commend him physically, though he was dressed in the height of fashion. He was short, of a puny build, and lacked any presence. His black hair was tousled and long and this served only to accentuate his pale, pockmarked face with its broad cheekbones, its long hawk nose and pointed chin. Because he was slightly short-sighted, he had developed a habit of contracting his eyebrows, screwing up his eyes, and pursing his thin-lipped mouth, and this made his appearance even worse. In manner he was old beyond his years and over the next few days Lady Overbury came to appreciate that any easy conversation with him was difficult. Despite the good fortune of his birth, he appeared to bear a grudge against the world for not recognizing his talents. Although he was outwardly sober, discreet and pious, Lady Overbury soon judged Mr Burnett to be shallow and selfish – a man interested only in his own welfare.

However, her heart immediately warmed to his companion, Tom Jones. He was tall and slender and very handsome in appearance, though his clothes lacked the quality of those worn by his companion. His hair was dark and curly, his eyes were a bright blue, and he had a perpetual smile that lightened the hearts of those around him and gave him an endearing charm. Lady Overbury thought that his intelligent and frank look and rather wild roguish manner reminded her of Henry Fielding when he was a young man. He even had the same air of authority in his voice. She knew instantly that there was not an ounce of malice or viciousness in this young man's character and she was to discover later that he always got things done without any fuss, although he gave the appearance of being idle and unconcerned.

After the introductions had been made, Henry Fielding departed, but not before he had urged both of the young men to take great care in guarding the house and told Lady Overbury that she must not hesitate to contact him if she required any further assistance. She thanked him profusely and then asked Joseph Graves to show both of the young men upstairs to the attic rooms so that they could each select a room. She subsequently learned that they had understandably avoided having the room that had been used by Miss Grey.

It was not long before the presence of the young men gave the household a new shape and Tom Jones's lively good humour soon helped dismiss much of the gloom that had descended upon the place. Lady Overbury took an early opportunity to find out more about them. 'Why are you here in Bath?' she asked curiously. 'Young gentlemen like you have no need of its waters.'

John Burnett, as the man of higher rank, replied first. 'I am here, Lady Overbury, in order to make some useful social contacts prior to undertaking some work for my uncle in London. When I was approached by Mr Fielding to protect you, I willingly agreed because I know that my uncle, Squire Woodforde, sets great store by his friendship with him. My only caveat was that Tom here should accompany me in the task. I did not think your protection warranted only a single volunteer.'

'You are most thoughtful, sir,' responded Lady Overbury, though she suspected that there was another reason for Burnett's insistence on having Tom Jones with him - if there were any danger, he would expect his social inferior to face it first. 'And what about you, Mr Jones?'

'I was only passing through Bath, your ladyship,' he answered, smiling at her. 'It was my intention to travel on to Bristol and take ship there for a new life overseas.'

'And what leads you to such a dangerous course of action?'

'My master, Squire Woodforde, has given me money to set me up in America because he no longer wants me to stay in this country.'

'And why does he want you to leave?'

Tom Jones blushed and Lady Overbury found herself wishing she were twenty years younger. He next exchanged a glance with his companion as if seeking guidance as to what he should or should not say. There was an uncomfortable pause. 'Come, sir, you can rely on my integrity,' interjected his questioner. 'I will not give away any secret you choose to share with me.'

'Very well, your ladyship, but I hope that what I have to say will not make you reject my role as your protector. Squire Woodforde wants me to leave because of my foolishness.' Jones hesitated again and then said apologetically, 'He is rightly angry at the way that I have recently let him down by overstepping the bounds of what is acceptable behaviour in a man in my position.'

'What did you do?'

'I'd prefer not to say, madam.'

'He expressed his love for the daughter of one of my uncle's closest friends,' interrupted Burnett, eying Jones with a jaundiced eye and smirking. ''Twas sheer folly on his part because she is destined for a far better marriage than Tom could ever offer her.'

'And who is this young woman?' asked Lady Overbury, looking into Tom Jones's embarrassed face.

'Her name is Miss Sophia Westbrook and I can assure you that she is one of God's loveliest creations,' he replied defiantly. 'She is a young woman of inestimable beauty and worth.'

'And a rich heiress because her father has no son,' added John Burnett, in a tone that implied his companion had less honourable reasons for being attracted to her.

'And your prospects, Mr Jones, are insufficient to warrant such a marriage?'

He hung his head rather sheepishly. 'I have no prospects, Lady

Overbury, other than what Squire Woodforde chooses to provide. I owe all that I have to his benevolent nature. He has given me a good education and made me the man I am.'

Burnett vigorously nodded his head in agreement. 'My uncle is a good Christian man who is blessed by both fortune and nature, but unfortunately Tom forgot his station in the matter of Miss Westbrook and my uncle was rightly highly displeased. Do you not think, Lady Overbury, that it is vital in these matters to keep to one's rightful social station?'

She ignored this barbed comment, choosing instead to ask Jones another question. 'What is your precise relationship with Squire Woodforde?' she said, wishing that Henry Fielding had explained to her more about the young man's background.

'None by blood. I owe everything to his and his sister's charitable nature because, twenty-one years ago, it made them take pity on a poor abandoned infant.'

'You intrigue me, sir! Tell me more.'

'At that time Squire Woodforde had just returned home late after many months away on business in London. After a short supper, he retired much fatigued, to his chamber. Imagine his surprise when he pulled back the bedclothes and beheld an infant wrapped in some coarse linen cloth and fast asleep. Once he had overcome his initial shock, he rang for his housekeeper. When she arrived, she was understandably not amused and she told him that some strumpet must have left the child in the hope that he would care for it. She told him that he should let her take the babe away and lay it at the door of the churchwarden.'

'It was correct advice,' interjected Burnett.

'But not advice he took?' said Lady Overbury, ignoring the patronising interruption.

'No. He said that he was afraid that I might catch a chill if she did that at such an unseasonable hour. She replied that it would be very fortunate if I died in a state of innocence before I had a chance to grow up to inherit the sins of my parents. Fortunately for me Squire Woodforde rejected such stern counsel and ordered her to procure clothing for me and send out for a woman who could provide pap.'

Lady Overbury tried to disguise her surprise. 'He was certainly behaving in a very Christian manner for few gentlemen would have acted so.'

'Yes, and the next morning he proved even kinder. He presented me as a gift to his sister, Miss Bridget, and asked her to take charge of my upbringing until he could discover more about my parentage.'

This time Lady Overbury could not hide her amazement. 'A rather startling present. Most brothers would give an item of jewellery if they wished to please their sister!'

'That is true, but Miss Bridget was no ordinary woman. She agreed to care for me and commended her brother's kindness to a deserted child.'

'And did they discover more about your parentage?'

'An investigation was undertaken by the housekeeper into the characters of all the female servants in the house but this proved fruitless. Then enquiries were made among the inhabitants of the parish and the finger of suspicion came to rest on a young girl called Jenny Jones, who had been employed to help nurse Miss Bridget through a recent illness. When accused, she admitted to being my mother and to depositing me in Squire Woodforde's bed. Miss Bridget was very taken aback, saying that she had esteemed Jenny as a very sober and upright girl and no wanton trollop.'

'And who was your father?'

'That Jenny Jones refused to say, but it was assumed it was the local schoolmaster – a man called George Partridge. He had been giving her lessons and the two were known to have become very friendly.'

Burnett sniffed to indicate his moral disapproval. 'I have been told that Mr Partridge stoutly contested his innocence but none believed him. My uncle dismissed him from his employ as a schoolmaster and arranged for Jenny Jones to have employ as a maid in a neighbouring county so that she could make a fresh start.'

'I hope that she made the most of this opportunity to redeem herself.'

Burnett took pleasure in shaking his head. 'No, the common harlot disappeared shortly afterwards and none has seen her since.'

Jones looked pained at these words and was unsure how to soften the harsh image that had been generated by his companion. In the end he simply said, 'I would like to report that my mother's later behaviour justified this act of kindness, but with regret I cannot.'

'She never made any attempt to contact you?'

'No, but her want of natural affection for me only seemed to make Squire Woodforde and his sister all the more determined to show me every kindness. He named me "Thomas" after himself and became my godfather and Miss Bridget brought me up almost as if I had been her son.'

'A woman can sometimes find pleasure in adopting a child when she has none of her own,' replied Lady Overbury, thinking that the squire's sister had done well to obtain such a handsome son, whatever his parentage.

'That is probably true, your ladyship,' said Burnett rather coldly, 'but I think you should know that Miss Bridget did have a child of her own. I am her son, born just over a year after these events.'

Lady Overbury apologized profusely for her error. She was understandably cross at herself for having committed such a blunder but even more annoyed with Henry Fielding for not having provided her with the proper details of John Burnett's parentage. As a result she decided to drop the conversation about the two men's backgrounds. Instead she asked them to undertake a further search of the house. It was therefore only later in the day that she managed to catch Tom Jones alone and resume the topic, asking him to properly explain his relationship with John Burnett. 'I am not clear,' she said, 'whether you act as his servant or whether you are friends?'

'I am neither his servant nor his friend, your ladyship, though we have known each other since infancy. He sometimes avoids my company altogether, but there are occasions – this being one of them – when he finds me a useful person to have with him.'

'I think, Mr Jones, I need to know a little more of your history together if I am not to cause needless embarrassment to you both.'

Jones nodded his agreement and gave her the explanation that she sought. 'It was scarce a few weeks after my arrival in Squire Woodforde's house that Miss Bridget announced to her brother that she wished to marry a captain in the dragoons called John Burnett. None viewed it as a wise choice. This soldier was handsome enough but he had not a penny to his name and his appearance reflected that. His dress was plain and out of fashion and it was known that he was rather too fond of drink and, when under its influence, rather vulgar in his behaviour. Miss Bridget was then about forty years old and lacking in any beauty so Squire Woodforde was under no illusion that it was her fortune rather than her person that he was after. He told Miss Bridget that the captain would be prepared to wed the witch of Endor if he thought it would bring him wealth.'

'That was hardly a tactful way of expressing the matter!'

'Perhaps so. It made no difference. Miss Bridget insisted on the marriage, judging that she should be entirely answerable only to herself for her conduct in the matter.'

'And were the couple happy?'

'I am told that, once they were married, he showed no affection for her and she treated him with complete indifference.'

'Yet a child was born?'

'Yes. Just over eight months after the wedding she gave birth to a son a month before its full time. He was named John after his father. It may have been her insistence on treating me so well that led to problems in her relationship with her husband. He had no desire to see his son brought up with a base-born child.'

'But that happened?'

'Yes, and, fortunately for me, Captain Burnett's opposition proved short-lived. He unexpectedly suffered an apoplexy whilst taking an evening stroll and died. This meant that I was educated alongside John, though our schoolmaster always distinguished between us. He treated John with kindness but argued that my innate sinfulness required regular use of the rod. I grew up with John sometimes treating me as a friend and sometimes as a servant and sometimes as an unwanted nuisance. I think he has always resented the fact that his mother often showed more affection to me than to him.'

'And is she still alive?'

Tom's eyes suddenly moistened. 'No. She died recently and I still deeply mourn her loss.'

'If what you say is true, then why should Squire Woodforde not set you up so that you can marry Miss Westbrook? He and his sister have obviously welcomed you into their family and he has a great fortune and no heir of his own. Even if he wishes the bulk of his estate to go to his nephew, he could still make a rich man of you.'

'There was a time when I dared hope that might be the case. But that is now out of the question because I have shown myself unworthy of his benevolence and unworthy of Miss Westbrook.'

'In what way?'

'By my actions.'

'And what actions were those?'

'I prefer not to say, your ladyship.'

Lady Overbury did not press the matter, but his reluctance to tell her the entire story left her concerned. What sin had he committed? It must have been something terrible to make his benefactor turn against him. Was Mr Jones, despite his charming manner, an appropriate person to protect her?

3

ENTER BEAU NASH

In the afternoon Henry Fielding called on Lady Overbury to see if everything was all right and to announce that he had found a new housekeeper. She immediately took him to task for not telling her enough about the two men he had sent to protect her and sought information about what crime Tom had committed.

'Forgive me, madam,' replied Fielding, looked very embarrassed. 'I should have told you more about his position. He is a good lad but one prone to get into scrapes. The daughter of Squire Woodforde's gamekeeper – a saucy trollop called Molly – became greatly enamoured of young Tom and, to be blunt, she used every opportunity of throwing herself at him. The poor youth clearly thought it wrong to seduce her but the hussy got the better of his good intentions. A young man's flesh will only stand so much. Shortly afterwards she showed signs of being with child. Tom wanted to do the honourable thing and marry her despite being told by his friends that she was unworthy of him. Happily he unexpectedly caught the jade in bed with another man, which cast understandable doubts on not only her character but also the paternity of the child.'

Lady Overbury shifted uneasily in her chair and then tried to cover her shock by saying awkwardly, 'Mr Jones is obviously well rid of the slut!'

'Yes, but Squire Woodforde understandably took the whole affair very ill, judging that his support for the illegitimate Tom had been scant rewarded. I tried to make him see that Molly had played the main part and, as a consequence, made him view the matter in a slightly better light. He has now decided that he will pay Tom's passage to America and so give him the opportunity of creating a new life there, rather than cut him entirely adrift.'

'But that could amount to a death sentence for the poor young man!'

'It might also make his fortune,' parried Fielding.

'And what of his love for Miss Westbrook?'

'He must put that behind him.'

'Does she love him?'

'I think Miss Westbrook still reciprocates Tom's feelings for her, despite what has happened, but she faces insurmountable opposition from her father. Mr Westbrook has told her in no uncertain terms that he will disinherit her and turn her out of doors stark naked and without a farthing if she does not abandon her idea of marrying Tom.'

Their conversation came to an abrupt end as Sarah Darr burst into the drawing room with the news that no less a person than Beau Nash, Bath's Master of Ceremonies, was at the door.

'Show him in, Darr. We cannot keep the great man waiting!' exclaimed Lady Overbury, casting a quick glance at herself in the mirror.

Beau Nash entered the room in a manner that belied his advanced years. Lady Overbury's gaze initially focused on his flamboyant dress – the white frilly shirt, the unbuttoned flowered waistcoat, the brown coat edged with lace, and, above all else, the cream-coloured tricorne hat, which was pulled so far forward that it grazed his right eyebrow. Then, as he pulled off his hat to greet her, she looked into a face whose features were striking if not attractive – large, watery blue eyes, an overly long nose, red plump cheeks, a small but sensuous mouth, and a strongly dimpled chin. The black wig that hung in curls to his shoulders belied his years for the wrinkles and lines on his face showed he was obviously in his sixties.

'My dear Lady Overbury,' he said, bowing graciously despite his years, 'I am so sorry that your first night in Bath has been such a terrible one. I want you to know that I will use whatever influence I have to ensure that we resolve this most cruel crime. I have already sent a messenger to inform Sir Robert of his housekeeper's death and I hope that I will soon be able to send him news that we have caught her killer.'

'You are too kind, sir,' she returned.

'In the meantime I hope that you will consider moving to a safer place. I would recommend either the White Hart or the Bear Inn or, if you prefer a lodging-house, the home of Mrs Hodgkinson. The latter has fine views over the river.'

Lady Overbury was slightly offended by the patronizing manner in which he said this and she shook her head. 'I have no intention of leaving this house until the poor woman's murderer is caught. Mr Fielding has provided me with two excellent young men to ensure that none can hurt me if I stay here.'

Nash shrugged his shoulders. 'I do not decry Mr Fielding's temporary measures but perhaps when you are more acquainted with me you will more readily heed my advice.'

'I already feel I know you, Mr Nash. I have heard so many talk about you.'

'I hope to my credit, your ladyship.'

'Oh yes, sir. Who has not heard sung the praises of the man who, for forty years, has been this city's undisputed Master of Ceremonies?'

He ignored the irony in her voice. 'You flatter me, your ladyship.'

'What brought you to this place?' she said, curious to see if she could acquire a greater insight into his true nature.

'Do you want the truth, madam?'

'Yes, sir.'

He chuckled. 'Then you are unusual because few women do!'

'I think you will find, Mr Nash,' interrupted Fielding,' that Lady Overbury is no ordinary woman.'

'Then we will be well matched for she will find I am no ordinary man.'

Lady Overbury smiled at the man's wit, but that did not prevent her saying, 'You have not answered my question, sir.'

'But I will. As you may know, I was from my youth a professional gambler and I first came here in 1702 when many nobles were accompanying Queen Anne on a visit to the city. I hoped to make their stay an enjoyable one for them and a profitable one for me!'

'Do you then take pride in fleecing the young and inexperienced?'

Nash ignored the gibe. 'One should always take pride in one's work, whatever it may be,' he replied.

Henry Fielding laughed. 'Don't let him deceive you, madam. Beau Nash is not ruled by greed. He will take money from those who have too much, but many a young innocent fool can vouch for the fact that the Master of Ceremonies has protected him from losing too much. Indeed there have been occasions when he has taken on the other professional gamblers, who have fleeced the inexperienced, and won back their money for them.'

'You make me sound like a modern Robin Hood!' retorted Nash.

'Judging from your clothes, sir, you strike me as a man more suited to the city than the forest,' replied Lady Overbury with a slight chuckle of amusement. 'You must like Bath very much to have stayed here so long.'

'I love it now but I hated the place when I first saw it. All the lodgings were mean and contemptible. Their walls were covered with unpainted wainscot and their floors with soot and small beer to hide the dirt. The furniture within most rooms was a ramshackle collection of shoddy items that paid heed neither to fashion nor comfort. Even worse for someone used to London society like myself, the amusements of the place were neither elegant nor conducted with delicacy. There were no proper dress codes and no rules about where or when people could drink, smoke, gamble, or dance. There was not even a central meeting place for the inrush of visitors, just a canvas marquee.'

'Then I am truly surprised that you stayed.'

'That is easily explained. I won a thousand pounds in just over seven weeks and I recognized that I could be a big fish in Bath's small pond. I decided that, rather than chasing around the country after men to dupe, I could stay here and encourage the dupes to come to me.' He gave a beguiling wink and, for the first time, Lady Overbury suddenly realized why this man had been so successful. She imagined what the corpulent Beau Nash might have looked like when he was thinner and forty years younger and decided that he had probably cut quite a dashing figure all those years ago. 'I and another gambler called Webster began suggesting ways of making a stay in Bath a more pleasurable experience,' he continued. 'When Webster was killed in a duel, I took on the role of being Bath's unpaid Master of Ceremonies and I used my authority to begin introducing significant changes.'

'Such as what, sir?'

'You have only to look around you, Lady Overbury. I determined to make the city attractive. That meant paving the streets so that they were less muddy in winter and less dusty in summer and creating new flower-edged promenades from what had been just cattle routes. It meant registering sedan-chair operators so that they did not charge unreasonable rates to their customers, and inspecting lodgings to ensure that they reached a certain standard and were not exorbitant in cost.'

'You may not think it because of what has happened in this house,' added Henry Fielding, 'but Bath is a remarkably safe city because of Mr Nash's endeavours. It was he who encouraged Bath Corporation to ban the wearing of swords and to become much tougher in dealing with unwanted beggars. It was he who saw to it that better night watchmen were appointed to patrol the streets and who created the cage where night walkers and disorderly persons can be locked up.'

'You flatter me, Mr Fielding. I have to say that none of that would have made Bath the success that the city is today had I not also recognized the power of women.'

'It has been my experience that women have no power in this man's world,' commented Lady Overbury with a wry smile.

'I beg to differ. You only have to look at how many men come here because their wives and daughters demand it. That is why I have encouraged women to view Bath as being the best place to see the latest fashions and the best place to acquire a husband.'

'Then you know the weakness of women, not their strength!' she countered.

Beau Nash laughed. 'I know human nature, madam. When I came here men and women chose to wear nothing special. So I told the men to stop wearing riding boots as if they had forgot their horse, and to dress smartly, and I told the women to stop wearing their everyday white aprons, which made them appear no different in status from a common whore. As a consequence both men and women began to dress only in the height of fashion and this made Bath the place to be seen. '

'He also did something else that was very clever,' added Henry Fielding. 'He recognized that nothing ruins fun as much too much snobbery and so he encouraged everyone to mix regardless of their social standing.'

'Even the most nobly born like the occasional bit of fraternization with their inferiors.'

'And what if someone objects?' asked Lady Overbury.

'I chivvy them on. As Master of Ceremonies I can say things that others cannot,' he replied enigmatically.

'Give me an example, sir.'

Beau Nash smiled very slightly. 'If I notice a noblewoman declining to properly touch the hands of those of lesser status in a dance, I will go up to her and say in no measured terms that if she cannot behave with ordinary politeness she must leave the room.'

Lady Overbury warmed to the man's impertinence, but this did not prevent her asking, 'Are there not others who have also contributed to this city's development?'

'Of course there are. No one can anyone dispute the importance of

John Wood and Ralph Allen in creating such beautiful new buildings as these in Queen Square. Men like George Trim, Richard Marchant, Thomas Greenaway and John Thornborough have invested heavily in creating places for visitors to stay and Bath owes much to John Harvey, who built the Pump Room, and Thomas Harrison, who built the two Assembly Rooms, where all can meet to play cards or take tea or dance. However, I can assure you that none of these would have done what he did had I not first increased the number of people wanting to come here. I only hope that those who follow me will not undo what I have achieved.'

'What do you mean, sir?'

'I fear others must now take on the mantle of ensuring that Bath offers appropriate entertainment for its many visitors. The government's recent ban on gambling is destroying my power.' Nash paused and looked her in the eye. 'My heyday as Master of Ceremonies is already over.'

For the first time Lady Overbury felt she glimpsed the vulnerability that lay behind the man's outward show. 'I am sorry to hear it,' she said quietly.

'Whatever the government thinks, the ban is a mistake because it runs counter to human nature. Rather than take their pleasure in enjoying the fruits of what they already have, the rich prefer to seek yet even greater wealth. Gambling offers a way of achieving that.'

'I fear you are right, Mr Nash.'

'I usually am,' he fired back and some of his earlier haughtiness reappeared. 'And I am pleased to say that my influence is not yet over. Rest assured that I will use it to do all I can to catch Miss Grey's murderer. And, while I am doing that, I hope you will discover that Bath has many delights.'

Lady Overbury recoiled at this suggestion. 'Sir, I can hardly go out enjoying myself while Miss Grey's body is scarce yet cold!'

'Nonsense! Her death has nothing to do with you and Sir Robert will be mortified if he feels that your stay here has been ruined. You will benefit no one by locking yourself away inside this house. You need to go out and have your mind diverted by happier things.'

'Like what?'

'Seeing the walks and shops, hearing the music playing in various venues, exchanging conversation with the fashionable all around you. Of course there are various subscriptions that will ensure you fully enjoy the city – these include half a guinea to subscribe to a library, one guinea to relax in a house near the Pump Room and another to enjoy the gardens of the Assembly Rooms, and two guineas to the entertainment fund to attend the balls and routs.'

'You have a slick tongue, sir, but it sounds to me as if you expect all visitors to keep their purses constantly open!'

'Don't go through the whole list, sir,' intervened Henry Fielding, sensing that Beau Nash's words were having a negative impact. 'Leave it to me to guide Lady Overbury through the maze of charges that open up Bath's pleasures. I will judge when the time is right. For the present I suggest that you focus on the investigation into Miss Grey's murder. Whilst you are embarking on that, I will escort her ladyship to Bath Abbey where together we can pray for the soul of the murdered woman.'

The smile on Lady Overbury's face at the start of his speech faded at its conclusion. 'I am not so stupid that I cannot see what lies behind your suggestion, Mr Fielding. You think that I will not be able to avoid seeing some of what Bath has to offer if I go to the abbey.'

'It is true that some of the attractive sights cannot be avoided.'

'Nor I suppose can curiosity!' she said and sighed at her own weakness. 'I will not deny that I am keen to see more of Bath than I have so far achieved. However, I want you to know that our prime purpose must be to pray for the dead woman.'

'I am pleased at your decision, Lady Overbury,' observed Nash. 'However, before I go I would like your permission to interview Joseph Graves to see if he knows anything about who might have killed Miss Grey.'

'You have my permission, but I want to stay and hear what he has to say.'

He frowned. 'It is not normal for a woman to be involved in questioning a man.'

'In Sir Robert's absence I am accountable for whatever happens in this house.'

Beau Nash had no enthusiasm for letting her remain but conceded to her request as graciously as he could. 'You may stay on the condition that you let me do all the talking.'

'You must know, sir, that asking a woman not to talk is asking the impossible, but I will do my best to remain silent.'

He grinned. 'Then I can ask no more, madam.'

It was left to Henry Fielding to ring the bell and instruct Burnett that they wished Graves to be brought before them. When the old servant appeared, he looked extremely apprehensive, especially when he saw the Master of Ceremonies standing like a judge before him. Nash eyed the man up and down and did not like what he saw. 'We have sent for you because we are investigating Miss Grey's murder.'

'I know nuthing about the murder, sir,' stuttered Graves.

'That is for me to judge,' replied Beau Nash sternly. 'Tell me, Graves, how long have you been employed here?'

'Since the 'ouse was built, sir. More 'an ten years.'

'And do you enjoy your work?'

'I'll be 'onest, sir. This 'ere is an easy job compared to others I 'ave 'ad. The family are only 'ere for part of each year and, since Lady Benson's death, Sir Robert 'as largely avoided the place.'

'But the house is sometimes offered to guests and that must generate work for you?'

'It doesn't 'appen very often, sir.'

'It was offered to me as a special favour because Sir Robert was once very friendly with my father,' commented Lady Overbury, fidgeting with the necklace round her neck and forgetting her promise to be silent.

'Is it normal for only you and Miss Grey to run the house?' continued Beau Nash, ignoring her intervention.

'Yes. Sir Robert brings 'is servants from 'is London 'ouse if he comes to Bath.'

'I have been told that you return to your home each night rather than staying here. Was not Miss Grey afraid of being in this house on her own?'

'No, sir. Miss Grey weren't a woman who were easily scared.'

'Yet you told Lady Overbury that Miss Grey had been frightened recently,' interrupted Fielding. Joseph Grave's face began to twitch and he looked very uncomfortable.

'Damn it, man! Tell us what you know!' shouted Nash. 'Or else I will have you whipped from one end of this town to the other!'

Every vestige of colour drained away from the servant's face and he wiped the mounting sweat from his brow. 'Well, sir, she came to me a week ago and she asked if I would sleep in the 'ouse. She said she were too nervous to do it alone anymore.'

'Did she say what had scared her?' asked Fielding.

'She said she'd seen a man 'anging round the 'ouse and she were convinced that someone were getting inside at night. She could 'ear doors creaking and the sound of footsteps on the stairs.' Graves sniffed and chewed his lip, searching his interrogators' faces for any sign as to how they were taking his story.

Fielding was making no attempt to hide his contempt but Nash's face showed no hint of what he was thinking. 'So did you stay?' he said.

'I did for one night, sir, but I didn't like it. I 'eard the same noises that Miss Grey had 'eard, but, when I tried to discover their source, I could find no one. I also found that the doors that I'd locked at night were some'ow unlocked in the morning.'

'So what happened then?'

'I told Miss Grey that I thought the place were 'aunted and I weren't prepared to spend another night 'ere.'

'And what did she say to that?'

'She said that I were a coward and that she'd deal on 'er own with whoever the intruder was if he dared return again.'

'Your behaviour was outrageous!' interrupted Lady Overbury, thinking again of the poor murdered housekeeper's body. 'Why was the matter not reported?'

'Neither Miss Grey nor I wanted to appear fools. She'd no proof that there really were any intruder and I feared people would laugh at my story of the 'ouse being 'aunted.'

'But did you not think it unfair to let Miss Grey stay here undefended?'

'It were 'er choice, your ladyship. I tried to dissuade 'er, but she were always a stubborn woman. That day we received a letter saying to prepare the 'ouse for yer arrival. I suppose I 'oped that the presence of guests might put an end to the matter.'

'And what about any risk to Lady Overbury?' roared Fielding, incensed at the servant's cowardly behaviour.

'I warned Lady Overbury more than once that the 'ouse were 'aunted, sir.'

'Ghosts do not slit a person's throat, Mr Graves,' interjected Nash sharply. 'Whoever disturbed this house at night was flesh and blood. Damn it, man, I'm sure you know more! If you want any future employment in this city, tell us what you have so far hidden!'

Graves stared at them in despair and appeared to struggle with himself over what to say. Finally he muttered, 'Believe me, sir. I never dreamt that she'd be killed, or I would 'ave taken what she told me more seriously. I thought she were just making up a tale to cover up her clumsiness.'

'What on earth do you mean?' commented Lady Overbury, holding her body stiffly as she tried to contain her anger at his weakness and stupidity.

'Two days ago, sir, I left the 'ouse during the a'ternoon to order provisions for Lady Overbury's arrival. When I returned I found Miss Grey in a 'ighly agitated state. She began to cry and sob and I 'ad to stop 'er by giving 'er a good shake. I asked 'er what were the matter and, once she'd composed 'erself, she told me that a man had attacked 'er. She said that after my departure she'd decided to go down to the kitchen and clean some of the porcelain dinnerware. She were so engrossed in 'er task that she didn't 'ear a man enter the 'ouse and so it were a huge shock when he came from behind 'er and seized 'er arm. She screamed and in 'er panic struck out at him with the dish that she'd in 'er 'and. It shattered against 'is face and, as he recoiled, she wrenched 'erself free and, 'urling another dish at him, ran upstairs. The man started to give chase, but then, for reasons that she didn't understand, he abandoned the task, shouting after 'er that if she valued 'er life she must quit 'er position. He then left the 'ouse.'

'Why have you not told us this before?' said Nash angrily.

'I were too ashamed, sir. You see, I didn't believe Miss Grey. I thought she'd made up the story to cover up 'er clumsiness in breaking a dish. I told 'er not to expect me to support 'er cock-and-bull tale when the master discovered what she'd broken.'

'Did she describe this man?'

'To be 'onest, I didn't give 'er much opportunity to do so. I told 'er that the master would be very angry at what she'd done and that she should clear up the mess.'

'But she must have said something about the intruder!' said Lady Overbury, once again forgetting that she was supposed to say nothing.

Graves wrung his hands together, a picture of remorse. 'All I can recall, your ladyship, is what she said about 'is right hand. She said that when 'e grabbed 'er and she looked down at 'is 'and on 'er arm, he'd only four fingers. There were no thumb, only a scar where it once 'ad been.'

'You are a fool, Graves,' stated Henry Fielding, angry at the servant's total mishandling of the situation. 'You preferred to believe in ghosts rather than see that there was a human agency at work in this house and, as a result of your stupidity, Miss Grey is dead. Do you appreciate the enormity of what you have done?' Graves abjectly nodded his head.

'Leave us and return to your duties,' commanded Beau Nash. 'I know not what your master will say when he hears this, but I know what I would do. I'd dismiss you on the spot!'

All three stayed silent as the poor man left them until Fielding spoke what they all felt. 'This damned matter gets ever more mysterious,' he said. 'Why should this stranger threaten Miss Grey?'

'I will set in motion an investigation to find this man who lacks a thumb on his right hand,' replied Beau Nash. 'We can be sure that Miss Grey will not have been the only person to notice such a deformity. If we can discover his whereabouts and catch him, then I am sure all will be revealed!'

'I hope so,' commented Lady Overbury. 'I thank you again, Mr Nash, for your assistance in this matter.' He nodded and bowed courteously in her direction before taking his leave. Once he had gone, she turned her attention back to Henry Fielding. 'Give me a few moments to go upstairs so that Darr can help me dress appropriately. I think that the walk you offered outside would now be most welcome. Miss Grey was so determined to set aside my fears that she hid her own. If only she had been honest with me she would still be alive. I really must pray for her poor soul.'

Half an hour later Henry Fielding led Lady Overbury out of the house. It was an exceptionally fine day for that time of the year and the blue sky was virtually cloudless. She breathed in the chill but fresh air, glad to be free for a time from the oppressive atmosphere that had permeated the house since the housekeeper's death. The afternoon sun made all the honey-coloured stonework in Queen Square glow so brightly that the buildings appeared even more beautiful than they had the night before.

'This delightful weather could make a vagrant of me,' she said, looking across at the exquisite proportions of the north side of the square and then at the lofty obelisk that stood in front of it. She walked over to where it stood and read the inscription. It stated that it had been erected by Nash in honour of a visit made by the Prince of Wales and his consort seven years earlier.

'I have been told that the poet Alexander Pope wrote the words,' commented Fielding.

'But the inscription is not in verse.'

'Mr Nash had hoped for a clever verse from the poet, but Mr Pope told him that he had no idea what poetry to offer because he had received so few favours from royalty that he was unacquainted with how best to thank them!'

'I am pleased Mr Pope would not produce poetry just because Mr Nash thought he should. The man is too full of himself at times.'

'Do not be too harsh on Mr Nash,' pleaded Fielding. 'Beneath the brash and sometimes pompous exterior he has a good heart. I said earlier that he sometimes came to the rescue of inexperienced gamblers. He has also often saved naïve young girls in danger of ruining themselves by listening to the false promises of men. And he has done much charity work in this city. He seeks out those in want and gives them aid uninvited. This city would never have raised the money for the Mineral Water Hospital without his fund-raising endeavours.'

The walk from Queen Square to Bath Abbey proved a very short one and, when they reached its spectacular west front, Lady Overbury looked with stunned amazement at the superb stone carving that surrounded its huge oak-carved doors. She had seen nothing quite like it before. Directly above the doors was a fine statue of Henry VII and far above him was the risen Christ and to either side of these were depicted angels ascending and descending ladders. She gazed at the cleverly wrought figures for some time but, to her mortification, she could not work out what message lay behind the choice of subject. Nor could she understand why to the side there was also a carving of an olive tree supporting a crown. 'What does it all signify?' she asked.

'I am no scholar in these matters but I believe this was the last great medieval church to be built before this country's break with Rome,' responded Fielding. 'The country was emerging from years of civil war and Oliver King, who was Bishop of Bath and Wells, chose to rebuild the great cathedral that had stood here since Norman times and dedicate the new building to the new Tudor monarchy that was being created. The façade, therefore, depicts the dream that made him think that. Just like Jacob in the Book of Genesis, he saw angels ascending and descending by a ladder to Heaven and he had a vision of an olive tree supporting a crown. He heard a voice say "Let an olive establish the crown and the crown establish the church".'

'Why an olive tree?'

'The olive tree is an emblem of peace and plenty.'

Lady Overbury stared again at the fine sculptures and the other intricate carving that surrounded the figures. 'Is it as beautiful inside as it is out?' she asked.

'I am afraid the interior does not match it. The dissolution of the monasteries meant that it was never properly completed. I have been told that the architect intended it to have a beautiful fan-vaulted ceiling but all it possesses is a rather dull wooden one. For that reason I suggest that we should enjoy looking at the rest of the outside first.' Fielding said this with an ulterior motive. He knew that there were interesting shops in the Orange Grove at the rear of the abbey and he hoped to tempt her to visit some of them and so divert her troubled mind.

His plan failed miserably. The nearest shop belonged to a seal-engraver called Wicksteed and it carried a large stock of china and giftware. Lady Overbury took not the slightest interest in it. Next came a toyman's called Sperrings and then two shops run by jewelers, one of whom was descended from a French Huguenot called Goulet. She resolutely declined to enter any of them. 'Can you not see, sir, that I am not in the mood for these or any other shops. When I think of what has happened I cannot enjoy looking at their contents. I have no time for jewellery, however fine it may be, or for anything else you care to show me, be it perfumes and pastries or tinctures and toys or fans and feathered muffs.'

'Then at least let me tempt you to enter the bookshop of Mr Warriner. It is the largest shop in this row and it has a fine circulating library. You cannot return to the house in Queen Square without something to read,' said Fielding, fast running out of options that might amuse her.

'I suppose that might make sense,' Lady Overbury reluctantly conceded.

'Bath has two excellent bookshops. This one and one round the corner which is run by Mr Leake in Terrace Walk. I prefer the latter because Mr Leake is the most extraordinary of all the coxcomical fraternity of booksellers and so a man well worth seeing in his own right.'

'Why do you say that?' she asked.

'For two reasons. First, because, having no learning himself, he is resolved to sell it as dear as possible to others. And second because, although he looks upon every customer as a friend, he will only speak to people in rank order. That means, for example, that he will not speak to a marquess whilst a duke is present. How he treats us will therefore depend entirely on who else is already inside his shop.'

Fielding expected her to find this amusing but instead it irritated her. 'Then I think I will forgo the pleasure of his acquaintance. I am not in the mood for snobbery!' she muttered. 'And what you have said makes me also wish to postpone visiting Mr Warriner's lest he be no better. I am sure I can find something in Sir Robert's library that will suffice to occupy me.'

Fielding looked at her grim visage and sensed that he had

overplayed his hand. 'As you wish,' he agreed reluctantly. 'Let us just go inside the abbey for us both to pray.'

Nothing more was said and an uncomfortable silence settled on them as they returned to enter the church. Lady Overbury found the inside far less attractive. The building's many windows meant that it was exceptionally well lit but the nave was cold and smelly and any grace that the inside might have had was marred by the galleries that ran along its walls and by the timber barrel vaulted ceiling that had replaced the original fan-vaulted design. More to her taste was the richly sculpted stone pulpit and the magnificent east window over the altar. Most people seemed to be using the church merely as a short cut to the Orange Grove and so Lady Overbury chose to make her devotions within a well-proportioned chantry that had the most wonderful delicate carvings of birds and foliage. Fielding waited outside. She sat quietly for a while trying to collect her thoughts and then she prayed most fervently that Miss Grey's killer might be found and punished.

4

THE MYSTERIOUS INTRUDER

After returning to the house in Queen Square, Lady Overbury said goodbye to Henry Fielding and ate the light supper which had been prepared by her maid. Shortly afterwards she decided to retire very early to bed. She felt exhausted. In part that was a physical reaction to two days of travelling followed by a disrupted night, but in the main it was caused by the emotional impact of the murder. No one attributed any blame to her for Miss Grey's death, but that did not prevent her feeling partially responsible. She felt somehow that she should have questioned the housekeeper more and so averted the tragedy. It took her quite some time to compose herself enough to fall asleep, but, when she did, she slept heavily. It was five in the morning when she was woken by a loud bang. For a brief moment she lay frozen with terror, but then her inherent courage returned and she forced herself to get out of her bed. As she did there was a knock on her door from her maid.

'Are you all right, my lady?'

'Yes. And are you?' she said, opening her door.

'Yes, but I am certain that no good will come of us staying here any longer. I fear that someone has been shot and possibly killed!'

The maid was clearly terrified and at her wits' end and even Lady Overbury was frightened about what she should do next. Danger seemed to dwell in every recess and shadow. It was a relief to both women when Tom Jones appeared in the corridor, having dashed down the staircase from his room. He was only half-dressed in clothes that he had hastily donned. 'Are you both unharmed, Lady Overbury?' he gasped.

'Yes.'

'Then I insist that you both go back to your room, lock your door, and stay inside until I tell you it is safe to come out. Leave it to me to explore the house and find out what has happened,' he commanded.

Even in the circumstances in which she found herself, Lady Overbury was annoyed at his presumption in dictating what she should do. 'Where's Mr Burnett?' she asked.

'I don't know. He's not in his room. It was his turn to stay awake and guard entry to the house downstairs.'

'Lead the way. I'll not hide in my room if that poor man lies harmed somewhere.'

Her courage was not matched by that of Sarah Darr. 'I cannot go, your ladyship. I am too scared!' she moaned, trembling with fear.

'Don't you realize that any intruder is bound to flee if he hears more than one person descending the staircase?' responded Lady Overbury, trying to bolster her own courage as much as that of her maid. Seeing the terror in Darr's eyes, she immediately realized that she was going to get nowhere. 'Never mind! We don't need you. Go back to your room, you silly girl!' she stormed in frustration.

Jones looked dubious but did not try to gainsay Lady Overbury's decision to accompany him. However, before taking a step downstairs, he locked the door that opened onto the spiral staircase so that none could enter the corridor from that direction. Then he proceeded cautiously to make his way down the main staircase into the hallway. Lady Overbury followed him although with every step she felt her knees tremble. She held a candle as high as she dared to light their way. They entered first the drawing room and then the library but found nothing disturbed. Then they made their way to the spiral stairs so that they could descend to the kitchen. The body of a young man dressed in fashionable clothes lay absolutely still on the stone-flagged floor, face down. A pool of blood had already formed round his head and they both sensed that they were looking at a dead man rather than an injured one.

Jones leant over the corpse and turned it over. He had expected to see John Burnett's face staring back at him, but instead he stared into the eyes of a complete stranger. He beckoned to Lady Overbury to take a look and, reluctantly, she did. She also had never seen the young man before. Even as they stood there, amazed and dumbfounded, a groan emerged from the cupboard at the far end of the kitchen. Jones strode over to it. It was locked but the key was in the door. He turned it and the door immediately swung open. The body of John Burnett tumbled out onto the floor. He struggled to rise and it became immediately apparent that his hair was blood-soaked and that a very ugly bruise was developing down the left side of his face. Lady Overbury hurriedly fetched him a chair and helped him into it while Jones lit the candles in the room so that the extent of his injuries could be more clearly seen. It was immediately apparent that the copious bleeding had stemmed from a savage blow to the top of his head.

'What has happened to you, Mr Burnett?' enquired Lady Overbury as she took a cloth and began gently wiping away some of the blood from his face.

'I heard a noise coming from upstairs in the hall, your ladyship, and so I went up the stairs. As I entered the main hallway I was struck a blow that all but cracked open my skull. It was followed by another blow to the side of my head. I must have collapsed into unconsciousness.'

'Did you see who struck you? Was it the man who lies dead on the floor?'

'I did not even get a glimpse of my attacker so I honestly cannot say if it was the man who lies over there. If it was, I am glad he is no more.'

Lady Overbury saw him flinch from the pain of his battered head and turned to Tom Jones. 'I think you had better go for a doctor at once. I know it's very early in the morning but I do not think we should wait to have this injury attended to properly. Once you have commissioned a doctor to come to the house, then go to where Mr Fielding is lodging and say we need his immediate advice and assistance.'

'I do not think I should leave you unguarded, my lady. For all we know, the attacker may be still inside this house.'

None would have guessed Lady Overbury's inner fear from the calm way in which she replied, 'It makes sense that you should search the house first, but, if you find no trace of the perpetrator of this deed, then I insist that you go for the doctor and find Mr Fielding. You will not be leaving me entirely alone. I have both my maid and Mr Burnett, even if one is a coward and the other injured.'

Jones undertook a thorough search but he found no hidden intruder. He therefore headed off immediately for Mr Fielding's lodgings with the intention of summoning a doctor en route. Once he had gone, Lady Overbury returned upstairs to upbraid her maid and to insist that she attend Burnett until the doctor arrived. She suggested that in the first instance a poultice should be made for his injured head. She then added, 'I suggest, Darr, that you put the poor man onto the bed in your room. He has sustained too great an injury to contemplate getting him to the top of the house.'

The two women had scarce got the injured man upstairs before they heard a knock at the main door. Lady Overbury sent Sarah Darr to answer assuming, rightly, that this indicated the arrival of medical help. The maid returned with the doctor in tow. He informed them that his name was Dr Cleland in a tone that implied they were fortunate to have a man of his standing. Lady Overbury did not take to him because he had a rather furtive appearance. His eyes were small and beady, his nose unpleasantly long, and his mouth smugly pursed. She also thought she could smell that he had been drinking although it was still very early in the morning. However, she felt any doctor was better than none. She urged him to undertake a full analysis of the injuries that Burnett had sustained and to spare no expense in treating them.

'How is he, Doctor?' she anxiously whispered once Dr Cleland had completed his examination.

'Better than he would have been if I had not been called, though 'tis a pity I was not summoned earlier,' he replied in a ponderous voice.

'I hope his skull is not fractured.'

'No, there is no fracture but I deem such a laceration as he has suffered to be just as dangerous.' He paused as if to make sure she understood the gravity of the situation. 'People who know nothing of medicine think all is well if the skull is not fractured, whereas I had rather see a man's skull broken than meet with some other wounds I have met with.'

Lady Overbury looked at him suspiciously. 'I had hoped that his injuries were minor. Surely he shows no symptom of any life-threatening injury?'

The doctor gave a sniff. 'I have stopped the haemorrhaging, but symptoms may change and what appears favourable one moment may soon become unfavourable. To say whether a wound is likely to prove fatal is a contentious point at the best of times.'

'Surely Mr Burnett's youthful age must help free him from danger?'

Dr Cleland looked as solemn as if he had just come out of a confessional box. 'Who is there among us who cannot be said to be at risk whatever our age?' he pontificated.

'So what can you tell me?' snapped Lady Overbury, frustrated at the doctor's unhelpful manner.

'That it is well that you sent for me and that it would have been even better if you had sent for me earlier,' he replied rather truculently.

'There is no point sending for you at all, Dr Cleland, unless you tell us what we should do to help him recover!'

He glared back at her but then responded to her command. 'I advise that you should keep him quiet and make sure that he drinks and eats only a little. I think a little chicken broth or some water gruel would be best. I will call back later today and see him again.'

'And may I send my maid out for some jellies for him?'

'Aye. Jellies are good for healing injuries. They promote cohesion.' And with that last comment ringing round the room, the doctor picked up his bag and went downstairs to examine the corpse. Lady Overbury followed him, leaving her maid to attend to Burnett's needs.

Dr Cleland was still engaged in his investigation when Henry Fielding arrived. 'My dear lady, how much you have suffered,' he said solicitously, raising her hand to his lips. His gaze held hers, communicating both kindness and reassurance. 'I should not have let you stay in this house.'

''Twas my insistence that led to me staying,' she replied, greatly relieved to have his presence with her. 'I have suffered neither as much as poor Mr Burnett, who has a very nasty cut to his head and bruise to his face, nor to the extent of an unfortunate stranger in our midst who has lost his life.'

'He is not any one that you know?'

'No, though his clothes are of sufficient quality to indicate that he is no commoner.'

Fielding looked at the body and asked the doctor peremptorily, 'Have you assessed the cause of death?'

'To fully answer that would require me to undertake a proper autopsy.'

'But I am sure you can hazard an opinion!' declared Fielding sarcastically.

The doctor's eyes darkened with angry pride. 'Opinions are not scientific, sir,' he replied.

'Damn it, man! Even I can see from here that he has been shot at fairly close range. If you want any payment for your services here I suggest you answer my question and stop prevaricating.'

'Very well, sir,' replied Dr Cleland, glowering at this affront to his professionalism but fearful of losing his fee. 'As far as I can see at this juncture the ball entered his shoulder, then passed through his heart, and came out through his lower back. I doubt whether he felt any pain. Death would have been almost instantaneous.'

'This is Dr Cleland,' said Lady Overbury, suddenly conscious that no introductions had been made.

The name caused Fielding to wince. In his haste to find a doctor Jones had found one whose reputation was one of the worst in the city. Cleland had been sacked from the Mineral Water Hospital the previous autumn and Fielding recalled how the news of this had been blazoned across the local broadsheets. Two women patients had accused Dr Cleland of professional misconduct on account of his repeatedly engaging in vaginal examinations. Fielding could not recall all the details but he remembered that one of the nurses had given testimony how the doctor had insisted she leave the room and then bolted the door so none could see what he was doing. His dismissal had caused upset in medical circles because it was feared that other doctors might respond to the decision by becoming reluctant to examine any lady above the shoestrings or below the necklace.

'I am quite ready to undertake a fuller examination of the victim. I can easily arrange for the body to be collected,' said Dr Cleland, unaware of Fielding's train of thought.

'That will not be necessary, sir. I have informed Mr Nash of what has occurred here and he is on his way. I am sure he will undertake the appropriate steps for this young man's removal. Your services are not required.'

Dr Cleland might have taken issue with this curt dismissal had not the thought of meeting Beau Nash filled him with horror. Instead he rapidly made his exit, pausing only to say to Lady Overbury, 'I will return this afternoon to continue Mr Burnett's treatment, your ladyship.'

'Has that man attended to Mr Burnett properly?' asked Fielding as soon as the doctor was out of the room.'

'As far as I can tell. I did not find him the easiest man to understand.'

'We may get a second opinion if necessary,' muttered Fielding, choosing not to alarm Lady Overbury about the nature of the doctor whom Tom Jones had found. He looked more closely at the dead man again. There was something about the man's coat that seemed familiar. At first he could not think what it was and then it dawned on him. It was the buttons on it. They matched the one that had been found grasped in the dead housekeeper's hand. On closer inspection he could even see where a button was missing. He pointed this out to Lady Overbury, saying, 'It looks as if we have found the murderer of Miss Grey even if we now have to discover who murdered him.'

'Have you indeed!' said an unexpected voice, as Beau Nash descended the stairs to the kitchen followed by a man from the night watch and Tom Jones. 'I came as quickly as I could once I received your message about what had happened.'

'We are very pleased to see you, sir,' replied Lady Overbury.

As Beau Nash drew near to the corpse he gave a startled gasp. From the look on his horrified face it was obvious that he, unlike them, recognized who it was. 'It is Lord Kearsley, the son of Sir Robert,' he declared, having mastered his surprise and dismay.

'Then the mystery certainly thickens,' responded Fielding. 'Why on earth would Lord Kearsley choose to break into his own family home on two successive nights? And why would he wish to kill his father's housekeeper? And who has now murdered him?'

'I assume it was the same person who struck John unconscious and locked him in a cupboard,' interrupted Jones.

'And could that be the man without a thumb who threatened Miss Grey?' added Lady Overbury. 'The man who has been killed has no such deformity.'

'I see no point in speculation at this stage, your ladyship,' commented Nash. He looked at her half-dressed condition and determined to introduce some order into the proceedings. 'This must all have come as a terrible shock and I think that you should return upstairs to your maid and try and get some rest in bed while I see to the removal of Lord Kearsley's body. Rest assured. They say that every cloud has a silver lining. In this case the status of the victim will ensure that our magistrates take the matter very seriously and more so than when I reported Miss Grey's murder.'

'I can assure you that rest is out of the question given what has happened, but I will retire to my bedroom so that the body can be removed and I can dress appropriately. I would then like to discuss with you in more detail what might have happened here.'

He bowed politely. 'As you wish, madam.'

Lady Overbury returned to her room and Sarah Darr began assisting her to dress but in a very clumsy fashion because of her agitated state. She looked like a frightened rabbit caught in the glare of a poacher's lantern. Her increasingly exasperated mistress finally ordered her out of the room, saying she would be better served by her tending to the injured Burnett. Lady Overbury completed her own toilet, surprised at how shaky she felt. The second death weighed heavily on her, even though she had never met Lord Kearsley. What could she possibly say to Sir Robert? It was bad enough that his long-serving housekeeper had been murdered, but his son's death would be a devastating blow!

It seemed an eternity, but it must only have been a couple of hours later that Tom Jones knocked on her door to say that, if she still wished to see them, Nash and Fielding were awaiting her in the drawing room below. Lady Overbury told him to tell them that she would be down almost immediately. When she entered the room, the two men rose courteously to greet her. 'Well, gentlemen, have you any light to shed on this matter?' she asked.

Henry Fielding was the first to reply, but he did so with a look of embarrassment written across his face. 'I regret to inform you, Lady Overbury, that Mr Nash has talked to Tom Jones and he is not content with his story about what happened here earlier this morning.'

'Why?'

'I find the idea of two intruders in one evening a little far fetched! It would make more sense to me if either John Burnett or Tom Jones had killed Lord Kearsley.'

Lady Overbury's mind struggled to come to terms with the implications of his comment. 'I do not understand, sir,' she said.

'I am sorry if I upset you by what I say, but I wish to offer you an alternative version of events, Lady Overbury. The angle of the bullet that killed Lord Kearsley indicates it is likely that he was shot by someone who was standing above him on the staircase. I would suggest that Mr Burnett heard the noise of an intruder and, coming down the stairs, fired at him. When he saw that the dead man was no petty criminal but a finely dressed gentleman, he panicked. Rather than face a murder charge, he persuaded his friend, Mr Jones, to provide him with an alibi. It was therefore not a second intruder but Mr Jones who hit Mr Burnett and then locked him up in the kitchen cupboard. Mr Jones then ran upstairs to arouse the house as if he had been in his bedroom when the killing took place.'

Lady Overbury was sufficiently astute to recognize that Nash's account could be true, but her emotions told her it was false. 'I grant you that what you say is possible,' she replied, 'but I refuse to believe that they would deceive me in this way.'

'I am not implying that they plotted a murder, your ladyship. I am merely suggesting that Mr Burnett may have shot Lord Kearsley by accident and understandably feared the consequences of his action. Hence the contrived tale designed to make us believe that another intruder was responsible.'

'I am sure that John Burnett is not always straightforward in his dealings with others,' intervened Fielding, 'but I can assure you that

Tom Jones is as honest a lad as you could possibly wish to meet. I would not have entrusted Lady Overbury to his or Burnett's care had I not been entirely certain of Jones's integrity as well as his courage. I knew that he would more than make up for any shortcomings on Burnett's part. I assure you that from my perspective he will be telling us the truth and so I believe that there was someone else in this house. Moreover, I think that there may be a way I can prove it.'

'How?'

'I suggest we engage in a search for the murder weapon. There has been no time to dispose of it. If we cannot find a gun we can assume an outside murderer took it with him.'

Beau Nash immediately saw the sense in Fielding's suggestion. 'I will instigate a search with Lady Overbury's permission.'

'I grant you permission, but I think you are wasting precious time while the real murderer is escaping. Tell me what you both know about Lord Kearsley. I think that might prove a more fruitful line of enquiry.'

'Lord Kearsley has been building up a bad reputation for himself in recent months by mixing with some notoriously immoral men,' replied Nash, 'and he is therefore regarded as the black sheep of his family. It is possible that Sir Robert may not be distraught at the news of his son's murder because Lord Kearsley was ruining the family's reputation by openly supporting the restoration of the House of Stuart to the English crown. Had the young man not disappeared a couple of weeks ago, he would almost certainly have been arrested for treason.'

'The poor lad must have had his head entirely turned to be so rash!' sighed Lady Overbury. 'It is almost sixty years since this country deposed King James II for his shameful Catholic beliefs. I am aware that there are some in Scotland who have risen to support the House of Stuart and that the rebels have seized control of Edinburgh, but Lord Kearsley should have known there is no demand in England to replace our Protestant King George with either the son or grandson of that long removed monarch.'

'Bravely said, your ladyship, but I regret to say that it is not as straightforward as that,' replied Henry Fielding. 'When the father of our current king was invited to become our monarch there were Englishmen who were prepared to take up arms for the House of Stuart and call themselves Jacobite after the Latin word for James that once was inscribed on our coinage. Surely you have not forgotten the Rebellion of 1715?'

'No, I have not, though I was but a young girl when it happened. But the rebellion occurred at a time when we were offering the crown to a German prince who did not even speak English. Even in that situation most people rejected the Pretender's claim to the throne. Thirty years have passed since then and the House of Hanover is now accepted in this country.'

'Would it were that simple!' continued Fielding. 'There are more than you think who still raise a secret glass to the so-called "king over the water" and there are enough of them to breed a dangerous hope among this country's enemies that there will be another Jacobite rising. As you know, that Old Pretender has a son to whom the Highlanders in Scotland have now sworn allegiance. They have named him Bonnie Prince Charlie. We ignore this Young Pretender at our peril. When he left Italy and arrived last spring in Paris, he managed to obtain from King Louis XV a promise of between twelve and twenty thousand French soldiers to help put either himself or his father on the English throne.'

'I have heard of the French king's perfidy but I do not understand why he has chosen to support the Young Pretender.'

'I can assure you that it is not for any love of the House of Stuart,' commented Fielding. 'It is purely because the French want to see this nation embroiled in a civil war. For the past thirty years our Hanoverian monarchy has been entangling this country in the affairs of Europe and, as you will be aware, this has led us to support the Austrian empress in her war against the French. King Louis XV sees support for the Young Pretender as a way of getting back at us – a useful diversion that will prevent us continuing to be a nuisance to him.'

'But any action the French take will serve only to unite us,' retorted Lady Overbury.

Beau Nash could not help but admire her loyal words, but he felt it essential that she should understand the reality of the political situation. With a grim face he continued, 'When news first came of the French army gathering at Dunkirk, our government passed a loyal address to King George II, but there would still have been a civil war had the French army landed here. That is why the government breathed a sigh of relief when a storm wreaked havoc on the fleet that had assembled to carry the French soldiers across the Channel. So many ships were lost that King Louis XV had to abandon his plan.'

Lady Overbury's face went white with shock at this startling information. Fielding gently took her hand in his. 'And the danger is not over yet,' he said softly. 'No one expected the Young Pretender to land in Scotland this summer. Nor did we think that the Highlanders would rally to the cause of a man who literally arrived with only a few men at his side.'

'But surely the fact that he has only a Scottish rabble behind him means that any danger to England is over,' responded Lady Overbury, her natural optimism asserting itself.

'No, I am afraid not,' replied Fielding immediately. 'In some respects he has now proved a greater danger because he has come without the French. Many in England might join him who might not have done had he come with an army of foreigners.'

'Yes,' added Beau Nash. 'By all accounts this traitorous prince possesses the attributes that easily win over hearts. He is tall and handsome in appearance and courteous and good-humoured in manner. Much therefore now depends on how quickly we can crush the Highlanders who have rallied to his cause. It is a huge blow that Edinburgh has fallen to them already.'

'And what has all this to do with Lord Kearsley?'

'The Young Pretender is keen to know on which Englishmen he can rely if he invades England from Scotland. We believe that Lord Kearsley may have been drawing up a list of those who would join the Prince. The authorities will therefore be glad to hear that they need not concern themselves anymore about his treasonable activities. I am tempted to see it as a good omen that he was killed on this particular day.' Lady Overbury and Henry Fielding looked puzzled. 'Have you forgotten that today is the fifth of November, the day we recall the death of that other traitor, Guy Fawkes?'

'I'm not sure I would remind anyone of that connection,' said Fielding. 'It might also encourage them to recall that the gunpowder plotters held meetings in Bath. We do not want anyone to view Lord Kearsley's presence here as evidence that the city once again acts as host to treason.'

Lady Overbury expressed her confusion. 'Why should that connection be made when the two events are so far apart in time?'

'Because of what happened here in Bath at the time of the first Jacobite Rebellion in 1715.'

'Aye, and I thought I had erased the memory of it!' muttered Nash.

The puzzled Lady Overbury looked at both men and saw that they were obviously deeply worried. 'I do not understand,' she said. 'Please explain.'

Nash and Fielding exchanged glances and Nash spoke first. 'At the time of the last rebellion information came into the hands of the government that the Jacobites were intending to use either Bristol or Bath as a potential rendezvous for the rebels in the southwest after the Old Pretender had landed with a French army in Plymouth. Troops were sent to ensure that this did not happen. Some were placed under the command of the Earl of Berkeley, who was Lord Lieutenant of Gloucestershire, and he used them to seize control of Bristol. Other troops were placed under the command of Major General George Wade, a distinguished soldier who had served under the Duke of Marlborough in the wars against France. It was Wade's deputy, a man called Colonel Pocock, who uncovered a Jacobite arms cache here in Bath. It contained enough swords and guns to equip at least two hundred men, plus a mortar, three cannon and moulds to create more. Two hundred horses were also seized. This was sufficient for Pocock to declare that Bath was the main Jacobite centre in the west.'

'And what happened then?'

'As you know, the Jacobite rebellion ended in fiasco. The Old Pretender abandoned landing in Plymouth and instead went to Scotland. The Highlanders there rallied to his cause – just as they are rallying to the young prince this year - but they were soundly defeated. Unfortunately Bath's attempts to distance itself from Jacobitism were undermined when a second Jacobite arms cache was discovered at Badminton in 1718.'

'Why should that be linked to Bath?'

'Because Badminton was the home of the Duke of Beaufort and he was a well-known figure in Bath,' interjected Fielding.

'It was very fortunate for this city that my friend Ralph Allen managed to persuade Major General Wade to come and live here and become our MP,' continued Beau Nash. 'Wade's presence put an end to rumours that might otherwise have ruined the ability of this city to attract visitors.'

A lesser woman might have been overwhelmed by the information being thrown at her, but Lady Overbury's response was to want to know more. 'How was Mr Allen able to persuade a big military figure like Wade to come to Bath? I thought that he was just the man responsible for discovering the architectural talents of John Wood and promoting the use of Bath stone as a building material?'

'Back then Ralph Allen was a deputy postmaster in Bath,' responded Nash. 'The service operated from the disused church of St Michael near the Westgate. He used his position to betray the Jacobite correspondence and in particular the role that had been played by Sir William Wyndham, the chief Jacobite in the west, and by his friend, Lord Lansdowne, whose seat is at Longleat. Both these lords were arrested and imprisoned in the Tower of London. Wade rewarded Allen by making him the country's Postmaster General. The wealth that he derived from this role enabled him to purchase the limestone quarries at Combe Down and to start the rebuilding of Bath.'

'In short,' interposed Fielding, 'this city's prosperity has rested on Mr Allen and General Wade establishing that Bath no longer has any link to Jacobitism. The idea that Lord Kearsley may have been working under cover in the city could easily undo their work overnight.'

'I now see, gentlemen, why you are concerned.'

'If we are to prevent harmful gossip, we have to find out as quickly as possible why Lord Kearsley came secretly to Bath and stole into his father's house like a thief.'

'And why he killed Miss Grey,' added Lady Overbury.

'If he did,' said Beau Nash.

'But a button from his coat was found in her hand!'

'It could have been planted there to mislead us. The man with a missing thumb may be behind the deaths of both victims.'

Whilst Lady Overbury was coming to terms with this latest concept Tom Jones burst into the room, looking distinctly frightened. 'I think the murderer may be locked in one of the rooms upstairs,' he exclaimed. 'I decided to return and have a short sleep in my room and, as I started going up the spiral staircase, I realized that there was someone ahead of me. I shouted and the person turned and ran up the stairs. I followed as quickly as I could and the person darted through the door of one of the rooms on the second floor.'

'But that is impossible! All those doors are locked and no one here has a key.'

'I am afraid that is not the case, Lady Overbury. When I tried to follow I heard a key turn on the other side of the door and the intruder thus blocked me entering.'

'My apologies, your ladyship,' said Beau Nash, 'I was obviously wrong in thinking it unlikely that there should be two intruders.'

'We must apprehend him,' interposed Fielding. 'You and I may be old but, with Tom's help, I am sure we three can break down a door and catch our man.'

'I'm not sure it was a man, sir. The figure was cloaked. It could have been a woman.'

'Man or woman, it does not signify. We just need to ensure that this murderer is caught!'

They bade Lady Overbury stay downstairs, saying there was no way they could guarantee her safety against someone armed with a pistol. However, yet again she refused to comply with their wishes. She was insistent that they permit her to be present at the arrest of the mysterious intruder and the men reluctantly agreed. Jones led the way upstairs, followed by Nash and Fielding, and she brought up the rear. On their arrival on the landing outside the room Beau Nash took charge. 'Come out!' he commanded. There was no response. 'Damn it, come out before we have to break this door down. You cannot escape!' Again, there was no response. Nash beckoned to Jones and the two men charged at the door. Lady Overbury heard the wood splinter. Fielding replaced Nash and joined Jones in another charge. This time the lock shattered and the door swung back into the room. The three men entered followed closely by Lady Overbury, though it took her all her courage to do so. The room was full of covered furniture and storage boxes but there was no sign of any intruder.

'I assure you, sirs, that I saw a person enter this room,' said Jones.

'Then we must search it and search it well. Unless the intruder can fly he or she cannot have escaped except by some secret passage.'

After half an hour they gave up. They could find nothing. 'I must leave and inform Mr Allen of what has happened,' said Beau Nash. 'I am expected at his house this afternoon because he is holding a big celebration at Prior Park to mark the fact it is Guy Fawkes Day.'

'Yes, I also have an invitation,' said Fielding.

'Then I suggest you use the opportunity to mix with all those who attend. See if you can pick up any clues as to what Lord Kearsley might have been doing.'

'May I go too?' asked Lady Overbury. 'I can listen to what the ladies are saying. Their tongues are often looser than those of their husbands and brothers.'

Beau Nash hesitated and then agreed. 'Use my name and you will be welcomed when you arrive.'

5

A VISIT TO PRIOR PARK

Lady Overbury had scarcely time to dress herself in her finest clothes before Henry Fielding arrived outside the house later that day in a small carriage. On their way to the mansion they travelled along Stall Street which was the main thoroughfare leading to what had once been the city's south gate. This area of the city was far less attractive and contained a mass of tall houses packed tightly together. From their style they appeared to date back mostly to the late sixteenth and early seventeenth centuries when large areas of medieval Bath had been rebuilt. Many had shops at ground floor level but these obviously catered for the city's residents and lacked any of the glamour offered by the shops that Lady Overbury had seen on her visit to the abbey the previous day. There was no trace left of the ancient south gate because it had been destroyed during the Civil War, but beyond where it had once stood lay the less congested Horse Street. This took them to a crumbling medieval bridge in the centre of which stood an ancient chapel dedicated to St Lawrence. Having crossed this, they turned to the left and a village called Widcombe. Along the way she could see the wagon road that conducted the stone from Ralph Allen's quarries on Combe Down to the wharf at Bath.

The carriage soon came to some new terraced houses. Fielding informed her that Allen had built them to attract skilled masons from Yorkshire and carpenters, joiners, and plasterers from London. The wisdom of such a move was evident when, having ridden up a very steep hill, she caught her first glimpse of his mansion standing on a terrace high up in the wooded combe above Bath. Not only was the house itself very grand with its central pedimented portico supported by Corinthian columns, but also on either side were two symmetrical semi-circular wings to provide offices, stabling, and other facilities. This gave it a vast imposing façade.

The carriage drew up under a pavilion that had been erected on the west side of the mansion and Lady Overbury saw Ralph Allen for the first time. He was greeting his guests as they arrived. He did not cut a grand figure because he was rather heavily built and only of middle height and he was dressed in very unfashionable clothes made from simple materials. His plain coat of dark broadcloth appeared almost worthy of a Quaker. His face was equally unprepossessing. His eyes were unattractively small, his nose rather fox-like, and his mouth thin-lipped. However, Lady Overbury was predisposed to like him when she saw how warmly he greeted Henry Fielding and how courteously he received her. There was an unexpected natural dignity in his manner and he exuded a rare serenity. By his side was his wife, who was no fashionable beauty but quite reserved, short in height and rather plain. Fielding later whispered to Lady Overbury that Allen's first wife had been a daughter of General Wade and a more fashionable and formidable person. Allen had only been married to his second wife for a couple of years but her pleasant, kind nature had made him very happy.

The mansion unfolded its pleasures to its visitors literally step by step as they entered it. Lady Overbury particularly admired the well-framed panels that had been created to display paintings in the central hall and the nearby chapel with its rounded apse and its second floor gallery. To the left of the central hall was a gracious dining room, which had the most intricate and elaborate stonework. Beyond this was the drawing room and a great staircase that led to a spectacular long gallery on the second floor, as well as to bedrooms. Henry Fielding told Lady Overbury that the architect John Wood had given the servants' rooms at the top of the mansion breathtaking views by breaking the entablature with little windows.

As they walked around the building Lady Overbury kept overhearing snippets of conversation. One young man was holding forth to a friend about his disappointment at seeing so many elderly women everywhere. 'I never saw so many ugly faces as here in Bath,' she heard him say, 'I think most of the ladies look worse because of the pains they have taken to adorn themselves. I have seen ladies without teeth, ladies without eyes, ladies without shape, and ladies with a foot and a half in the grave, all still aping youth and dressing themselves as if they were forty years younger.' 'Don't worry,' said his friend, 'there are some beauties around.' Most of the talk among the women was either about the latest fashions and gossip, or about rheumatism in the shoulder, sciatica in the hip, or gout in the toe and Lady Overbury quickly grew tired of it. Far more interesting was the talk of Ralph Allen and others about the threat of a Jacobite invasion from Scotland. She hoped that she might hear something that might provide a lead into why Lord Kearsley had come to Bath.

'I think it is very unfortunate that those who are honest and loyal in Scotland should have their persons exposed to the most horrid insults and their fortunes subjected to the depredations of these rebels,' voiced a man with a large bulbous nose and popped eyes.

'I agree, sir,' said his companion. 'These savage inhabitants of moors and mountains who support the Pretender are no more than outlaws, robbers and cutthroats, who live in a constant state of lawlessness.'

'The Highlanders have joined him in their thousands not because they have any attachment to the Stuart cause but because their chiefs have called them out,' contributed Ralph Allen. 'A chief's declaration of war is binding on all the clan and, if any man objects, he is ruthlessly punished. The Scottish chiefs view the Act of Union as a betrayal. They never wanted a union between Scotland and England and so dress their grievances in the livery of the prince. They see supporting him as a way of restoring their ancient rights and winning wealth and power.'

'Aye, these Jacobites cloak ambition, avarice, revenge, malice, envy, and every bad passion under the guise of patriotism,' uttered the man with the bulbous nose, 'and they count on obtaining the support of the Papists in this country.'

'Do not condemn all Catholics, sir!' voiced an elderly man. 'Most of them in this kingdom will not be persuaded by their priests to participate in what is happening.' This evoked a storm of disbelief, but the man stood his ground. 'They will not wish to see their religion forced on this country by a banditti of robbers and cut-throats.'

'I wish I had your faith in them, sir,' replied the man with the bulbous nose. 'For my part, I think they are only biding their time. Sooner or later we will hear how the Catholics are seeking our destruction. Today's Guy Fawkes' celebrations remind us of an earlier wicked papist plot to blow up Parliament and of the need for constant vigilance against all of the Roman faith. We must never forget that they give their allegiance to a foreign power. The cause of King George is the cause of liberty!'

This statement produced a round of patriotic comments and Lady

Overbury moved on to where another group were discussing the rebellion.

'We would be foolish to treat these rebels with contempt,' said a pale-faced man with large red lips and a pointed nose. 'They may be bandits but they are well armed and bold. It is said they number close to six thousand troops.'

'But I hear that the army of General Wade at Newcastle is about eleven thousand strong and other troops are now being formed to deal with the menace,' replied the man standing next to him. 'I am reliably informed that the troops which are to march to the borders of Lancashire under General Ligonier will consist of seven regiments of foot and that these will be accompanied by nine troops of cavalry with the Duke of Richmond serving as lieutenant general.'

'Even where our forces smaller, I would be confident of victory if the Pretender invades,' remarked the man opposite him. 'Our cause is just and our desire for liberty and the true faith add weight to our courage.'

Deciding that none of this talk of war was going to give her any insight into what Lord Kearsley had been doing, Lady Overbury opted to take some fresh air outside. The poet Alexander Pope had lent Ralph Allen a fine gardener called John Serle to enhance the site's natural beauty not only by creating a great lawn and engaging in an extensive tree-planting programme but also by creating water cascades. Though the landscaping was not yet finished, Lady Overbury thought the view down to Bath was enchanting and she happily sat down on a seat in an arbour to gaze upon it. She fully understood why the architect had encouraged Ralph Allen to build his mansion on one of the natural terraces surrounding the city.

Scarcely had she been there for a few moments when she saw two women walking in the nearby avenue of newly planted trees. One was a very young woman with an air of innocence and vulnerability. Her long neck and luxuriant black hair set off a face worthy of an angel – a fine forehead, a well-shaped nose, lily-white oval cheeks, and a rich-lipped mouth with beautiful ivory teeth. Her black eyes had a lustre that captivated the onlooker. Her shape was not only exactly proportioned but also extremely delicate and, whenever she spoke, her hands fluttered with every nuance and expression. She bore herself with that natural gentility that stems from having received a good upbringing, but there was an air of misery in her manner. Whatever problems she faced, Lady Overbury doubted not that her character was as sweet as her appearance. The older woman was much taller – almost six feet in height – and a far more dominating figure. By her dress and deportment it was obvious that she was used to moving in the highest social circles. However, there was a harsh look to her eyes and many of the wrinkles on her face were a product of a tendency to grimace and scowl at anyone who incurred her displeasure.

Unbeknown to Lady Overbury she was looking on Miss Sophia Westbrook, the young woman who had so captured Tom Jones's heart, and her aunt, the formidable Lady Crowthorpe. The latter was the perfect mistress of all high society's manners, customs, ceremonies, and fashions, and, although she had never in her life flirted with a man, she knew how to instantly recognize that activity in others. She noticed at once when a lady sought to give encouragement or conceal liking. No species of affectation or disguise escaped her attention. As a consequence she was under no illusion about her niece. She knew that, whatever Sophia might be saying to the contrary, she was hopelessly in love with Tom Jones. This distressed her greatly and the scowls she directed in Sophia's direction bore testimony to that. She was determined to squash her niece's unwelcome passion.

Unaware of Lady Overbury's presence, the two women began talking freely with each other and the first sentences of their conversation immediately betrayed who they were to the hidden listener. 'My father wishes me to marry Mr Burnett,' said the younger of the two in a voice that was soft and cultured. 'He has told me that he has proposed the match to Squire Woodforde and that they will be seeing Mr Burnett shortly. Dearest Aunt, can you not prevent this? I know Mr Burnett is heir to a great estate but the man is such a sanctimonious bore!'

'I will not be lied to or thought a fool. What you mean by that, Sophia, is that he is not as attractive to you as Mr Jones. Is it possible that you are still thinking of disgracing this family by seeking to ally yourself to a bastard? Can the blood of the Westbrooks submit to such contamination? Your pride in our family should have prevented you from giving the slightest encouragement to so base an affection! Mr Burnett is a far better match for you.'

'Mr Burnett is not agreeable to me and I hope that you and my father will not make me the most wretched person by insisting that I marry him against my inclinations.'

'Inclinations! How can a young unmarried woman talk of inclinations when we are resolved that you will marry him and nothing that you can say or do can prevent it? Indeed, if your father has his way, there will not be a moment's delay in announcing the engagement and fixing the day for the wedding.'

'Surely you will give me time to get used to the idea and to overcome my current disinclination to this person,' pleaded her niece with a note of increasing emotional intensity in her voice.

Lady Crowthorpe's scowl deepened. 'Why should we give you time? You have already shown that you are a foolish young woman by entertaining an unworthy alliance with an amorous coxcomb. Young girls never know what their best interests are and you are as wild and wanton as a colt on a common. I put the blame for your monstrous infatuation entirely on Squire Woodforde for breeding up a bastard to be like a gentleman. When a princess of France is married to a prince of Spain the arrangement is a match not between two persons but between two kingdoms. This is a match between the Woodfordes and the Westbrooks and that is what matters.'

'Can you be so unmoved? Will you kill me by condemning me to a loveless marriage?'

'Pooh! What nonsense! Kill you indeed! Marriage will not kill you.'

'Such a marriage is worse than death,' wailed her niece. 'It will make me become a burden to my friends and a torment to myself. It is not that I am indifferent to Mr Burnett. I hate him.'

The corners of Lady Crowthorpe's mouth pulled down as she clenched her teeth with rage. 'Spare me such commonplace cant!' she stormed. 'It is impossible for you to hate a man from whom you have received no injury. I am as resolved as your father on this match. He will rightly cut you off from the family without a penny if you persist in this nonsense. Believe me, child, I know about these things and you should obey your father. Romance is not fashionable. This city is full of wives who dislike their husbands and who lead very comfortable and genteel lives.' Her eyes flashed angrily at Sophia. 'Let me hear no more about your foolish feelings. Think only of what matters to your family.'

Her niece refused to be cowed. 'I hope that I shall never do anything to dishonour my family but my family's opinion on this matter cannot make me love Mr Burnett. Marrying him would be like turning vice into a virtue. Whatever the consequences, I am resolved against him and no force or threat can prevail in his favour.'

Lady Crowthorpe inhaled sharply. 'Impertinent hussy! I think you will find that you will have to do as we say. And there's no point pining for Mr Jones. He's headed for the colonies and I expect he'll be dead within a few months of his arrival there.'

This stark image plunged Sophia into floods of tears. Unfortunately this only served to further enrage her aunt. 'I'll hear no more of this. I am going back indoors. Rejoin me when you have composed yourself. Remember for once that you are a Westbrook!'

Lady Crowthorpe marched away. As soon as she was sure that the aunt was out of hearing, Lady Overbury emerged from the arbour in which she had been concealed and went to comfort the poor sobbing girl. Sophia Westbrook's embarrassment soon gave way to excitement when she discovered that Lady Overbury knew Tom Jones and had a high regard for him. It proved an easy task for the older woman to persuade the younger one to sit in the arbour with her and exchange stories about him. Lady Overbury told her all about the events that had happened since her arrival in Bath and Sophia took a pride in Lady Overbury's account of her lover's brave actions.

'I have known Tom and John since we were young children together because my father and Squire Woodforde are life-long friends. John was always a mean-spirited creature, prone to complain at the slightest excuse, whereas Tom was always a good-natured boy. I remember how on one occasion Tom sold a small horse that he had received as a present from the squire so that he could offer help to the gamekeeper's starving family. John got Tom into trouble with his uncle by making out that he had got rid of the horse for other reasons.'

'That hardly was the act of a friend,' commented Lady Overbury.

'Though the two boys were brought up together, there is no love between them,' replied Sophia in a tremulous voice. 'John used to encourage their schoolmaster to treat Tom very harshly. I think it was his way of getting revenge for nature having given Tom all the good looks that he lacked.'

Lady Overbury tutted. 'I am aware from my limited dealings with them which is the better man.'

Sophia grasped her hand affectionately at this implicit commendation of the man she loved. 'My affection for Tom took a deeper hold a couple of years ago following a riding accident whilst we were out hunting. My horse had a mettlesome spirit that required a more skilled rider and it began to prance and caper in such a manner that it threatened to throw me. Tom saw my predicament and rode to my rescue. He leapt from his horse and caught hold of my beast's bridle. However, my horse reared its back legs in such a manner that I was hurled from the saddle. Tom somehow managed to catch me in his arms and broke my fall with his own body. It was only when I saw that his left arm was dangling at his side that I realised he had broken his arm in saving me from a fall that would surely have crippled me for life. The combination of seeing his bravery and his uncomplaining suffering made me realize just what a fine young man he was. Until then I had let his poor birth deter me from making him an object of my love, but now I judged him a true gentleman, whatever his origins.'

'And what of his affair with the gamekeeper's daughter?' ventured Lady Overbury.

'I am sorry that you have heard about that wicked jade who seduced him. I am sure that he would not have been so importunate had not my father made clear that marriage with me was an impossibility.' She paused and tears formed in her eyes. 'I also think that I am partly to blame because I should have let Tom know how much I love him.'

'Having spoken with him I am sure that it is only you that he truly loves,' replied Lady Overbury.

Sophia smiled but her eyes remained dark with worry. 'So what should I do? You heard what my aunt said. My father will never accept Tom and I am to be forced into marriage with John Burnett. I am expected to abandon the handsomest, finest, most charming man in the world for a droning, moaning fool or face being disinherited.'

Lady Overbury smiled back reassuringly and, reaching out, gently placed both her hands around the poor girl's face. 'Miss Westbrook, no father in England could force me to marry against my wishes. What signifies your inheritance if it prevents you marrying the man you love?'

It was as if courage seemed to flow from Lady Overbury's fingertips. Sophia straightened her drooping shoulders and looked her straight in the eye. 'You are right! I'd rather starve to death with Tom than live in luxury with John Burnett!'

Hearing this brave response, Lady Overbury vowed then and there that she would do all she could to help her and immediately promised to convey to Tom Jones how much Sophia loved him.

'Please give him the hope that we might one day be together,' urged the young girl, blushing at her own temerity. 'My greatest fear is that he will go to America and then I will never see him again.' She fought to keep the panic from her voice at such a prospect, but she could not prevent her skin going hot and cold.

'I am sure that will not happen,' reassured Lady Overbury, seeking to console her.

Sophia looked miserable. 'You do not know my father. Once he has determined on a course of action, he will let nothing stand in his way.'

'Then take some advice from an older and more experienced handler of men. See your father this very night and tell him that he must not proceed with his intention of seeing Mr Burnett. Say that you have heard that he has been injured and cannot receive visitors or invent whatever tale you think will best sway him on this matter. Once he speaks to him I think your father's sense of honour would force him to proceed with your marriage, whatever you might subsequently say.'

'You are right, Lady Overbury, and I will heed your most welcome advice.'

'I am gratified that you find my opinion helpful and I wish you every success when you meet your father this evening.'

Sophia lent over and gave the older woman a kiss. 'I would gain further wisdom from you but my aunt will begin to suspect something if I do not soon join her.'

'Then when shall we be able to meet again?' responded Lady Overbury, whose heart was completely melted. 'I would like to hear the outcome of tonight's discussion and I am sure that Mr Jones will wish me to bring a message to you.'

Sophia thought for a moment and then observed, 'Lady Crowthorpe insists on me joining her every morning in the King's Bath. Could we possibly meet there tomorrow at seven o'clock?'

'I have not yet experienced the waters of Bath. You have given me an excellent reason for wishing to try them!'

The two women exchanged kisses and Sophia Westbrook then dashed off in the direction her aunt had taken. 'Well,' said Lady Overbury to herself, 'I may not have discovered anything more about Lord Kearsley but I think that I have news that will be most welcome to Mr Jones!'

6

A THIRD MURDER ATTEMPTED

The departure of Lady Overbury for Prior Park meant that she missed the promised return visit of Dr Cleland that afternoon to re-dress Burnett's head wound. It was therefore Tom Jones who showed him up to the bedroom where the injured man was still fast asleep. The doctor was none too gentle in roughly awakening him. 'Sir, you have woken me from the sweetest sleep that I have ever had in my life,' mumbled Burnett once he had gathered his senses.

The doctor looked at him sternly. 'Many a man has dozed his life away, sir. Sleep is not always good and your pulse is disordered. I think you may be developing a fever and I propose to prevent that by bleeding you.'

Though his strength had not yet fully returned, Burnett shook his head emphatically. 'Damn it, sir! I'll lose no more blood. I already feel far better and I have no doubt that I will soon be fully recovered without any further treatment.'

'I wish I could assure you that you will be well in a month or two, let alone a few days. In my experience people do not recover quickly from such contusions.'

'Doubtless they do not if you bleed what little blood they have left. I tell you I will not be bled!'

Dr Cleland looked at him coldly. 'Yours is not the action of a responsible man.' He turned to Tom Jones, who only just managed to hide his amusement. 'Young man, I think you will have to persuade your friend here to heed my advice. If he is not blooded, I fear he will die.'

Seeing how much better Burnett already looked, Jones thought this highly unlikely. 'I hope, Doctor Cleland, that you would not have me hold him down while you bleed him against his will,' he replied with a wry smile.

Seeing that Jones was no ally, the doctor turned back to his patient. 'I demand of you, sir, one last time – will you or will you not be blooded?'

'And I answer you for the last time. I will not.'

'Then I wash my hands of you and I desire you pay me for the trouble I have already had. Two journeys at five shillings each and a dressing at five shillings more, and half a crown for my advice.'

'I fear that I have not got such a sum to hand, sir, but Tom here will ensure that you are paid in full.'

Jones led the unhappy doctor back downstairs and gave him the money he had requested, although from past experience he doubted whether Burnett would repay him. While he was doing this the patient resolved to get up. Although his head still hurt, his injury had been more superficial than it had looked because wounds to the scalp often bleed profusely. He went upstairs to his room, unlocked his portmanteau, and took out fresh clothes to wear. Once he had donned these, Burnett went downstairs and asked Jones to arrange for Sarah Darr to bring him something to eat. 'Have her bring it to the drawing room because no fire has been lit in the dining room and it is cold,' he concluded.

Half an hour later the maid brought in a tray on which was a tankard of beer and a large plate of bread and cheese. Hungry though he was, Burnett could not help admiring her beauty once more. Though he had as yet no desire for marriage, he was not devoid of manly appetites and the prospect of embracing such a lovely woman in his arms was an attractive one. When she placed the tray on a small table by the side of the sofa and looked to leave immediately, he leaned forward, grabbed her by the arm, and tried to kiss her. 'Don't go away, Sarah. I am in need of some company,' he said in a tone that was intended to sound amorous.

'You are too forward, sir!' she gasped. 'Surely you would not seek to ruin my reputation?'

'Why don't you come and sit beside me?' he pleaded.

The maid pushed away his hands. 'Lady Overbury ordered me to stay by your bedside until I could be sure that it was safe to leave you unattended, so I have sat beside you for enough of the day already, sir.'

'Ah, is not fate cruel to tease a man so? That I should be in a bed for most of the day and you so close by and yet not in it with me!'

'I fear, sir, that the blow to your head has affected your judgement.

This is not the time nor place for any dalliance,' she replied stiffly, trying to repress the repulsion she felt for him lest he take offence and cause problems for her.

'Then I fear perhaps I am having a relapse,' he said, stifling his irritation at her response. 'I must return at once to your bedchamber so you can nurse me further. The touch of your gentle hand is required.'

'My hand is required elsewhere. This house is hopelessly understaffed,' the maid replied, pretending that she had not grasped his purpose.

Burnett continued to stare at her lecherously. 'I am sure that Lady Overbury will understand if you tell her that you have spent your time attending to my needs.'

Sarah Darr's face flushed with annoyance. 'I think, sir, that your needs are best met by eating what lies before you.'

'But you are a far more delicious morsel! How can you treat a man with spiteful indifference when he loves you to distraction?' he said in a patronising tone, trying to cup her oval face in his hands.

'What you say sounds more like lust than love to me, sir, and I would have expected better of a man who lays claim to being a gentleman. Surely you can see that I am no doxy to fall into your arms at your slightest whim.'

'Then let me at least give thee a kiss for thy modesty,' he demanded, grabbing her arms and pulling her roughly towards him. No one could have been more relieved than the maid when a knock at the main door of the house put an end to his toad-like embrace. 'Damn! You'd better go and see who it is,' he said, releasing her. She left to do as he bid, readjusting her bodice and pleased to be free of his vulgar attention. A few minutes later she was ushering into the drawing room two men, announcing as she did, 'Squire Thomas Woodforde and Mr George Westbrook are here to see you, sir.' This duty accomplished she made a welcome escape back to the kitchens.

Though now somewhat worn in years, Squire Woodforde had always taken care of himself and he was still a handsome and good-natured man with a fine open brow, a clear skin, gentle blue eyes, and teeth that were discoloured but still sound. His tall, lean figure and erect carriage set off his clothes very well, though they were not of the latest fashion. His affable nature and open and honest manner stood out in sharp contrast to the less personable and more pompous stance of his friend, who was a short, stocky, more muscular man with an unhealthily florid face and a preoccupied air. Though more richly dressed, Mr Westbrook presented a far less attractive image. His eyes were bloodshot, his nose was broad and flat, his cheeks were pockmarked, and his mouth overly large. Given his wealth and connections, there was no reason why he should not have been a most happy man, but his manner conveyed only discontent and anger with the world around him.

'Uncle! Mr Westbrook! To what do I owe this unexpected pleasure?' said Burnett, trying to disguise his annoyance at their untimely arrival.

'Henry Fielding told me you were here to protect Lady Overbury,' replied his uncle, 'but by your looks you are in need of protection yourself.'

'We had two intruders this morning and I was attacked.'

'I hope you did more harm to them then they did to you,' barked Westbrook.

Burnett blushed. 'I am afraid, sir, I was struck so hard that I was knocked unconscious and locked into a cupboard. None of us knows what happened next except that Tom Jones found one intruder dead and the other gone. I assume the villains fell out with each other.'

'I would prefer you not to mention that young man's name in my presence!' boomed out Sophia's father, grinding his teeth together like millstones. 'Mr Jones is a villain and libertine who seeks to make lewdness fashionable!'

'Is Lady Overbury safe?' asked Woodforde, ignoring his friend's explosion.

'Yes. I gather she is currently enjoying herself at Prior Park.'

'That is where we should be, but instead we have come here to talk to you about your forthcoming wedding.'

A wave of confusion passed over Burnett's face. 'Forgive me, Uncle, but I did not know that I was getting married.'

'Then I think the blow to your head has affected your intelligence,' barked Westbrook. 'You are aware that I have long wished to see my family linked to yours and today I am offering you the hand of my daughter Sophia.'

Burnett's pallid face turned even paler, but his desire not to offend his uncle made his reply a politic one. 'Matrimony is a subject on which I have spent little thought as yet, but I am not insensible to the honour offered me and I am happy to submit to your pleasure.'

This rather cold response did not please Woodforde. 'Damn it, sir! Is that all you can say? Miss Westbrook is wondrously beautiful and highly intelligent. What more could you want in a wife?'

'I fear Miss Westbrook has a predilection for Tom,' stuttered back his nephew.

'I told you not to mention that man's name in my presence again,' shouted her father, thumping the table with his fist. 'Are you a fool, sir? Parents are the proper judges of matches for their children. My daughter will marry whomever I choose for her and it will certainly not be that bastard Tom Jones. You would be mad to refuse her. She is pretty enough to please anyone and she brings with her the promise of a large fortune as I have no son. I should not have to remind you that most men would jump at the opportunity of marrying her.'

This exchange did little to reassure Woodforde, who was at heart a romantic. He therefore turned to his friend. 'George, you know that an alliance of our families would bring me much joy, but I do not wish to see both parties dragged into a loveless marriage against their will unless they can grow to love each other.'

Before Westbrook could respond Burnett muttered weakly, 'I am sure that I could learn to love Sophia if it's what you want.'

This pathetic reply caused Tom Jones to burst into the room. Sarah Darr had informed him of who had arrived and he had been hovering outside the room listening with mounting horror to the conversation within. 'I love her already with a passion that knows no bounds!' he exclaimed.

'Damn your impertinence,' snarled Westbrook. 'Come closer and no one will prevent me licking thee as well as ever thou wast licked in thy life. Wretch that you are, you have tried to seduce my daughter with your good looks and your fancy manners, but I know thou art just a bastard, and I tell you I will see you hanged if you dare try to contact her again. Consort with your wanton hussies and be damned, but leave my daughter alone.'

'Sir, whatever abuse you heap on me, I will not be provoked or lift my hand against you,' replied the distraught Jones. 'I respect you as her father.'

'Respect me! I need no respect from filth like you,' roared Westbrook, his face livid with rage.

Fearing that his friend might resort to violence, Woodforde appealed to his former protégé's common sense. 'Tom, you behold how angry your presence makes Mr Westbrook. Do not tarry here longer. His anger is too inflamed for you to hold any sensible conversation. It is far better that you should leave the room. We will speak later of what you wish to say and, if I feel it is appropriate, I will convey your message.'

'I'll heed no message from him whoever chooses to deliver it!'

retaliated Sophia's father.

Jones did as his uncle requested and then fled from the house in a paroxysm of grief and despair. Once he had gone the two older men reopened the purpose of their visit with Burnett. Thus in Jones's absence, the marriage of John Burnett and Sophia Westbrook was formally agreed. The Squire and Westbrook then took their leave, the former not entirely sure that he had done the right thing and the latter entirely happy to have the issue resolved according to his wishes.

This was the state of affairs when Lady Overbury and Henry Fielding returned from their visit to Prior Park at dusk. They told Burnett that it had been an entertaining experience but not one that had added to their knowledge of Lord Kearsley's activities. In reply he told them not only of his forthcoming wedding but also of Tom Jones's disappearance from the house.

'The lad had no right to desert his post!' cried Fielding. 'I thought better of him!'

'I am sure he will return once he has composed himself,' retorted Lady Overbury, trying to appear unconcerned whilst mentally reeling at the news of what had happened. What was she to do now? Should she tell Tom Jones, once he had returned, of her meeting with Sophia Westbrook and convey the poor girl's love for him? Or was it better to let him live in ignorance that his passion was returned? Poor Sophia! Lady Overbury dreaded to think what would happen when Sophia broached the subject of her feelings with her father that evening.

'I will stay here until Tom Jones returns,' pronounced Fielding. 'I cannot leave you alone in this house with just John Burnett to protect you. You only have to look at him to see that he is not yet recovered from the injury he sustained this morning.'

'As ever, you are too kind, sir,' said Lady Overbury, gratefully seizing his hand.

He turned to Burnett. 'I suggest, John, that you go downstairs to the kitchen and eat your supper, which I see you have not yet consumed. If you feel up to it, stay on guard. If not, ensure all doors are securely locked and go back up to your room to rest. I will call you if I need you.'

'Ask Darr to bring us a cup of tea,' added Lady Overbury.

Burnett did as he was bid. Shortly afterwards, the maid arrived with the requested tea on a tray and, placing it on top of a small walnut table, she carefully poured them each a cup.

'Now go and make sure that Mr Burnett does not overtax himself,' commented Lady Overbury.

'I can assure you that I have no intention of letting Mr Burnett exert himself,' her maid replied, thinking of his horrid approaches to her earlier in the day.

'While we are waiting for Tom Jones to return, why don't we try and make more sense of the events of the past two days, Lady Overbury?' ventured Fielding once Darr had departed.

'A good idea, sir. However, I beg you to begin the process because I confess it has been a long day and your mind is sharper than mine.'

Fielding sat back in his chair, paused a moment to collect his thoughts, and then began expressing his views in a very measured way. 'We know more than half-a-dozen things for certain. First, that Miss Grey reported seeing a man hanging around the house and that a week ago she feared that he might be an intruder. Second, that Joseph Graves stayed overnight and also heard noises but attributed them to a ghostly rather than a human origin. Third, that Miss Grey refused to be intimidated into leaving the house on the day before you arrived. Fourth, that the man who attacked her lacked a thumb on his right hand and so was definitely not Lord Kearsley.'

'And it is possible this four-fingered man was the person who murdered Lord Kearsley.'

'It's possible, Lady Overbury, but let us stick to what we know before we enter into any surmises.' She nodded in agreement and he recommenced his list. 'Fifth, we know that you saw a man hanging around the house on the evening of your arrival, but we cannot be sure if this has any connection with the murders. Sixth, we know that there has never been any sign of a break-in and so it is probably safe to assume those responsible for what has happened possess a set of keys to the house. If you recall, Joseph Graves said that doors he had locked at night were sometimes open in the morning.'

'A careless intruder, then!'

'Or one who when disturbed did not have time to relock doors. But we are straying from the facts. Seventh, we know that we are dealing with more than one intruder because of Lord Kearsley's murder and, eighth, we know that Lord Kearsley was engaged in treasonable activities.'

'We also know that a button from his coat was found clasped in Miss Grey's hand.'

'But that button could have been planted.'

Lady Overbury nodded her assent. 'So what are the possible solutions?' she said, hoping that Fielding might be able to shed some light on the issues that she found totally inexplicable.

'One possibility is that Lord Kearsley thought the housekeeper was about to betray him and so he killed her, but that would not explain why he returned this morning or why he was killed.'

'Nor does it explain the presence of the man with the missing thumb.'

'Agreed. So another possibility is that Miss Grey was helping Lord Kearsley with his work for the Jacobite cause and that both were killed by someone loyal to the crown.'

'But why should that person resort to murder? He could simply have reported what they were doing to the authorities and had them arrested.'

Fielding could not help but admire the clarity of Lady Overbury's thinking. 'Agreed,' he replied. 'That is why I think a third possibility is the most likely.'

'And what is that?'

'There is something in this house that people want. That would explain why there was an attempt to frighten off Miss Grey. That would explain the noises over a succession of nights.'

'And if Miss Grey came upon the intruder that would explain her murder.'

'Yes. What it does not answer is who was doing the searching. Was it Lord Kearsley, or the man who killed Lord Kearsley? Or were both of them rivals for possession of what lies hidden in this house?'

Lady Overbury's eyes lit up with excitement. 'I think you have hit on something and, if you are right, there is every reason for not leaving this house until we find what has been so assiduously sought!'

Fielding winced that Lady Overbury's courage should be so much greater than her common sense. 'If I am right, then there is every reason for your ladyship not staying in this house another night. Unless the hidden object has been taken by Lord Kearsley's murderer, whoever stays in this house remains in danger. The intruder is likely to strike again.'

Lady Overbury had always hated being instructed. It was the main reason why she had chosen never to marry. The thought of having always to obey whatever a husband wished held no attraction for her. She struggled to retain her composure and answered very coldly, 'You know my view on this matter, Mr Fielding. I will not be driven out!'

'I am not going to argue with you at the moment, but I will say that it is unfair to put others at risk – not just John Burnett, who has already been injured, and Tom Jones, but also your maid and the temporary housekeeper that I have now found.'

'You may be right, sir, but surely Mr Nash can provide more men to protect all of us?'

'If he does, then the intruder will not return and we will never get to the bottom of this mystery.'

Lady Overbury saw the sense in his words and for a moment her desire to stay in the house wavered, but then a simple idea occurred to her. 'Not if we can find what was being sought. Tomorrow let us all search this house from top to bottom, using as many men as Mr Nash can provide.'

Fielding once again found himself admiring her. 'On that we can agree, Lady Overbury,' he said with a smile. 'So let us turn to lighter matters while we wait for Mr Jones to return. How about a game of cards?'

'I can think of no better way to while away the time,' she replied instantly.

At first the cards proved a welcome distraction but, as the evening drew on, both of them paid increasingly less attention to what they held in their hands. Though neither spoke of their mounting concern, both began to fear that something had happened to Tom Jones. Whatever the extent of his grief, each felt it was unthinkable that he would completely desert his duty. It was almost nine o'clock when their long wait was broken by the sound of a loud insistent knocking at the main door. 'I'll give the lad a piece of my mind for staying out so late!' muttered Fielding, feeling a mix of relief and anger that the missing man had finally returned.

They heard the sound of someone opening the door, but this was followed by a babble of voices. Fielding rushed out, fearing the house might be under attack. Burnett was standing in the open doorway. Outside in the street stood two soldiers carrying a litter on which lay a badly injured Tom Jones. He had obviously been subjected to some terrible ordeal because he was badly bruised and bleeding heavily and he was wearing the strangest of clothes. 'Don't just stand there! Bring him in!' commanded Fielding, pushing aside Burnett, who appeared to have been rooted to the spot at seeing Jones's condition. 'Take him upstairs, John. See to it that these men place him on the bed that you used this morning. Then go and fetch a doctor – preferably not the one who attended to you. Once you have done that, seek out Mr Nash. I don't care what he is doing, get him to come here at once!' He turned to Lady Overbury, who had turned white at seeing the extent of Jones's injuries. 'I will need to ask these soldiers what has happened once they have taken Tom upstairs. Can you and your maid or the new housekeeper tend to him until the doctor comes?'

She nodded and followed the soldiers as they carried the stretcher up the main staircase. The men were as gentle as they could be because none knew the extent of Jones's injuries. He appeared to be covered with cuts and bruises and some of the weird clothes in which he was covered were scorched. Lady Overbury clutched her hands together, her heart beating furiously. 'Heaven help us! What on earth has happened to you?' she exclaimed.

Jones reached out feebly and she grasped his hand. 'I know I should not have left the house, your ladyship. Please forgive me.'

'Never mind that. Mr Burnett has told us the cause. Tell me who has done this to you. Surely not Mr Westbrook?'

Even in his injured state Jones could not help smiling at such an idea. 'No, though he would not be sorry to see me in this state. When I left here my mind was in a whirl and I ran mindlessly, not caring where I went. I know not what I did but when I came to my senses I found myself outside the inn known as The Rising Star. I decided to drown my sorrows with a drink and entered. Inside I found the landlord serving beer to a large number of soldiers. Their sergeant informed me that their regiment was due to march against the rebels and that they hoped they would be commanded by the glorious Duke of Cumberland. I responded by wishing them well and urging all present to drink for the cause of liberty and the Protestant faith. I shouted out, "God save King George!" and the words were taken up on all sides. Then a man asked me to enlist in their company so I could play a part in safeguarding the throne. He said that the regiment would be only too glad to welcome such a gentleman as me. When I told him that I was already committed to protecting your ladyship it evoked much mirth among the soldiers because they mistook my meaning.'

'In what way?'

He blushed. 'They thought that you were paying me to be your lover.'

Lady Overbury gasped. 'Damn their impudence!' she raged.

Jones felt her embarrassment more keenly than his injuries and swiftly tried to reassure her. 'They asked me to drink a toast to my lady love's health, and I agreed, but it was Miss Westbrook's name that I shouted out, not yours.'

'You should not have shouted out any name!' chastised Lady Overbury. 'If Squire Woodforde hears what you have done, he will cut you off without a penny.'

'I knew it was wrong of me, but I could not help saying it.'

If Lady Overbury had any doubt about how much the young man loved Sophia, it disappeared at that moment. 'What happened next?' she asked.

'One of the soldiers said that he knew one Sophy Westbrook who had lain with half the young fellows of Bath and that it must be the same woman. I assured him that it was not and that the Miss Westbrook I knew was a lady of great virtue. To this he replied that half the regiment had enjoyed her favours. At this I told him he was a damned liar, whereupon he discharged a bottle full on my head, hitting me above the right temple and bringing me instantly to the floor. I think he would have done more damage had not a lieutenant intervened. I staggered outside and headed back here, but I had not gone far when the man who had hit me blocked my path and struck me unconscious.'

Lady Overbury saw how much the conversation was exhausting him and urged him to rest, but at that moment Henry Fielding appeared. 'I think you had better hear the entire story from him. If what the soldiers below tell me is true, the poor lad is lucky to be alive.'

'I'd rather wait than subject him to an interrogation,' she demurred.

Tom Jones squeezed her hand and croaked, 'No, let me tell you. Then I shall sleep better.'

'Very well, if that is what you want.'

His eyes hooded over as if to hide his pain, but he could not disguise how distressing the events had been. 'I heard a cacophony of sound all around me when I regained my senses but I found that I could neither move nor see properly. At first in my dazed state I could not understand why. Then I realized that someone had placed a stinking mask over my face. Looking through small slits that had been made in the material I saw a sea of people. They were all laughing and shouting and screaming. At first I could not make out what they were saying. It was as if my sense of hearing had not yet properly recovered from the blow to my head. Then suddenly the words became clear. They were chanting "Remember, remember the fifth of November, gunpowder, treason and plot!" I recalled it was Guy Fawkes' Day and that a huge bonfire had been built to mark the occasion.'

He paused and Lady Overbury felt a tightening in her stomach at what he might say next. 'A few of the crowd struck at me with sticks and I tried to shout out, but I could not,' he continued, obviously only keeping the terror out of his voice with difficulty. 'I suddenly realized that my mouth was taped. I struggled to escape but found that I could scarce move at all. My forehead and neck and body and legs had been bound to some kind of pole behind my back whilst my arms had been stretched out and strapped to some kind of crossbar. I was like some crucified man. Then I felt my whole body being moved and I saw people and buildings pass by. I knew I was on some kind of cart because I could feel the vehicle shake and hear the rattle of its wheels as it crossed the cobbles. The crowd roared as I passed and many began to throw objects at me. It was then I knew what I had been turned into and I tried to scream – oh, how I tried to scream – for help!'

'It's all right, Tom. I know. The soldiers just told me. You don't have to say more,' said Fielding, intervening gently. 'You were inside the costume that had been made for the Guy Fawkes effigy that was to be burnt.'

'My God!' exclaimed Lady Overbury. For a moment she thought that she was going to faint, but her determination not to cause Jones any further upset helped her recover. She dug her fingers into the palms of her hands and bit her lip as she awaited what would be said next.

Fielding's face was grim. 'He was pulled through the streets on the cart. The crowd subjected the dummy to all that you would expect. They spat at it, hit it with sticks, hurled stones at it. That is why Tom is so injured. He would be in a far worse state had not the costume been a padded one.'

Tears fell from Lady Overbury's pain-ridden face and dropped onto the victim of this outrage. 'That was not the worst, your ladyship,' the wounded man whispered. 'It was not just the helplessness of my position, it was the hatred that surrounded me. All the natural prejudice against Papists had been multiplied by drink into a frenzy of intolerance. I shut my eyes and prayed repeatedly to God to forgive me for all my sins. Eventually the cart stopped and I realized that I had been brought to my final destination. Some soldiers grasped hold of me and I felt the poles on which I was tied being lifted up. They took what they thought was a stuffed guy and stuck it at the top of the bonfire pile. I could see the flaming brands waiting to ignite it. The crowd roared their approval. Shouts of "Down with all papists!" filled the air. Desperately I struggled to make some movement that would show them I was no dummy but I was bound too tightly. My murderer had done his work too well.'

Once again the horror of his situation struck home and Tom Jones could say no more. He fell back wearily and Fielding took over his tale. 'The lad may not have shown the crowd that there was a man within, but his struggles did make the guy slip slightly from its central position as the bonfire was lit. A soldier was sufficiently stupid to clamber up the pile before the flames began to take hold of it in order to correct this. As he grasped the guy to reposition it he happened to look directly into its face and, to his amazement, he saw human eyes staring back at him through the slits of the hood.'

'I owe my life to him,' groaned Jones. 'A lesser man might simply have fled in horror but he yanked off the mask from my face and then threw me down the side of the bonfire, even as the flames began to lick at us both. The last thing I can recall before I fainted was him shouting out, "There is a man trapped within!"'

'Listen to me, Tom,' said Henry Fielding in a voice that shook with emotion. 'I vow that I will never ever rest until I have found who was responsible for this outrage!'

What more might have been said was lost because at that moment Sarah Darr arrived escorting a doctor. 'Mr Nash is below and asks if you will join him whilst the doctor attends to Mr Jones,' she announced.

Lady Overbury leant over Jones and whispered into his ear so that only he could hear what she said. 'Tom, I saw Sophia today. She is determined not to marry Mr Burnett because she loves you as much as you love her. She wanted me to tell you this. A battle may have been lost today in your struggle to win her, but the war is not over. Remember the old adage that while there is life there is hope.' Tom Jones smiled and some of the strain etched on his features visibly began to fade.

'What did you say to him?' asked Fielding, noting the remarkable change in his manner.

'Only words of encouragement,' she replied. 'Come, let us go and see Mr Nash.'

When they entered the drawing room they found both Burnett and Nash awaiting them. The latter rushed to greet them. 'You don't need to tell me. The news of what happened at the bonfire was brought to me. The poor lad has had the narrowest of escapes. If any man can ensure young Mr Jones makes a full recovery, it is Dr Oliver whom I have brought with me.'

'Who could possibly want to do this to him?' queried Lady Overbury, who was still deeply shocked by the whole affair.

'Well, it's obvious that Mr Jones was targeted from the outset. He must have been followed when he left here. The fight in the tavern was engineered and I suspect he would have been killed then and there had the lieutenant not intervened. As it was, the man followed him to finish the task. Heaven knows what led him to choose such a vicious way of achieving an assassination. Take heart that his cruel action will now ensure his arrest because we know who finished creating the guy – it was a soldier called Humphrey Watson. By escaping what was intended for him Tom Jones has sealed the man's doom. It is only a matter of time before we capture this Watson and find out what lies behind all this train of murderous events. Until then I have ordered that this house will be under constant surveillance. Whatever else you may do, Lady Overbury, you can sleep soundly tonight in the knowledge that you are entirely safe.'

7

DEAD IN THE WATER

The next morning Lady Overbury rose early so that she could go to the King's Bath and meet Sophia Westbrook. On her way back from Prior Park the previous day she had told Henry Fielding of her desire to bathe and he had been most helpful. They had stopped to purchase an appropriate bathing costume and he had made arrangements for her to be collected from the house by sedan chair. In her own mind Lady Overbury could not help feeling that she looked slightly ridiculous as she stared at herself in the mirror. The brown linen jacket and petticoats that she had purchased were far from flattering and she felt they looked even worse when she donned the chip hat that was designed to hold some handkerchiefs. It was no wonder that ladies hid themselves from public view by journeying under cover and when it was scarcely yet light.

When she emerged from the house she was rather taken aback by the vehicle that was to take her. It looked much like a black coffin and the thought of being enclosed within it was very unappealing. However, the biting cold of the early morning made her enter it speedily. Once inside she was disconcerted to find that its interior stank because the lining had been repeatedly impregnated with moisture from the wet clothes of previous occupants. How could the gouty and rheumatic possibly benefit from exposing themselves to such a horrible form of transport? Had she not faithfully promised to meet Sophia she would have immediately returned to the house and the comfort of her bed. As it was she said a prayer that she would not catch her death of cold and instructed the two chairmen to take her to the King's Bath as quickly as possible.

'Do not worry, yer ladyship,' said the older of the two men, smiling and exposing a mouth in which there was only the stump of one blackened tooth left. 'You'll be hoisted down into the water just as safe and as snug as a snail in his shell and, when you are done and your pores are all open, we'll bring you back before the cold morning air can nip you.'

This imagery and the jolting she sustained during the journey did little to calm Lady Overbury's mounting nerves. Her only comfort was that she had instructed her maid to follow the sedan chair so that she could have her assistance. Once she reached her destination there appeared to be chairs unloading and people shouting everywhere. Nevertheless with surprising speed Lady Overbury found herself being carried down a narrow and dark passage to a dungeon-like dressing room, where the only furniture was a rush-bottomed chair. A serving woman greeted her and, having given her some bath-cloths, asked whether she also wished to pay for her maid to bathe with her. Lady Overbury indicated that she did and the woman gave Sarah Darr some clothes into which she changed as quickly as her modesty permitted. The two women were then taken into the bathing area and attendants helped lower them up to their necks in the hot steaming water.

Lady Overbury discovered to her relief that her strange bathing costume did not expose her shape by clinging to her body but instead floated around her. The warmth of the water was initially welcome after the cold journey, but soon Lady Overbury started to perspire freely. Looking around her she saw a sea of equally flushed faces and noticed that the male bathers wore drawers and waistcoats made of the same canvas material as her costume. She could not help thinking that she and all the other bathers looked rather like ancient yellow water lilies that had seen better days and were long past their prime. However, of greater concern to her than everyone's ludicrous appearance was witnessing the ulcers, sores, and rashes that seemed to abound all around her. She wondered what terrible contamination she and her maid might be risking.

Her mind was taken off this alarming prospect by the sound of crude shouting coming from above her. To her consternation she discovered that the King's Bath had no roof. Looking down upon those in the water from the galleries and surrounding houses was considered one of Bath's delights. The shouts stemmed from some male bystanders who were keen to draw attention to Sarah Darr whose youth and beauty was at odds with the aged and ugly visages of most of the bathers. The saucy comments continued until two bath attendants drove them away.

Most of the bathers appeared unconcerned. They were too engrossed in gossiping to all and sundry. The shedding of their clothes seemed to have freed them from the social conventions that normally dictated to whom one could or could not speak. Lady Overbury exchanged pleasantries with those bathers nearest to her, but, as far as she was concerned, the sound of the orchestra striking up came as a welcome relief to the scurrilous gossip and lewd innuendoes that seemed to form the bulk of their conversation.

The musicians began playing a movement from a symphony. She recognized its main tune although she could not recall its composer. Once this was over they started performing the music to Purcell's popular song 'When I am laid in earth'. Seeing the decrepitude of so many of the bathers Lady Overbury could not help but feel the choice of song was particularly apt. She was relieved when, shortly after seven o'clock, she saw Lady Crowthorpe and Sophia Westbrook arrive. The latter spotted her immediately and engineered it so that she and her aunt entered the water relatively nearby. Once her aunt was deeply engaged in talking to other bathers, Sophia moved across to Lady Overbury, who, not wishing their conversation to be overheard by her maid, told Darr to go and occupy herself for a time in talking to whom she pleased. Her maid seemed more than happy to do as she was bid.

Sophia grasped Lady Overbury's hand and whispered so that no other person could hear, 'I am so very pleased to see you. I feared that you might not come.'

'I always keep my word, Miss Westbrook.'

'Please call me Sophia.'

Lady Overbury smiled. 'As you wish, my dear.'

'I am afraid that your plan that I should speak to my father before there was any formal marriage agreement came too late. When I returned from Prior Park to our lodgings here in Bath I discovered that he and Squire Woodforde had been that very afternoon to your house to tell Mr Burnett to marry me. My father says that he will have me locked away in Bedlam if I object any further to the match. Oh Lady Overbury, what shall I do? I have no one to whom I can turn.'

'Calm yourself, Sophia. The marriage will not take place immediately and you can count on my assistance to help see it never does. Together we will find a way to change your father's mind.'

'You do not know my father, Lady Overbury. Once he has an idea in his head it is almost impossible to dislodge it.'

'We will see about that, but for now I must share with you some other bad news and I must ask you to be very brave.'

The poor young woman felt a sudden chill run through her body despite all the hot water in which she bathed. 'Please don't tell me that Tom has already left for America!' she said, her voice barely a whisper.

'No, it's not that your Mr Jones has gone anywhere,' reassured Lady Overbury. She hesitated, not sure how to break the news of what had happened. 'He is fine now but he's been injured.' Again she paused to find the right words. 'I regret to inform you that someone tried to murder him last night.' Sophia Westbrook's face went a deathly white and for a moment it looked as if she might faint, but she proved of stronger stock. Anxious to get the whole story told, Lady Overbury proceeded to outline the events of the previous evening whilst trying to minimize the extent of Tom's injuries. Sophia listened intently, her face showing all her horror at what she was being told.

'I must go to him at once!' she cried when Lady Overbury had finished.

'No, Sophia, I believe that would be very unwise. Mr Burnett would have no hesitation in informing your father and that would lead to measures being taken to prevent you ever seeing Tom again. Rest assured that I have told your sweetheart how much you love him and I am confident that the knowledge of that will make him recover quickly. So I beg you to be patient in this matter. I will keep you informed of his progress and, if I discern a time when you can see him without others knowing, I will let you know.' She paused to let another bather pass them by and then reached out kindly to her distressed friend. 'Be comforted. I will use Tom's injuries to help your cause by encouraging Squire Woodforde to visit him. I am sure that if he sees the poor boy's sad condition it will reignite his former fondness. I will then try and persuade him to abandon the idea of a marriage between you and his nephew so that you can marry Tom instead.'

'Bless you, Lady Overbury,' sobbed the grateful young girl.

The older woman bit her lip to prevent showing how moved she was and then said gently, 'I know this wretched water is hot but there is really no point trying to cool it down with your tears, is there? Now go back before Lady Crowthorpe notices your absence. I will have to think of some way that we can keep in touch that does not involve us being boiled alive.'

As Sophia Westbrook made her way back towards Lady Crowthorpe, the orchestra began playing a popular tune by Arne written for Shakespeare's song 'Blow, blow, thou winter wind'. Lady Overbury reflected on the phrase in the song that ran *most friendship is feigning, most loving mere folly*. There was nothing feigned about her affection for both Tom and Sophia and she did not view their love for one another as mere folly. 'Damn it,' she said to herself, 'I'll see these two young people wed even if it means that I have to be shrivelled up by these infernal waters every day for a month!' She looked out to summon her maid and was surprised to find that she could not see Darr anywhere near her. 'Damn that girl! Where can she have gone?'

Even as she said this, a voice rang out, 'My God, there's a man bleeding to death here!' Lady Overbury looked across and saw that the water round the ornamental marble pump in the centre of the King's Bath was turning pink. An instant hush had fallen upon the scene but it was soon broken by a woman shrieking as she pointed to where the bloody water had begun staining her bathing clothes. Within seconds there was chaos with some bathers trying to get out of the water as quickly as they could and others trying to make their way to the man's aid. Lady Overbury suddenly became aware of Sarah Darr behind her. 'This way, your ladyship,' she said, sounding concerned. 'This is no place for us.' The maid quickly assisted her to clamber onto a stone shelf and both women then watched grimly as attendants lifted the man's body out of the water. They heard a voice say 'He's been murdered! Stabbed to death!' For once her maid's tendency to go to pieces in a crisis did not display itself. She organized their departure from the King's Bath with quick efficiency. No one dared stop any of the bathers leaving because detaining people dressed only in bathing clothes would have rapidly added to the death toll in the chill November air.

Once back inside the house in Queen Square and dressed, Lady Overbury tried to forget what had happened. As far as she was concerned investigating two corpses was sufficient without adding a third. When she entered the drawing room she found that Henry Fielding had left her a brief note. She opened it and read:

The new housekeeper will arrive this afternoon. Her name is Mrs Fleeting and she comes with excellent references. I have told her as much as she needs to know. I also arranged for Dr Oliver to see Mr Jones again this morning. You will be pleased to hear that the doctor has decided his injuries are ugly to look at but essentially superficial. He therefore thinks Mr Jones will be well enough to resume his duties within three or four days at most, although he is likely to be sore in some places for a week or so.

Lady Overbury was delighted by the news but it made her aware that she would need to get Squire Woodforde to visit the injured youth whilst all his wounds still looked at their worst. With that in mind she went back upstairs to her bedroom to write him a letter. Unknown to her, her plan was already being undermined as she wrote it. Lady Crowthorpe had also left the King's Bath quickly that morning and she had spent most of the time since then giving full vent to her feelings over what had happened to her brother. She had harangued him with a very dramatic and exaggerated version of her experiences and then tried his patience with an overly long invective against the incompetence of the attendants in permitting anyone to smuggle in a weapon. At the very moment that Lady Overbury was putting pen to paper, Lady Crowthorpe was also telling Westbrook about the incident that had happened the previous evening and how it showed that the authorities were losing their grip.

'I was reliably told this morning by fellow bathers that a man was almost burnt to death last night. Apparently the Guy Fawkes dummy had a real man hidden within it. He was literally pulled out of the flames at the last minute!' Lady Crowthorne paused to picture the scene, relishing in her mind the potential horror of what might have happened.

Her niece tried not to show how much this story affected her and feigned surprise.

'I am sure it was no more than a prank that got out of hand,' ventured Westbrook. 'He was probably a soldier who had had too much to drink. That would explain why he failed to get out of the costume earlier.'

'According to what I have been told he had been bound hand and foot and his mouth had been taped to prevent him shouting out.'

'Doubtless the work of equally drunken comrades! The sooner these soldiers leave and head off to fight those damned Jacobites the better.'

Sophia had intended to stay quiet during this further exchange but she simply could not suppress her feelings when she heard details of her lover's sufferings that Lady Overbury had chosen not to tell her. As a consequence she found herself blurting out in a distressed tone, 'The injured man was not a soldier and he was not drunk. It was Mr Jones and someone tried to cruelly kill him!'

'Zounds! Did I not say that I never wanted to hear that coxcomb's name mentioned again in this house!' yelled back her father, glaring at her. 'If it was him, I wish he had been burnt! The world would be well rid of such a scoundrel!'

'Father, how can you say such a thing?'

'How have you acquired this information?' stormed her father and she could hear the distrust in his voice. 'Have you been keeping in contact with this man despite my command to the contrary? If you have, I swear that I will disinherit you and have you locked away in an asylum. There you can live on bread and water.'

Sophia was unwilling to lie and yet equally unwilling to reveal Lady Overbury as her source. She tried to diffuse his anger by saying a partial truth. 'I heard his name mentioned whilst we were bathing.'

'Then let that be an end of the matter!' he interjected. 'I want no more said about this Mr Jones from either of you.'

'There is no need to take that tone with me, Brother!' snapped Lady Crowthorpe, rolling her eyes at him. 'You have a roughness in your manner that no woman should have to bear. I shall go to my room until you are in a calmer frame of mind.'

Sophia waited until her aunt had departed before ignoring her father's command by daring to continue the subject. 'Father, I have known Mr Jones since we were children. May I not go and see him and convey our condolences and sympathies now that he has been so cruelly abused?'

'Have you not heard what I said?' Westbrook shouted. 'I have no sympathy whatever for that infamous lad. Whatever burns he has suffered are just a foretaste of the agonizing pain that he will endure when he faces the fires of hell. And make no mistake – that will be his destiny!'

His daughter reeled under the savagery of his words. 'We cannot be in Bath and ignore what has happened to him! What would Squire Woodforde think?'

'Then we will not stay a day longer here. I will order our servants to pack at once. We will return home this afternoon and there you can prepare for your forthcoming wedding to Mr Burnett. I intend to get a licence as quick as I can.' Westbrook began furiously ringing the bell to summon his manservant. 'Go and tell your aunt that I want you both ready to leave the city by midday so we can be home before it gets too dark.'

The poor girl saw that there was no point trying to argue with her father in the mood that he was in, but she thought his cruel words were abhorrent. Why should she accept his command that she should not see Tom? Why should she let him force her into an unhappy marriage with John Burnett? Why should she and Tom not marry, even if it meant they were penniless? Poverty with a man she loved was infinitely preferable to riches with a man she despised and loathed! A weight seemed to drop off her shoulders as she determined that, whatever the cost, she would run away rather than obey her father's instructions. She chose her next words carefully because she knew she would have to feign acceptance of her father's wishes if she was to achieve her freedom. 'You know, sir, that I must not, nor can, refuse to obey any absolute command of yours,' she said in a voice that was both subdued and conciliatory. 'I was upset at the news of the cruel treatment bestowed on Mr Jones but you are right to remind me that his welfare is no concern of mine.'

'I am pleased to hear you say it,' responded Westbrook. 'But don't think that means we shan't be leaving Bath this day.'

'Of course not. I will instruct my maid to pack my case at once. The sooner we are home the better. I can then begin planning my wedding. My opposition to Mr Burnett has been a mere girlish whim. A daughter's father knows best whom she should marry.'

This sudden surrender to all that he wanted instantly dissipated all Westbrook's rage and he insisted on embracing and kissing her. A tinge of guilt at her deceit swept across Sophia's conscience but she renewed her determination by picturing in her mind Tom lying injured in the house in Queen Square. Knowing that she would require money, she clung to her father and said, 'My only regret at leaving Bath so soon is that I have not had time to purchase any new jewellery whilst we were here. I saw a very fine bracelet yesterday in one of the shops in the Orange Grove and it was very reasonably priced.'

'I know that you have felt that I have been overly harsh with you in recent months, but I have done everything because I want only the best for you. Now that we are in agreement you can have all that you want. Go and purchase it quickly, my dear, while the packing is taking place. I'll send one of the servants with you as your escort.'

'But I have no money and the jeweller is unlikely to take credit when I am wanting the bracelet immediately and he knows we are leaving town.'

'How much is it?'

His daughter named a sum and her father handed the money over to her. 'I know you love me,' she replied and she meant it. She began to leave the room but then turned and ran back into his arms to give him another embrace. She whispered into his ear, 'We never had a single dispute until this business of my marriage to Mr Burnett. I want you to know that whatever happens to me I do love you very much.'

Rushing upstairs, Sophia took refuge in her bedroom where a middle-aged woman was undertaking some sewing. She was rather gaunt and her thin nose and prominent cheekbones gave her a rather skeleton-like appearance, but there was a kindness in her dark eyes and a warmth to her smile that was immediately engaging. Though dressed very plainly, it was obvious that she took pride in her appearance because her clothes were immaculately clean and her greying hair well brushed. Elizabeth Newton was a widow who had served as her maid almost since Sophia's birth. It was therefore only natural that the young girl wished to confide in her all that had happened and to inform her of her determination to flee from her father that very day. The older woman listened with mounting concern because she was deeply attached to Sophia and saw only disaster in what she was proposing.

'You have long known my feelings about Tom and you have often said that you would help me should I wish to elope with him,' concluded Sophia. 'Will you not help me now?'

'Oh dear, ma'am, 'tis a great risk you take and I am frightened out of my wits at what might happen. Don't you think with time you could learn to love Mr Burnett?'

'Rather than submit to be his wife I'd plunge a dagger through my heart!'

'Lud! ma'am! You frighten me out of my wits. Let me beseech you not to suffer such wicked thoughts to enter your head. O lud! I tremble every inch of me. Dear ma'am, if you did that you would be denied Christian burial. They'd have your corpse buried in the highway, and drive a stake through you. If you hate the young gentleman so very bad that you can't bear to think of going into bed to him, then all that is required is that you must not wed him.'

'And if you have the friendship for me which you have often professed, you will keep me company if I flee?'

Mrs Newton's jaw dropped but she covered her confusion by quickly saying, 'That I will, ma'am, to the world's end, but I beg you to consider the consequence before you undertake any rash action. Where can you go?'

'I thought I might go to Lady Overbury's house, where I can be with Tom.'

'Oh dear, ma'am, you cannot go there. When she hears that you have run away from the master she will hand you back to him.'

Sophia laughed. 'You are wrong, Newton. I am sure Lady Overbury will both receive and protect me till my father can be brought to some reason.'

'Ma'am, I fear the master will call upon the authorities and forcibly take you back.'

Her mistress felt a sudden sinking sensation but refused to be cowed. 'Then we must flee Bath and hide in some inn. I thank God my legs are very able to carry me.'

The maid clasped her hands together and held them to her breast as if she were to pluck out her heart. 'Oh heaven! Do you know what you are saying? It will be dark before you have gone very far and would you think of walking about the country alone and at night?'

'Not alone. You have said that you will accompany me.'

'Yes, to be sure, I will follow you wherever you go, but you had almost as good be alone for I cannot defend you against any robbers or other villains. They would ravish us both!' The maid rolled her eyes as if she was already facing a terrible attacker and reached out to clutch Sophia's hands. 'Besides, ma'am, consider the time of year and how cold it is. We shall be frozen to death.'

'A good brisk pace will defend us from the cold and I will take a pistol.'

Her maid drew in her breath and visibly winced. 'Dear ma'am, you frighten me even more. I mortally hate firearms for so many accidents happen by them.'

Sophia could not help laughing. 'My dear Newton, you always fear the worst! I have money from my father and, once we have walked enough distance to hide our tracks, I will hire a conveyance to take us further. I promise you that you will be rewarded to the very utmost of my power if you will attend me.'

Seeing her mistress's determination, Mrs Newton ceased trying to dissuade her. To prevent Lady Crowthorpe becoming suspicious it was agreed that the maid would pack her mistress's clothes as if in preparation for the journey home. This left Sophia free to go to the jeweller's shop where she intended to deceive the servant who accompanied her into believing that she had spent the money her father had provided. It was agreed that they would endeavour to be away from the house by eleven at the latest, thus giving them at least an hour's start before their flight was discovered. However, no sooner had her mistress gone then Mrs Newton began to develop serious doubts about what she had promised to do. Reluctantly she decided that she might better serve her lady by betraying her intentions to Lady Crowthorpe. With that in mind she sought out Caroline Squibble, that lady's maidservant with the intention of asking her to arrange a meeting.

Squibble was quite a few years younger and certainly far prettier than Mrs Newton, but she was not an easy woman. She made no attempt to hide the fact that she thought herself far above the other servants. Already the more discerning observer could see that her beauty would soon be marred by her discontented mind and bad-tempered spirit. Only to her mistress did she put on a humble attitude. Before Mrs Newton could say anything, she began a diatribe against them all having to leave Bath. 'I would not mind if all this packing meant that my mistress was returning to London because when we are in the City we visit none but men and women of quality. But there is no pleasure in residing at Mr Westbrook's house. All he thinks about is hunting and farming. He does not even keep servants that a person of my experience can judge proper company. Of course, I do not speak on your account for you are a civilized woman, Mrs Newton. When you have seen a little more of the world, I should not be ashamed to walk with you in St James's Park.'

'Are you saying that you'd be shamed to walk with me now?' asked Mrs Newton incredulously.

'I think you will agree that there is some difference between you and me,' replied the maid in as superior a tone as she could muster.

'Yes, there is. I am no hoity toity upstart and I have a fine mistress unlike the ugly old cat you serve!'

Lady Crowthorpe's maid scowled back angrily. 'You common hussy! Your rudeness shows the meanness of your birth as well as your poor education, and both very properly qualify you to be the serving woman of a mere country girl.'

'Don't abuse m'lady,' retaliated Mrs Newton. 'I won't take that from you or anyone. She's ten thousand times better than yours in looks and manners.'

What more might have been said between the two maids was lost because at that moment Lady Crowthorpe entered the room. Seeing her mistress, Caroline Squibble burst into false tears and immediately looked to her for support. 'My lady, I have received such rude treatment from this woman and, although I could have despised all she said to me, she has had the affrontery to call you ugly – yes, madam, she called you an old ugly cat to my face!'

'How dare you speak of me in that fashion!' screeched Lady

Crowthorpe at Mrs Newton. 'If my brother does not instantly discharge you I will never sleep in his house again. I will go to him now and have you dismissed at once!'

'Dismissed!' cried Mrs Newton. 'And suppose I am? There are other places I can take. Thank heaven good servants need not want for work in Bath. And if you turn away all who think you plain, you'll not find a servant to replace me. Let me tell you that!'

Lady Crowthorpe swept out of the room with a countenance so full of rage that she resembled one of the Furies rather than a human being. The two maids being left alone began to exchange further words and this then led to a fight in which Mrs Newton emerged the victor, though not without the loss of some hair and a considerable amount of damage to sections of her dress. However, her triumph proved short-lived because Mr Westbrook then arrived on the scene. His ear had been well and truly bent by his sister and he was in no mood to debate the rights and wrongs of what had happened. He promptly ordered Mrs Newton to finish packing her mistress's bags and then be gone because her career as his daughter's maid was over.

'Don't worry, sir. I'll leave well before midday,' she replied. She did not add that it would be in the company of his daughter. All thought of betraying her mistress's plan to run away was now forgotten.

Westbrook stomped back downstairs and threw himself into a chair. It was only as time passed and his temper began to subside that he began to be worried about what his daughter might say about the loss of her maid. He was therefore pleasantly surprised to find that, on Sophia's return from her shopping expedition, she took it very well and did not oppose his decision. He took this as another encouraging sign of her newfound obedience to his wishes and relayed as much to his sister. Lady Crowthorpe was rather surprised that her niece had taken her side in the matter but welcomed the news. However, she made no indication of her gratitude and contented herself by saying to Sophia, 'Once that woman has completed your packing, tell her to be gone and not to expect any good reference from us.' To this acidic comment, her niece made no reply but simply nodded her acquiescence.

It came as something of a surprise to both brother and sister, therefore, when Sophia did not come down to the drawing room at noon as they had requested she should. 'Damn the girl, why is she keeping us waiting? The coach is now loaded with our luggage and ready to depart,' grumbled her father.

'It is a woman's right to occasionally make a man wait,' replied Lady

Crowthorpe, who was still feeling more favourably towards her niece.

Ten minutes passed and Westbrook decided that he could wait no longer. He summoned one of his servants to bring his daughter down immediately. Five minutes more passed and then the servant returned alone. Looking rather flustered, he bowed to his master and said, 'I regret, sir, that Miss Sophia cannot be found.'

'Not to be found! Zounds and damnation! What do you mean she cannot be found?'

'She appears not to be anywhere in the house, sir.'

'George, don't get yourself in a passion for nothing,' interposed Lady Crowthorpe, 'I expect the foolish girl was a bit upset when her maid left and has probably gone for a short walk in the garden before facing the confines of the coach. Have the man look out there.'

The servant once again did as he was bid and then returned to say that he still could not find her. Westbrook was furious and he began going round the house roaring her name and, when that failed to produce any response, he did the same in the garden, but all he achieved was to eventually make himself hoarse. He returned to the drawing room, threw himself dejectedly in his chair, and said despairingly to his sister, 'I think the minx has fled with her maid.'

Lady Crowthorpe hid her own discomfiture at this news by looking at him with disdain. 'I am sorry, Brother,' she said, 'but you have only yourself to blame. You always gave Sophia too much freedom. Have I not always told you that no daughter should be permitted to have a will of her own? Had I been entrusted with her education when she was a child I would have taken pains to eradicate any headstrong behaviour. Now her reputation and that of this family will be ruined because I expect her saucy maid has encouraged her to run off with that villain Mr Jones. This is all your doing for indulging her too often.'

'Blood and fury! Do not talk nonsense, woman! If thou wast a man I would have you horse-whipped. Have I not regularly threatened to disinherit Sophia and to confine her to a room on bread and water if she dared disobey me?'

'Would any man in his senses have provoked a daughter by such threats? Women are not to be hectored and bullied into compliance. They are best won over by gentle means. You have a roughness in your manner that no woman but myself would bear.' Lady Crowthorpe pursed her lips and muttered dismissively, 'I do not wonder that my niece has fled from you!'

'You seem to have forgotten your own constant chiding of her.

Perhaps had you not scolded her so frequently she would have listened to her father! And it was you who first suggested that she should marry that wretched Mr Burnett. You said he would make her a fine husband.'

'And so he will in fortune. He is Squire Woodforde's heir.'

'But had we selected a better man for her she might not have been so attracted to that coxcomb Jones. You were not present when the squire and I had to virtually demand that his nephew marry Sophia! What kind of lover is that to win her heart? It was an ill day that I ever listened to you on the matter! I had no trouble with my daughter until then.'

This was too much for Lady Crowthorpe. She drew herself up to her full height and glared at her brother as if, like a Medusa, she could turn him to stone. 'You dare to blame me for Sophia's wanton behaviour! The girl has shown herself to be no better than a common trollop. I have preached to her constantly against love. I have told her a thousand times that her fancy for her childhood companion was all folly and wickedness. I have told her repeatedly that her role is to do as her family dictates. Yet she has chosen love over the family's honour. Let her live on love if she can. Let her carry her love to market and see if she can exchange it for a loaf of bread or a rasher of bacon. I can scarce forgive myself for wasting so much time on her! As for you, Brother, I will not endure your bad temper any longer than she could. Please be aware therefore that I shall not be returning to your country house. Instead I will take the first coach I can to London.' And with that Lady Crowthorpe stormed out of the room like a ship leaving port.

'A good riddance too!' growled Westbrook after her retreating figure. For the next quarter of an hour he sat still and alone thinking solely of his daughter. Then he leaned forward and put his hands to his head and, though there was none to see it, shed bitter tears.

8

THE AGENT PROVOCATEUR

By two o'clock in the afternoon a highly agitated Westbrook was deep in conversation with Squire Woodforde at his lodgings in the city. Preliminary enquiries about where his daughter and her maid might have gone had proved fruitless. His wise friend advised that the news of Sophia's disappearance should as far as possible be hidden from all others, including John Burnett. 'Give out that she has gone with her maid to the house of a relative to discuss plans for her forthcoming wedding,' he advised. 'Once you have discovered her whereabouts I am sure this matter can be satisfactorily concluded with her reputation intact.'

'And how do you suppose that I can discover her whereabouts?' asked a bewildered Westbrook. 'No one said that they had seen either of them when I made enquiries around our lodgings.'

'Make some discreet enquiries in neighbouring inns and you will probably be able to find where she has gone,' replied Woodforde, giving his friend a reassuring look. 'You can be sure that she and her maid will have hired some form of transport and they will have given their proposed destination. You should then be able to follow and catch them.'

'And if I cannot?'

Woodforde cleared his throat before delivering in as calm a manner as he could an answer that he knew his friend would not like. 'Then I know who will help us find her. Sooner or later she will try and make contact with Tom and I am sure that I can persuade him to betray to us where she is.'

'Damn the man! I'll not go cap in hand to that coxcomb!' roared Westbrook, thumping the table at which they sat.

'No one is asking you to do that. While you seek for a lead on where she has gone, I will speak to Tom. I will go at once to the house in Queen Square on the excuse that I have heard of his injuries and wish to offer him my sympathy. Once in his room I will explain matters to him and why he must not permit Sophia to destroy her reputation. I will also make clear that he must give no hint to Lady Overbury of what has happened because I fear she would have the tale all around Bath by this evening. Believe me, he knows what he owes to my benevolence and he will do as I ask in this matter.'

'I wish I had your confidence, sir. I suggest that you make sure he understands his future is dependent upon his compliance!'

'Threatening him will not help our cause. It will only serve to antagonize him. If he has any feeling for Sophia he will understand that he has not the right to ruin her.'

Westbrook was not convinced and his manner showed it, but he reluctantly agreed to let his friend tell Jones about his daughter's flight. Then he promptly departed on his search for her. Within half an hour of his departure Woodforde was presenting himself at the house in Queen Square. The new housekeeper, who had taken up her duties just before his arrival, opened the door. Mrs Fleeting was a woman in her fifties and was not very striking to look at. Her face was plain and her figure rather squat and square, but she had an efficient manner and the air of authority that normally accompanied the role. She welcomed the Squire politely and led him into the parlour where Lady Overbury was sitting. After exchanging greetings, Woodforde requested to be taken up to Jones's bedroom. Lady Overbury asked the housekeeper to send her maid upstairs first so that the injured man could be alerted to the presence of his visitor. Once that had been done, Darr was to return and escort the squire to Tom's room. This was a deliberate move on her part because Lady Overbury thought it more likely that he would permit himself to be moved by Jones's plight if she was not present.

Woodforde was indeed deeply shocked at the sight of Tom's extensive bruises and injuries. Just as Lady Overbury had hoped, all his former affection returned. However, this did not prevent him from abandoning his mission. Once he had offered his sympathies, he told Jones how Sophia Westbrook had run away. Jones was delighted at the determination Sophia had shown in resisting a marriage to Burnett, but he was ashamed that her love for him had led her to take a step that threatened to dishonour her and wreck any chances of her future happiness. 'I will be honest, sir,' he said a trifle shakily. 'The thought of life without Sophia makes my future seem meaningless and the idea of her marrying John almost rents my heart asunder, but I will play no part in condoning her rash action. I am not so foolish that I cannot see that as a penniless man I can offer her nothing but ruin and beggary.'

'I am pleased that you see it that way, Tom,' replied Woodforde, impressed at such a manly response.

'I promise you, sir, that, once I am recovered, I will resume my journey to the colonies and thus I will fly forever from her sight. Should she try and contact me before then, I will beg her to forget me and to return home. All I ask in return is that you reconsider whether John is the right choice for her. I know he is your nephew but Sophia deserves the best and there are far better men than him.'

'Are you sure you can do this, Tom?' questioned his benefactor, ignoring the comment about Burnett. 'What will you say should she try and weaken your resolve?'

'If necessary I will make her believe that I have never loved her.' This brave resolution was said with honest fervour, although the prospect of such an eventuality made Tom Jones's heart begin to throb with anxiety.

'I am not sure that you could say such a thing to her face and make her believe it,' replied Woodforde somewhat awkwardly, because he knew how much it was costing the injured man to offer what he had. 'A letter saying that you do not love her might be preferable and would certainly be less painful than saying it to her face.' Hardening his own heart, he brought pen and paper to Jones from the desk in the room. 'Write what is necessary,' he commanded. In his weakened state Jones did as he was bid and Woodforde read the resulting letter:

Dearest Sophia,

I know the goodness and tenderness of your heart and I would avoid giving you any pain, but I have resolved to go to the colonies as soon as I can and fly ever more from your presence. Fate makes this necessary. I must have employment and your good name requires that you should forget a wretch like me. Think I never loved you and think how truly I deserve your scorn. It was presumptious of me to ever court your favours. I am unable to say more. May guardian angels protect you for ever!

'It is not entirely to my liking but it will suffice,' he said.

Shortly afterwards Woodforde took his leave and, once he had gone,

Lady Overbury rushed to Jones's room to discover what had been said between them. Swearing her to secrecy, he told her all, despite having been asked not to do so. In ordinary times Lady Overbury would have been deeply shocked by what Sophia Westbrook had done, but her heart had gone out to the young couple and she found herself weeping with the despondent lover at the tragedy that had befallen them. What she might have said or done was forestalled by Sarah Darr entering the bedroom. She informed them that Henry Fielding had arrived downstairs bringing news from Beau Nash that Sir Robert Benson was arriving on the London coach that very day. This news sent Lady Overbury into an understandable panic. She immediately returned to her room, demanding that Darr assist her to change her clothes before Sir Robert arrived. She also rang for Mrs Fleeting and asked for some light refreshments to be prepared.

When, sometime later, Lady Overbury entered the drawing room she found Henry Fielding in a highly agitated state. 'I have bad news, madam,' he said.

'I am not sure that I want to hear it!' exclaimed Lady Overbury. 'There is a limit to what my nerves can take. Has something terrible happened to Miss Westbrook?'

'Miss Westbrook? No, I know of nothing that affects her. Why do you ask?'

'Oh, no reason. Silliness on my part, that is all,' she muttered, trying to extricate herself from her unfortunate comment. 'What is your news?'

'The man murdered in the King's Bath this morning was Humphrey Watson. Whoever paid Watson to kill Tom knew that we would begin searching for his attacker and so has eliminated him.'

'But to kill the man in such a public place! It is the act of a madman!'

'Or a desperate one.'

'Whichever is true, what you are saying to me is that the real instigator of what has happened in this house is still free and our one clue to his identity – this murderous soldier – has been successfully removed.'

He blinked a little, unsure of how to respond. Deciding reassurance was necessary, he replied, 'Not entirely. We still are seeking the man who lacks a thumb. He may well be the assassin of all those who have died.'

Lady Overbury tried to draw some comfort from his words. 'Perhaps Sir Robert can help us identify this thumbless man?' she queried.

As if he was choosing his timing to fit these words, a knocking on the outside door indicated Sir Robert's arrival with Beau Nash. As Darr showed them in, Lady Overbury rose gracefully to greet them. Sir Robert was a man of medium height and slightly round-shouldered, but he bore himself with all the grace of a born aristocrat. Sometimes those who met him for the first time were put off by the way he kept turning his head from side to side and by the tendency of his right eyelid to droop, but any such reaction was speedily overcome by his good humour and ready wit. Lady Overbury had a great respect for him, but on this occasion his grim, unsmiling face showed how much he was currently weighed down by overwhelming grief at the loss of his heir. Nevertheless, his forthright gaze commanded respect and his large, greenish-grey eyes displayed both intelligence and good sense. He bowed to Lady Overbury and then acknowledged the presence of Henry Fielding with a circumspect courtesy and no hint of condescension.

'I want you all to know that my son was no traitor,' he said, addressing them all in a tone that brooked no denial. 'I grant you that appearances may look otherwise but what can appear true is often false. All three of you need to know the real truth if you are to help me find my son's killer. However, I must caution you that what I have to say is told to you only in the strictest confidence.' He paused and both Nash and Fielding nodded their acceptance of this condition. Lady Overbury hesitated and then also agreed. Lord Robert remained standing but beckoned them to sit down. All three did as they were bid and then listened to what he had to say with mounting astonishment.

'Last November Lord Kearsley was approached by one of those closest to His Majesty. He was told that the government had discovered that for many months a man called James Butler had been relaying information about the strength of Jacobite feeling in England to the French king. Butler had successfully avoided discovery for so long because ostensibly he had been touring the country to purchase bloodstock in his capacity as King Louis XV's Master of Horse. It had subsequently emerged that among other things he had held meetings with no less than twenty to thirty members of the Corporation of London in early August and held private talks with the Lord Mayor, Robert Willimot, and many other leading figures. Butler reported back to France in October 1743 that there was a great zeal for a revolution against King George.'

'So that explains, my dear sir, why the French king in recent months has been prepared to back Bonnie Prince Charlie!' Fielding exclaimed earnestly.

'I am afraid so,' corroborated Sir Robert. 'My son was told that British spies in Paris had uncovered the fact that another French agent would be sent out this year to obtain firm promises of support from English Jacobites for a rebellion. The government agent asked my son to begin voicing open support for the Young Pretender in the hope that the French spy would contact him. At worst he might be able to unmask the traitor, and at best he might gain access to the entire list of English Jacobites and convey it into the government's hands, along with whatever plans they had made. My son recognized that the task he was being offered was extremely dangerous but he did not hesitate to accept.'

'Lord Kearsley played his part exceptionally well, sir, because there can be few who have not heard of his outrageous attacks on leading government figures,' commented Fielding.

'Aye, he played it so well he even deceived his own father!' snapped back Sir Robert. 'I raged at him for his traitorous behaviour, especially after I heard the shocking news in February about the planned French invasion. That news was leaked to the government by a senior clerk in the French Foreign Office, who sold the names of some of the Jacobite traitors, including the Duke of Beaufort, Lord Barrymore, and Sir Watkins William Wynn. They were arrested but there are many more whose names we do not have.'

'But in response the House of Commons passed a loyal address,' chimed in Lady Overbury, anxious to show that she was not entirely without some political awareness.

'Yes, but almost a third voted against it. In the wake of that you can imagine the row that I had with my son! I think I would have disinherited him on the spot for being a traitor had not news quickly followed that a storm had scattered the French fleet, causing the invasion to be cancelled. As it was, I merely threatened him in the hope that he would see reason. You can imagine my dismay when weeks later I heard how the wretched Young Pretender had landed in Scotland and won support there.'

'I understand your feelings, sir. There is no doubt that the prince will launch an invasion from Scotland if he can be sure of enough English Jacobites joining his cause.' Nash reflected on how much he had personally lobbied for Lord Kearsley's arrest for that precise reason. The government's reluctance to imprison such an open critic was only now understandable.

'Exactly, sir,' responded Sir Robert. 'Lord Kearsley was this country's main hope in uncovering those whom we cannot trust. Unfortunately my son had overplayed his hand by being such an outspoken critic of the government. Jacobite plotters approached him, but his sympathies were judged to be too well known for them to make him a safe repository of their plans. It was in this situation that my son came to me for my advice last month. It was not at first a very happy meeting because I was in too much a hurry to condemn him to hear a word he said and I said much about his character that I wish I could now unsay. But eventually I stopped my flood of invective and he persuaded me to listen. The more he spoke the calmer I became. By the end I was a prouder father than I had ever been before.' Tears sprang into the father's eyes. He bent his head and covered his face with his hands until he had composed himself again. 'I wish now that I had dissuaded him from doing anything more but, alas, I did not,' he muttered.

'You must not torture yourself, sir,' whispered Lady Overbury, full of distress at the memory of seeing the poor man's murdered son lying on the kitchen floor.

He acknowledged her sympathy with his eyes and then, turning to Nash and Fielding, he commented, 'My son had discovered that a series of meetings was to be held in Bath between a Catholic priest, who was acting as the agent of the French king, and various nobles. Out of those meetings would come a list of those who would rally to the Young Pretender if he invaded England.'

'Why Bath and not London?' queried Lady Overbury, now beginning to feel out of her depth in the conversation.

'For reasons we know all too well,' interrupted Nash. 'Bath is a city of countless meetings. It is a place to which any man may come without arousing suspicion. It offers the perfect cover to any group of plotters. It has in the past and doubtless it will continue to do so in the future.'

'Quite right, Mr Nash. I suggested to my son that he offer this house as a meeting place and make clear that he would not be present in Bath while these took place. In that way he could allay any concerns that might be felt about bringing him into the full picture of what was going on.'

'I do not understand. If he was not to be party to what was happening, how would that help uncover the traitors?' asked a perplexed Nash.

Sir Robert paused before replying, as if judging exactly how much he should and should not tell them. Then he answered quietly, 'I knew that we could rely entirely on the loyalty of my housekeeper, Miss Grey and I urged my son to bring her into his confidence. He agreed and we asked her to play the role that my son could not. We told her to win the confidence of the Catholic priest sufficiently that she might somehow obtain his papers and copy not only the list of traitors but also any plans that were being drawn up by them. In that way the cursed Jacobites would not know that we had discovered their plans and my son's loyalty to the government would not be revealed. We also told her that I would invite Lady Overbury to take up residence in the house in early November so that the plotters would know that they only had a finite time to engage in their work.' He turned to face Lady Overbury, who had been taken aback by this latest revelation. 'I am sorry, madam, that I have exposed you to such dangers. I really thought that by the time of your arrival everything would be over.'

'Whatever inconvenience I have faced is nothing compared to the loss of your son,' she replied graciously.

Sir Robert tried to smile but his mouth began to quiver with emotion. 'It is indeed a most grievous loss to me and to the country,' he finally managed to say.

'It was a highly dangerous task to set your housekeeper,' said Fielding grimly, reluctant to voice how unwise he judged their action.

'Yes, and I appreciate that now more than I did then. What I did not foresee was that, Miss Grey, in her determination to defeat this country's enemies, would eliminate one of the men we most wanted to capture and interrogate.' He pulled out of his pocket a letter. 'This was the first intimation we had of this. Let me read it to you. It is addressed to my son:

"My dear Lord Kearsley,

Please return to Bath as soon as you can. I have much valuable information to provide you with. As you requested I have kept a list of the names of those who have visited this house over the past week. I think you will be surprised because some of them are men of great status and power in the land. Unfortunately trying to see the papers of the Popish priest has proved more difficult. The man remained far too suspicious, despite all my attempts to make him trust me.

When I told him that the time had come for Lady Overbury's arrival at the house as the guest of Sir Robert and he would have to hide elsewhere, he expressed annoyance but did not suspect that anything was amiss. He announced this morning that he would have to attend a meeting at a nearby house so it could be agreed where he should go next. In his absence I entered his room. He had locked it with a key that I had provided but, of course, he was unaware that I held a duplicate. Searching his belongings took me far longer than I had anticipated because I had to make sure that I put back everything exactly where it had been before lest he discover what I had done. In the end I found papers hidden in the lining of one of his jackets. I had brought the necessary pen and paper and ink with me and I sat at the desk in his room and began to copy everything. Unfortunately I was so engrossed in the task that I did not hear his unexpected early return until I heard the sound of his feet on the stairs. As I quickly thrust all the papers, both original and copied, into my apron pocket I heard him put his key into the lock and try to turn it.

When he realized the door was not locked he stormed in and, when he saw I was there, he demanded to know what was I doing in his room. I told him that the room required some cleaning and I had thought to do the work while he was out. He asked me how I had got into it when he had left it locked. To this I replied that as housekeeper I had spare keys to all the rooms in the house. This did not please him. He said that in future he did not want anyone in his room unless he had given his express permission. I said that I was sorry if I had inadvertently offended him. He then demanded that I give him the spare key.

I reached into my apron pocket and drew out my bunch of keys in order to unhook the requisite key. Unfortunately, as I did so, he saw that I had some papers in my possession. Before I could say or do anything he plunged his hand into my apron and pulled out them out, screaming "What is this, woman? Have you been spying on me?' He grabbed hold of my right arm and twisted it behind my back, demanding that I tell him for whom I was working. The pain was excruciating and in my agony I grasped a stone paperweight from the desk with my other hand and swung it behind me and against his head. The unexpected blow caused him to let go of me and I turned and pushed him as hard as I could. He fell backwards and I ran from the room.

I expected him to follow, but, to my surprise, there was no sound of pursuit. Part of me urged continued flight but curiosity eventually overcame caution and I climbed the stairs and entered the silent room. The priest was still lying on the floor and a pool of blood was gathering around his head. I looked to see the cause and realized that in falling he must have hit his head on the sharp corner of the fender of the fireplace. It had punched a hole through his skull. My first thought was horror that I had killed a man, but then I thought of all those who would have died if this man's treachery had won the day and I saw in his death the hand of God. I hope that you will agree with me because I have no desire to hang for what I have done.

Over the next few hours I sought to remove all the evidence of what had happened as best I could. I managed to lift the priest's body into a trunk. Then I mopped up all the blood that I could find and scrubbed the floor clean. I took the priest's belongings and burnt them in the kitchen fire. I am confident that when Lady Overbury arrives she will not see anything amiss. The only thing I have not burnt are the documents that I was caught copying. They contain all the information that you want about those who are seeking to betray the king. I will give the documents to you as soon as you can come. Please do not delay. I will require assistance soon because it will only be a short time before the stench of the priest's body will begin to permeate the house. I have not the strength or means to dispose of it and I am not sure that I can trust that old fool Graves.

I will say to any who come seeking the priest that he has left and that he would not say where he was going. I hope that they will believe me. I hope the presence of Lady Overbury will keep them out of the house. If you cannot come soon, send someone you trust and let him carry a sign that he comes from you. I suggest one of those pretty French buttons with a fleur-de-lis that I have always admired.

Your most loyal servant
Agnes Grey"

'The poor brave woman,' said Lady Overbury. 'I would never have guessed what she had done from the calm way in which she greeted me. I assume that whoever killed her gained admittance by showing her the button. For some reason she must have then become suspicious and refused to hand over the document. That person killed her and it explains why after her death he was forced to continue searching the house.'

'It is not as simple as that,' interrupted Henry Fielding. 'We have searched this house from top to bottom and the one thing I can assure you is that there is no body hidden here. Where has the priest's corpse gone? Who disposed of it? Nor is that the only mystery. I do not understand how Miss Grey's murderer came to know the significance of the button or, for that matter, Sir Robert, why you or Lord Kearsley did not come sooner to the house once you had received Miss Grey's letter?'

'I cannot answer what has happened to the body or how our enemies came to discover that the button was a signal, but I can answer your question as to why we delayed coming here. Miss Grey directed her letter to my house in Leicester Square, but neither my son nor I were there: we were staying with friends in Oxford. As a consequence her letter was not immediately opened. Once it was my son set off for Bath but with the deadly outcome that we know. He must have entered the house by night expecting to speak to Miss Grey without Lady Overbury knowing of his presence.' He paused and then added in a voice that cracked with emotion, 'Unfortunately a murderer was awaiting him.'

A hush fell on the room as if each of those present were paying their last respects to the unfortunate Lord Kearsley. 'The only clue as to who this killer might be is Joseph Graves's statement that Miss Grey had felt threatened by a man who lacked a thumb on his right hand,' remarked Beau Nash, breaking the sombre silence.

'Do you know, Sir Robert, of anyone of that description?' asked Henry Fielding. 'So far all our attempts to find him have proved useless.'

'No. I am not aware of anyone who has that deformity, but I agree with you that finding this man is absolutely imperative. I intend to stay here in this house until you produce him. I am sure that Lady Overbury will not object to me joining her here – indeed, I am sure that my presence can only make her position safer. I can have my servant, who is bringing my bags, set up my room with the assistance of this temporary housekeeper who has been appointed.'

Lady Overbury nodded her agreement.

'Do not worry, my lord, everyone in this house will be safe from now on,' said Beau Nash. 'And, if this thumbless man is still in Bath, he will not escape us.'

'He had better not or else there will be those in government who will think this city is still Jacobite at heart!' replied Sir Robert with a fierce glint in his eyes. Then he stared at Nash and, in a chilling tone, added, 'And there will be others, like myself, who will judge Bath to be no longer a safe place if three murders can go unsolved, especially when one of them involves a man of my son's standing!' This latter comment was an unstated threat and Nash recognized it as such. Sir Robert was influential enough to put an end to Bath's popularity if he chose to wield his power in that direction. Both the safety of the nation and the status of Bath now rested on finding the man without a thumb. But who was he? And where was he? And what on earth had happened to the priest's corpse?

9

A SECRET UNCOVERED

When Sophia Westbrook left her father's lodgings in Bath she was still unsure of where she should go. However, she assumed that her best hope of escaping capture lay in leading her father to believe that she was going to London. For that reason she gave out the name of that city as her ultimate destination when she procured a young guide and some indifferent horses to take her and her maid as far as Chippenham. It was only after they had left Bath that she asked the guide to turn off the London road. By then she had given the matter further thought and so she asked him to take them to Chipping Sodbury. She had a vague recollection that she had heard of a reputable coaching house there called the Squire Inn. This, she hoped, would offer a safe place to stay until she could decide what was her best course of action.

'Master ordered me to take yer to the inn at Chippen'am and I'll lose me place if I go anywhere other than where he told us to go,' muttered the rather gangly youth, peering at her through a mop of ill-cut hair and rubbing first the sides of his thin nose and then the stubble on his chin with a remarkably dirty hand.

'But I will expect you to go no further than the agreed distance and then you can return. Your master will not know what you have done,' she replied.

'He's a way of finding out things and nothin' pains 'im as much as being crossed. He'd make me suffer terrible like.'

'Please do this for me,' pleaded Sophia, trying to make her whole countenance smile affection at him, despite his unprepossessing looks and churlish manner. She looked at him with doleful eyes, fluttering her long eyelashes in such a way as to discharge a volley of charm in his direction. To this, however, he seemed immune because he looked solely at the road ahead and commenced whistling a tune. Unsure what to say next, Sophia resorted to repeating her plea in a curious mixture of command and entreaty.

He stopped his whistling and looked first at her and then at Mrs Newton. 'It's a sinful thing to ride the master's horses on a road other than what was agreed, miss. Gentlefolks like yerself don't consider us poor folks when they demand sich a thing.' Once again he rubbed his chin, depositing yet more grime on a spot-ridden face that showed little sign of having been washed for days.

'I'll give thee a guinea, or two, if one is not sufficient,' responded the increasingly desperate Sophia, deciding the promise of money might prove more effective in changing his attitude.

He smiled at her offer, revealing a mass of blackened stumps where there had once been teeth. 'It's honestly worth three when I run sich a risk for your la'ship,' he replied, tapping the side of his nose. 'For three I'll venture to take thee to The Cross Hands at Old Sodbury. It's not quite as far and it's a good inn.'

'Very well, take me there and let us make it three.'

'O lud, ma'am! How do you know that this wretch may not lead us to a den of thieves and cutthroats?' groaned Mrs Newton, astonished that her mistress had surrendered to his audacity. 'The very fact that he's asked for three guineas shows he's untrustworthy. Three guineas is more than enough even if he were to lose his job for doing this.'

Some tears ran down Sophia's cheeks because she was inwardly very frightened, but, in a tone that brooked no opposition, she voiced her determination to continue. 'We have no choice in the matter so please accept my decision. We simply cannot afford to proceed to Chippenham because I am sure that my father would come in pursuit once he discovered we were going there.'

Mrs Newton was not convinced but could not bring herself to say so. Instead she glowered at their guide and muttered, 'All I can say to you, sir, is that I hope the guineas may provide you with enough money to have a decent wash, because from the smell of you that's long overdue!'

The youth merely laughed at her jibe. 'No point wasting money on water,' he said.

The bargain having been struck, they turned off the London road and commenced riding at speed in the direction of Old Sodbury. The guide recommenced his whistling and the ladies were happy to have no more conversation with him. After about nine miles they reached their destination. To Sophia's relief The Cross Hands was not the robbers' den that Mrs Newton had feared. Instead it was a large and obviously reputable ancient coaching inn that clearly dated back to medieval times and whose traditional exterior was partially covered with ivy. It seemed to exude an air that promised warm hospitality. Once they had dismounted, she paid her mercenary guide what she had promised so that he could depart with the horses back to Bath whilst there was still light.

Just as she had completed this transaction, a tall, elderly man came out to usher her and Mrs Newton inside and out of the cold. Although his hair was grizzled and he had thin lips and a gaunt, grey face, there was intelligence in his eyes and a natural kindness and trustworthiness in his manner that was most reassuring. 'Whom do I have the honour of welcoming?' he asked in a most courteous fashion.

Mrs Newton took it upon herself to respond first. 'Have you ever heard of a Mr Westbrook? He is a man of wealth and quality. This noble lady is his daughter and heiress to all he possesses.'

'Newton, we are supposed to be travelling incognito!' whispered Sophia, angrily poking her maid to make her be silent. 'Is your brain so addled by the cold that you have forgotten?' She turned to the landlord, her face puckering with anxiety, and added in a very formal tone, 'Sir, I would have you know that we are on secret business and I must ask that you forget the name that my maid has provided. All I require is a room for the night and privacy. Once the room is ready, I would be grateful if you could send up some refreshments as we have not eaten anything since breakfast.'

'I am sure that a woman of your quality will have her reasons for wishing to remain anonymous,' he replied tactfully as he led the two women inside, 'but I think it only fair to inform you that your name is not unknown to me.'

'How so, sir?' replied Sophia, genuinely puzzled.

He grinned. 'There is a young man called Mr Thomas Jones who is in the habit of stopping here for refreshment when he goes hunting and he never tires of singing the praises of a Miss Westbrook. I suppose that you are the woman of whom he speaks because there cannot be two of the same name and description. He has often said that you are the finest lady in the world, and, if you will pardon my presumption, now that I have the pleasure of meeting you, I can see why he should think so.'

The colour rose in Sophia's pale cheeks but this served only to enhance her beauty. Part of her was slightly shocked that Tom had talked about her to a landlord but mostly she was flattered. 'What else has this Mr Jones told you?' she enquired, blushing even more.

The landlord gave a slight chuckle as he encouraged the two women to sit beside the inn's fireplace and warm themselves after their journey. 'I hope that you will not be insulted if I tell you that he says he loves you to the bottom of his soul.'

'What a saucy fellow! He's no right to say such things about my mistress!' broke in Mrs Newton, outraged at Jones's behaviour.

'Indeed he has not,' said Sophia, but in such a tone that it was obvious she was pleased rather than annoyed.

'I can only attribute his imprudence to passion and an open heart,' replied the landlord, and a smile lit up his wrinkled face. He turned and summoned a pert young girl called Polly who was wearing a crisp starched apron. He gave orders for a room and meal to be prepared whilst simultaneously thinking what he should do. It seemed obvious to him that Sophia must have fled from home with the intention of eloping. Many a less scrupulous man would have judged there was an opportunity to make some money out of the situation either by helping the lovers or by betraying them, but the landlord was an honest man and ill nature or hardness of heart were not among his vices. Instead he felt concern at the potential impact on the young woman's reputation and so he made bold to advise Sophia against what she was doing in a tone that was both measured and gentle. 'Miss Westbrook, forgive me but I must ask you to reflect on the wisdom of running away with Mr Jones. Consider your reputation and what you are about and whither such a step will lead you!'

'You misjudge my purpose and do me wrong sir,' answered Sophia angrily. 'I have made no arrangement to meet Mr Jones, though I confess in confidence that I have run away from home because of my father's ill-treatment.' She proceeded to outline what had happened the night before, including how Jones had been seriously injured and how her father had not only prevented her going to see him but also insisted on her immediately marrying a man of better birth and fortune. 'I do not share my father's view that Mr Burnett is the preferable man,' she concluded. 'He lacks that generosity of spirit which is the sure foundation of all that is noble in human nature. Since we were young together I have seen a selfishness in him that I despise and I know he is a man capable of base designs. I have therefore chosen to flee rather than to marry him.'

'I am truly sorry that young Mr Jones has been so grievously injured, but that does not prevent me asking whether your father's opposition to him is not based partly on some misbehaviour.' He paused and then added reluctantly, 'I regret to say that I received the impression when he was last here that he had got himself entangled with some common jade.'

His words made Sophia wince but she countered them bravely. 'The matter to which you refer was not Tom's fault, sir, and I can assure you that my father's opposition to him was very marked long before that incident. It is the circumstances of Tom's birth and his lack of any money that make him an unsuitable suitor in my father's eyes.'

'And in that your father is correct,' sniffed Mrs Newton, unable to stay quiet any longer. 'Mr Jones may have a charming manner, but possessing a whore for a mother and a father who has fled the scene isn't the right background for marriage to one of your birth and fortune.'

Sophia stiffened as if she had been slapped in the face. 'Pardon my maid, sir. She places circumstance before character out of her deep love for me.'

The landlord made no immediate response because he found himself in a quandary. He possessed information about Jones's parentage that might help the young couple but it meant speaking about a dreadful time in his past, the memory of which he had long tried to suppress. What made his decision even harder was that he knew that what he had to say might serve only to raise false hopes and so cause in the long run more pain. He looked again at the young woman in front of him, who had dared so much for love, and decided he had no option but to share with her what he knew.

'You have been very open with me, Miss Westbrook,' he said, 'and so in return I will tell you what I have told no other, not even Mr Jones. It may surprise you to hear that for years I viewed him as the greatest enemy I ever had, although he knew me not and never intended me any wrong.'

'I do not understand sir,' she replied, her curiosity evident in her expression.

'He was but an infant when he grievously injured me.'

'How could that be? You speak in riddles!'

'Then I will unriddle the matter by telling you my real name. Men now call me George Peartree but once I was known as George Partridge and I was a highly respected teacher. Unfortunately I had the misfortune to be named as Tom's father. Overnight my reputation was ruined and it led to my ignominious dismissal.'

For a moment Sophia was rendered speechless. It took her all her powers of self-control to restrict her response to one simple statement of fact. 'I have heard of you, sir. Tom believes that he is your son.'

'Well, I can absolve him of all filial duty because I am not and never was his father, though Squire Woodforde believed I was.'

'But surely no false suspicion could have led to such certainty of your guilt!'

'What is false can sometimes appear true, Miss Westbrook. All those years ago I foolishly thought my innocence would be my defence.' He tried to smile but his expression contained only evidence of his suffering. 'It proved otherwise. Jenny Jones refused to name the real father, although I begged her to do so. Her silence was taken as proof of my guilt.'

'Then who was Tom's father?' She felt a chill of apprehension at what he might say.

He shrugged his shoulders. 'That is where I cannot help you. Only Jenny Jones knows and I have long lost touch with her. The last that I heard she was in London and had joined the Methodists.' There was no anger or blame in his face as he said this.

Pity at the undeserved treatment the landlord had received flashed across Sophia's mind, but this emotion was quickly superseded by a desire to know more. Her eyes sparkled with newfound energy. 'Then we must find her and discover Tom's real father.'

'What makes you think she will tell you?'

'If this Jenny Jones has hidden the father's name out of love, then maybe she will respond to the love I have for her son.'

The landlord admired her courage but he had no desire to encourage false hopes. 'I am sorry to disappoint you but I would not count on her proving co-operative even should you find her. She stood by and let me be driven out, though she knew my innocence. Why should she be kinder to you, a stranger?'

'Even if she did, ma'am, doubtless she would name some scoundrel far worse than this schoolmaster as the father,' interjected Mrs Newton, who already feared what this new intelligence might lead her mistress to do.

'On that point I am not so sure,' continued Partridge. 'Jenny was a very virtuous girl. It came as a great surprise to me when I heard what had happened. When she lost her virginity I think it would have been to no common man.'

'But 'twas a man lacking in honour, because he never came forward afterwards,' snapped back the irrepressible maid, determined to crush Sophia's foolish urge to seek out Jones's mother.

'All I know is that Jenny must have had good reason to protect him.'

'Is it possible that it was Squire Woodforde?' asked Sophia tentatively.

'No, he was absent in London and he had little to do with Jenny.'

The conversation continued for a little while longer but none of them could make any progress in surmising who might be Jones's real father. Partridge promised to arrange transport for them so they could travel to London in search of Jenny Jones and Sophia decided to retire to the room that had been prepared and stay there so as not to risk attracting attention from other guests who were due to arrive by coach. It was fortunate that she did so because later that evening her father alighted from his horse and banged on the inn door. After making various enquiries in Bath, he had eventually found the place where his daughter had hired her transport and unfortunately, whilst he had been interrogating its owner, her young guide had returned with the horses. It had not taken him long to persuade the youth to divulge where he had taken her. Westbrook had then immediately set off to seize his errant daughter, riding at great peril to himself through the moonlit night.

When Partridge answered his frantic knocking, Westbrook thrust his way inside, demanding to know where his daughter was. 'If she be in the house, take me up to her, and, if she be gone away before, tell me which way she has gone that I might follow her,' he declared, and with that he pulled out a handful of guineas and cast them on the counter.

'What does your daughter look like?' asked Partridge, seeking to buy some time while he thought how best he might deal with this unexpected crisis.

'She has dark eyes, lily-white skin and black hair and, as far as I know, is dressed in a purple gown.'

''Tis a description that can be applied to many, sir. There is a woman here whom it might describe, but she is with her husband and they have already gone to bed.'

This news made Westbrook go pale but he commanded peremptorily, 'Damn it, sir, show me to their room at once.'

The landlord pocketed the coins and led him upstairs to his largest guest room. Finding its door locked, Westbrook flung himself at it with such violence that its lock broke and it burst open so suddenly that he fell headlong into the darkened room beyond.

'What is the meaning of this! How dare you break into an honest man's room!' roared the occupant of the bed.

As Westbrook's eyes adjusted to the gloom he noticed a gown on the floor surrounded by stays, petticoats, garters, ribbons, and stockings. Then he realized there was a woman hiding under the bedclothes alongside its male occupant. In his disordered state of mind he feared this was indeed his daughter and he launched himself upon the bed, yelling he would murder them both. A fierce battle ensued between the two men whilst the terrified woman screamed out murder, robbery and rape. The landlord had not expected such a terrible outcome and had no recourse now but to join in the struggle. Soon they were joined by a third man, because the occupant of the next room, hearing the noise, entered to provide assistance. It took the efforts all three men to eventually pin down the infuriated Westbrook.

'What the devil is the meaning of all this?' gasped the battered occupier of the room.

'Villain! You have debauched my daughter and got her into bed with you!'

'My wife is no daughter to you, sir!' declared the husband and, turning to Partridge, he shouted angrily, 'This man's a madman!'

At that moment Westbrook spotted the lady in question and was confounded to see that she was indeed not his daughter. The enormity of his mistake came rushing upon him and his anger dissipated as rapidly as it had erupted. He knew not what to say in his embarrassment.

'I assure you, landlord, I am not this man's daughter,' sobbed the distraught woman.

'I thought this was a respectable inn,' said her injured husband, looking furiously at Partridge. 'Instead I find you harbour a man intent on robbing or murdering us! This is worse than a bawdy-house, sir!'

'I apologize, sir, but this madman more or less forced his way into my inn demanding his daughter.'

'And I was wrong, sir,' added Westbrook, finally finding voice to apologize. 'In my haste to find my daughter I mistook the situation.'

This did nothing to appease the man who had been attacked. 'If you fear that your daughter is with a man, sir, then all I can say is that you come from a family of little honour and I suggest you leave us at once. Landlord, I want your assurance that we will go unmolested for the rest of the night. As for any bill in the morning, you can go hang!'

'Aye, that goes for me too,' said the occupier of the next room icily, mopping some blood from a cut lip with the sleeve of his shirt.

Partridge made what excuses he could and escorted a humbled Westbrook downstairs. 'May I suggest that I provide you with a room and bring you a meal. We have some excellent mutton pie and I will select a bottle of my best wine. You can do no more today because night has already fallen. I think whatever information you were given was falsely given because your daughter is certainly not here. I suggest an early night and then you can return first thing in the morning to Bath and discover where she has really gone.'

Confused and embarrassed, Sophia's humbled father readily acceded to this request. The emotion of the day and the journey he had undertaken had combined with the fight to leave him utterly exhausted. He promised that he would compensate the landlord for his losses and for any damage he had inadvertently caused before he left in the morning to resume his search. Partridge expressed his thanks and then, having issued orders for a meal to be prepared, took Westbrook to the guest room that was furthest away from the one in which he had placed Sophia. Once he was sure that Westbrook was not going to re-emerge, he ran over to her room and sought admittance. She had heard the noise of the fight and recognized the unmistakable sound of her father's angry voice so she and Mrs Newton were already dressed and ready to depart.

'I beseech you, sir, if you have any compassion, please do not betray my presence here!' she begged.

'I never betrayed anyone in my life and I will not commence now. Having seen the unreasonable nature of the man my only surprise is that you have not run away long before this! I suggest that you stay hidden in this room until your father is gone.'

'Your advice may be sound but I dare not risk it. He might resume his search here in the morning. It is a clear moonlight night so there is light enough for us to see as we walk until we can find some alternative accommodation. Just set us on the right road and Mrs Newton and I will make our escape long before my father rises.'

'What you suggest is a most dangerous course of action. Outside it is bitterly cold and there is no guarantee that you will find somewhere to stay. Should the sky cloud over you would be quickly lost in the dark.'

'I would rather risk that than be caught by my father in the morning,' replied Sophia.

'I insist, Miss Westbrook, that you do not attempt to walk outside. It is sheer folly. You will appreciate that I cannot leave this establishment unattended for too long, not least in case your father makes a reappearance downstairs once he has slept off his initial weariness, but I will try and take you in my cart as far as Wotton under Edge tonight. Gloucester is about another twenty-five miles or so beyond that. With luck you can be there the day after tomorrow and there is a regular coach from there that will take you to London.'

Sophia burst into tears as she conveyed her gratitude at Partridge's kindness. He was as good as his word. Once he had prepared his cart, the two women climbed aboard and he covered them with as many blankets as he could to protect them from the ice-cold night air. Then he drove northwards. However, the pace at which they could travel was very slow because the road was badly potholed. Partridge had to take extra care in the limited light provided by the moon not to overturn their means of transport. After they had been travelling for a couple of hours he reluctantly pulled his cart to a stop at a fork in the road.

'What is wrong?' asked Sophia, sticking her head out of the blankets.

He pointed to the clouds that were beginning to appear in the sky. 'I think they will bring rain before the night is much older and, before that happens, they will block out all the moonlight, then I will not be able to drive this cart. It is imperative that I turn back now if I am to get back to Old Sodbury this night. I told Polly, my serving girl, to say that I have gone to visit a neighbour should your father leave his room and ask for me, but that story will not hold if I do not return. He will then know that I have been helping you and your chances of escaping him will be very poor. Though it pains me to say it, I think it therefore wiser for you to walk the rest of the way so I can instantly set about the return journey. I can assure you that it is not much further from this fork to Wotton under Edge.'

Sophia and Mrs Newton understood his reasoning and clambered out of the cart. Sophia thanked him profusely and he, not without a heavy heart, turned around and, with a wave and prayer for their safety, set off back where they had come from. The two women, each still with a blanket over her clothes, watched till the cart disappeared round a bend and then set out on foot. In silence they walked for about half an hour, acutely aware that the cold night air was increasingly seeping into their bodies. Suddenly they became aware of a low moaning sound and there sprang up a sudden wind, which blew keen and hard. This was soon accompanied by the fall of raindrops that increased in size and quantity with every passing second.

'Madam, this is sheer madness,' complained Mrs Newton, trying hard not to shiver uncontrollably as the increasingly heavy rain began to soak through her clothes. 'I am already almost frozen to death and I fear that I will lose a piece of my nose unless we find a place to stay.'

At that instant the clouds covered the moon and the resulting darkness was so dense that neither woman could see a hand in front of her. Fortunately Mrs Newton espied a glimmering light through the trees ahead and began stumbling towards it, crying out, 'I think Heaven has heard my prayers and brought us to a house. Come this way before we are wet through entirely.'

'We cannot just knock at any strange door at this hour of the night!' shouted back her mistress.

'We can when the alternative is to die in this sudden storm. I beseech you not to despise the goodness of Providence. If the owners of this house are Christians, they will not refuse entry to people in our miserable condition.'

Such was her weariness that Sophia surrendered to her maid's entreaty and also approached the place whence the light issued. With each step nearer to the house their tired spirits rose. However, when they reached its porch and knocked loudly and repeatedly on its door, no one appeared. 'O lud, have mercy on us! Surely the people must all be dead,' sighed Mrs Newton, all hopes of rescue fleeing from her mind.

'Do not be so foolish. It must be nearing midnight. They have long gone to bed and I dare say they are understandably fearful of opening their door to strangers at such an ungodly hour.'

As if to prove the truth of this, a casement window was opened above them and a small, thin old woman stuck out her head, exposing a lined and wrinkled face that revealed a mix of fear and curiosity. 'Who's there? What do ye want?' she shouted.

'We have missed our way in the dark and require a bed for what remains of this night else we will perish in the cold,' replied Sophia with a slight tremor of her lips.

'I'll have no whores in this house!' the old woman said waspishly, shaking her fist at them.

'I'll have you know that my mistress is a woman of quality,' remonstrated Mrs Newton in an injured tone.

'I am surprised then to see sich a person journeying on foot at this time of night. Even a dog lies quiet by the fireside in freezing weather like this! How do ye come to be here at this hour?'

In response Mrs Newton began to feign that she was crying. 'Please help us,' she sobbed. 'We should have got to the inn where we were staying before it got dark but our escort somehow lost the way. After travelling in what direction I know not my mistress's horse stumbled and threw her. I got off mine to assist her and, while I was attending her, both our mounts took fright and fled. Our escort rode after them but he did not return. We waited and waited till it got dark and then we realized that we had probably been deceived. The man must have deliberately got us lost in order that he could later seize the moment to steal our horses.' Mrs Newton paused in her inventive tale in order to wail even more loudly. 'We've been reduced to walking in circles for many hours and are now so lost that we've no idea where we are.'

Sophia was rather taken aback by her maid's version of events but she squeezed her arm in gratitude for her quick thinking. She had the sense to add on her own accord, 'We are both exhausted and will die if we do not find shelter. Please help us. I will give you half a crown if you give us shelter for what remains of this night.'

Whether motivated by pity, curiosity or greed, the old woman signified her assent and shortly afterwards they heard her unbolting the door to give them entry. Clutching a worn but clean gown around her, the old woman looked out warily at her unexpected visitors and was at once shocked to see the extent of their sodden and frozen condition. Her natural kindness immediately asserted itself. 'Come in, come in,' she urged. 'Come sit by the fire at once and take off yer wet clothes so that I can hang 'em to dry or else ye will catch yer death of cold. Dear me, what ye must have been through! I'll bring ye some warm blankets from upstairs and I'll make ye something hot to drink. Then, once ye have warmed up, I suggest ye both get as much sleep as ye can. Ye both look exhausted.'

The house proved to be modest and plain in its furnishings but very neat and tidy. The old woman quickly put some fresh wood on the embers of the fire in the hearth and beckoned them to sit on the oaken settle that stood nearby. Within a very short while both Sophia and Mrs Newton looked like two embalmed figures so snugly were they wrapped up in front of the flickering fire. As they felt the warmth slowly returning to their hands and feet, they became aware of just how tired they were. However, before they fell asleep Sophia insisted on informing her hostess of how vital it was that they should make their way towards Gloucester the next day. The old woman replied, 'Set yer mind at rest, m'lady. When me son arrives here tomorrow morning I will ask him to take ye in his cart to Stroud and from there ye can hire fresh transport. Now go to sleep and may God's angels watch over ye.'

The next morning the old woman's son turned out to be a deep-chested, broad-shouldered man named Peter. His face was dominated by his large eyes and bushy eyebrows, a hawkish nose and a firm-set jaw. He was a man of very few words but whenever he did speak, he tended to wave about his long arms, which made them very conscious of his unusually large hands. Though not prepossessing in appearance, he had an air of honesty about him that helped reconcile Sophia, though not Mrs Newton, to the discomfort of his vehicle as they travelled the twelve miles to Stroud. It did not help matters that many sections of the road they took had been reduced to a quagmire by the heavy rain that had fallen throughout the remainder of the night. Sometimes this made the cart slide and more than once they thought it was going to overturn into a ditch. More frequently the wheels got stuck in the mud and on such occasions both women had to clamber out in order to lighten the load. Even then it usually took the strength of all three of them to haul the cart back onto firmer ground. As a consequence the state of their clothes got progressively worse.

The journey was particularly hard on Sophia who was not used to labour of any kind, but she bore it all uncomplainingly. The same could not be said for Mrs Newton, who periodically gave voice to the stupidity of the journey they were undertaking. After they had been travelling for a couple of hours, Sophia decided that it might be a good idea to see if the old woman's son could tell her anything about the Methodist movement that Jenny Jones had joined. All she knew about Methodists was that her vicar hated them and chose to repeatedly condemn their horrid enthusiasm. He had often lambasted the preaching of one of their leaders, a Gloucester-born clergyman called George Whitefield. 'Do you know anything of a Mr Whitefield?' she enquired of Peter. 'Or about the Methodists?'

'Aye, ma'am, I've met Mr Whitefield and I knows a few who call 'emselves Methodist.'

'I have heard that he is a fanatic and that all his followers are caught up in a strange madness. Is that true?'

'There are them, ma'am, as would say a person has to be afflicted with madness to want to spend part of each day praying and reading the scriptures when attending church once a week is sufficient for even most clergy.'

'And is that all these Methodists want to do? Surely they must be doing other things than praying and reading to have brought on themselves such frequent condemnation?'

'Methodists are condemned round 'ere because they dare to preach in the open to those who nivver enter a church and who know nothing of God.'

Sophia adjusted where she was sitting to try and reduce the jolting that arose from the cart passing over a particularly bad stretch of road. 'That hardly seems enough to condemn them unless what is preached is seditious nonsense.'

'I speak as I do find, miss, and I tell ye that I've heard Mr Whitefield preach a number of times and, if ever a man speaks like an angel, he does. These Methodists go out of their way to 'elp the poor and those who're sick. The clergy say their behaviour is madness but, if 'tis, then I confess 'tis a condition I wish more shared.'

Sophia appreciated that this was quite a speech for the usually silent man. 'I begin to believe that it is wrong that these Methodists should be so vilified. Who do you think I should speak to if I want to find a woman who has joined them and who is now in London? Her name is Jenny Jones.'

'I know nothing of 'er or London but I tell ye that finding her will depend on which group of Methodists she's with. Some still look to Mr Whitefield, but others now follow Mr John Wesley and his brother, Mr Charles Wesley.'

'And why is that?'

'I've not had the schooling to follow their arguments, miss. All I know is that Mr Whitefield thinks most of us are headed for damnation, whilst the Wesleys preach God's salvation is for all who are prepared to accept it.'

'Then I think I prefer what the Wesleys have to say. Where can I find these men?'

He shrugged his shoulders. 'I dunna know, miss. Like Mr Whitefield they travel the country encouraging the creation of religious societies.'

'If yer ask me,' interrupted Mrs Newton, lifting her head and pushing back a stray hair, 'those societies are just a cover for promoting political discontent. The lot of 'em are probably secret Jacobites!'

The cart fell silent and Sophia's thoughts turned increasingly to how her injured lover might be faring. She wondered whether Tom knew that she had fled for his sake or whether that was being kept from him. Her reverie was broken only by their arrival at the cloth-making town of Stroud. The place had little to commend it, but she was grateful to be able to purchase new clothes for herself and her maid after the rigours of two days of travelling. Once this was done their driver drove up a steep hill to a coaching inn called the Bear of Rodborough, which stood on land overlooking the town. Sophia thanked him profusely for his assistance and handed over some coins in generous payment. Within a very short time of his departure, she and Mrs Newton had managed to find not only a room for themselves at the inn but also had paid to be transported to Gloucester the next day.

Both women welcomed the opportunity to wash and change into their new clothes and then to enjoy a proper rest after the exertions of the day. The previous night Sophia had been first too frightened that her father might capture her and then too exhausted to think much about what condition her lover might be in, but now, as she relaxed, her thoughts turned increasingly to how Tom Jones was lying injured in the house in Queen Square. She wondered whether he knew what she was enduring for his sake or whether that information was being kept from him. Did he think that her failure to visit him stemmed from her new position as the bride to be of John Burnett? The very thought brought tears to her eyes. That night, lying in bed her last thought before going to sleep was a fervent prayer: 'May God ensure your speedy recovery, my dearest love, and may I not rest until I have found out whose son you really are and hopefully proved you are not an unworthy match for my hand!'

10

JACOB'S LADDER

Tom Jones spent the days immediately after Sophia's flight gradually regaining his strength after the ordeal that he had faced. Lady Overbury insisted on staying in his room most of the time and personally nursing him, despite the protests of her maid that it would have been a role better played by her. However, on 11 November, even such a strong-willed person as her ladyship could not prevent him eventually rising from his bed in order to resume his duties, although by then Henry Fielding was beginning to conclude that, in the absence of any further incident in the house, whatever danger had existed was over. Sir Robert Benson had already returned to London with the body of his son, infuriated that no progress had been made on either finding the whereabouts of the man with no thumb or discovering his identity.

That evening Beau Nash brought information that had just arrived in the city. There were reports that the army of the Young Pretender, Bonnie Prince Charlie, had entered England three days earlier. The news had clearly rattled him. 'I fear these Highlanders will prove a difficult enemy,' he concluded, after telling them what he had heard. 'They stick close to their ancient ways and, because they are inured to hard living, they are strong and highly dangerous. That is why they think themselves superior to any man living south of their wild hills. They will not easily turn back because ties of blood and name bind them together and they will follow their chieftains to the death.'

'I am not so sure that they will pose a long-term threat, sir,' responded Henry Fielding. 'These Highlanders may be very brave but all the reports indicate that they lack discipline and they are not as well armed as our soldiers. Facing them in open battle should pose no problem. If our soldiers keep their courage and stand their ground then they will not penetrate our line of blue, white and scarlet and we will destroy them easily.'

'Why are you so confident?' asked Lady Overbury.

'We have superior firing power. We will use our cavalry to protect our flanks and in the centre we will place our infantry in serried ranks so that they can fire their muskets in rolling volleys rank by rank until the Highlanders are stopped in their tracks by the sheer number of dead and wounded.'

Jones, who had been listening to this conversation with mounting interest, now spoke up. 'There is not a true-blooded Englishman who will not rise up to repel these invaders. I for one will sign up and join our country's defenders rather than go to America. It is up to every able-bodied man to show these wretched Jacobites that there is no support for their cause.' He turned to Burnett and added, 'Why don't you join me in this cause?'

'I have no love for a soldier's life, Tom. When they are not fighting, it is nothing but drinking, cursing and fornicating.'

'But on this occasion they will fight for the true faith. Does that not matter to you?'

Burnett looked at the floor, avoiding eye contact with anyone. 'I wish them success but why should I join when it might lead to my death?' He paused and, looking up, added more defiantly, 'Besides, I am sure that the scriptures are against fighting. You can never persuade me that a man can be a good Christian while he sheds Christian blood.'

These statements did not impress Jones, whose patriotism had been thoroughly roused. 'We might fall in battle but does that matter? We know not what lies before us any more than a miser knows the path to Heaven. And, if we die young, then at least we will have died for a good cause. Did not our schoolmaster teach us when we were young that none can escape the grave?'

Burnett frowned. 'I do not deny that all must die, but I prefer to think I will live for many years to come. It is wicked to tempt death before a man's time.'

'Not even if it protects us against papist heresy and brings our king victory?'

'What matters a royal victory if I am dead? What will all the ringing of victory bells and lighting of celebratory bonfires signify if I am buried six feet under the ground?'

Jones' face showed his anger at this reply. 'I think, sir, you speak as a coward.'

His companion merely shrugged his shoulders. 'If wishing to preserve my life makes me a coward, then I profess to being one. I prefer to think that I simply speak as a man of common sense.'

'Common sense tells me that there will be enough soldiers to defeat this rebel Prince without either of you getting involved!' interposed Lady Overbury, who had no desire to see either man risk his life. 'Is that not so, Mr Nash?'

'I fear it is too early to say, your ladyship. Like Mr Fielding I am sure that victory will be ours but as far as I know our forces are not yet gathered in sufficient numbers to quickly crush these traitors. It is taking too much time to move our troops from the Continent where they are currently engaged in fighting. It is possible that our country will require some volunteers of Mr Jones and Mr Burnett's calibre, but I think they should not be importunate and make unnecessarily precipitate decisions about enlisting. It is easy to be rash and usually one then ends up deeply regretting the outcome. Though it was over a completely different matter, I did that once with one of my servants, a good Irishman named Bryan.'

'In what way?'

'A fellow gambler said he would bet me two hundred pounds that Bryan could not run to London and back in just two days. I rashly took up the challenge and ordered Bryan to undertake the venture. He succeeded in winning the bet for me but died three days later as a result of the over-exertion involved. I gave my winnings to his widow but it did not make up for the folly of my action.'

'I also advise you, Tom, to think carefully before immediately joining the army,' interjected Fielding. 'We still require your services here. I recommend that you at least delay your decision about joining the militia until Lady Overbury has returned to London. It is only a few days and by then we may well know more about the danger posed by this invasion. It may even be the case that by then our current fears may have proved false and the prince will have already returned to the north, disappointed at the lack of English support shown for his cause.'

'I will do as you say, sirs, but I confess that I chafe under the strictures that you lay on me.'

Beau Nash laughed. 'The only way to rid yourself of restraint is to persuade Lady Overbury to make you her coachman. Then you'll have the whip hand,' he joked.

Fielding saw that this jest was taken ill, and, judging that a more considered response was necessary, intervened to give further sound reasons as to why Jones should accept their advice. 'Tom, I beg you not to think that a soldier's life is a glamorous one. Think what enlisting actually means. As a soldier you will have to abandon all your freedom for a mere sixpence a day and, though your scarlet uniform may look wonderful when first donned, it will shrink at the first shower of rain, making you look like some ill-garbed scarecrow. You will eat bread and water for breakfast and slops for the remainder of the day and, if you seek to drown your sorrows in beer, you can expect to awake robbed of whatever money you had. You will have to march endlessly where you are told and any disobedience will be met with flogging by the nine-tailed cat, anything from twenty-five strokes upwards. You will have to stand in battle against all that is meant to destroy you – from the deadly thrust of a sword to the sweep of grapeshot and cannonball. If you decide you have had enough and try to leave, you will be hanged for desertion, and, if you stay, you will more than like be eventually mutilated or maimed in conflict, at which point you will be cast out to become a beggar. No, sir, there is no point in rushing to become a soldier!'

'You paint a bleak picture, sir, and one that omits comradeship and loyalty and pride in one's country, but rest assured that I will indeed heed your advice for the moment.'

Even as he said this the sound of raucous shouting could be heard in the square. Jones looked out of the window and saw hordes of drunken young men pouring past. That the news of the Jacobite invasion had spread rapidly was evident because they were singing a patriotic song whose chorus included a rousing call to arms. 'As you can hear, there will be enough cannon fodder without you adding to the number!' said Nash grimly.

'I'll go downstairs and check the house is safe,' replied Jones, annoyed by Nash's cynicism. When he got to the kitchen he found no one in it except for Joseph Graves because the housekeeper and Sarah Darr were upstairs tidying up Sir Robert's bedroom after his departure. Graves was sitting crouched in a chair next the fire and Jones was shocked to see the intense agony that was writ on his face. He laid his hand on the troubled man's shoulder. 'What's the matter? Are you fearful of this news of an invasion, or are you afraid of the mob outside?'

'No, sir.' Graves tried to smile but there was no pleasure behind the action and there was a cold and tormented look in his eyes.

'So what is the matter? You look as if the Devil himself was about to seize you!'

'I think he may, sir, because I deserve no better.' The poor man's sense of hopelessness was palpable as he said this.

'Do not be ridiculous, man!' responded Jones.

Graves took in a deep breath and bit his lip. Then he groaned and there was in the sound such a heart-rending agony that Jones knew not what to say or do. The old man looked at him. 'I am a traitor to my country, sir, and there's not a man out there who wouldn't tear me to pieces if he knew what I've done!'

'Tell me what all this is about.'

'I can't, sir. I dare not!'

'Does it concern what happened in this house to Miss Grey and Lord Kearsley?'

Graves nodded and covered his face with shaking hands. Again he gave a groan that came from the depths of his tortured soul. 'I meant no 'arm, sir. Truly, I meant no 'arm.'

Jones pulled away the man's hands and stared him in the face. 'Then you need not fear telling me the truth,' he said gently.

Graves wept soft tears of utter despair and began massaging his eyes with the lower palms of his hands as if somehow he could wipe away the imaginings and fears that were generating tension in every nerve of his body. Finally he looked up and, between gritted teeth, whispered, 'I told the truth, sir, when I told yer all that I thought this 'ouse was 'aunted. I did think that. For days I heard noises in rooms that were supposed to be empty and sometimes doors that I locked at night were mysteriously unlocked in the morning. But I lied when I made Lady Overbury believe that I still thought the 'ouse was 'aunted when she first came here. I didn't. I simply 'oped to scare her from staying 'ere. By then I knew the true secret of this place.'

Graves paused as if he was suddenly unwilling to say more. Jones was desperate to hear what the old man knew, but he waited quietly for him to continue, somehow intuitively recognizing that it would be foolish to say anything that might deter him from continuing with his confession. His patience was rewarded when, with a jerk of his head, the servant resumed his tale. 'I discovered that a papist priest was holding secret meetings in this 'ouse with those who were considering betraying their country and I confronted Miss Grey over what she'd done in enabling this to 'appen. She told me to ignore what was going on and I agreed on one condition.' Again he paused.

This time Jones could not refrain from speaking. 'And what was that?' he asked.

'That I should be paid for my silence.'

'You should not have lied to us about this.'

'That was not the worst I did, sir. Before Lady Overbury arrived I helped Miss Grey dispose of the priest's body. She hadn't wanted to tell me about his death but he was beginning to smell and so she was forced to seek my aid. I helped her wrap up the corpse and I carried it away at dead of night, telling her that I would bury it where none would find it.'

'And where was that?'

'I didn't do as I had promised. You see, I'd recognized some of 'em that had attended the priest's meetings and so I took the body to 'em. I knew it was wrong of me but I 'oped for a reward.'

'And did you get it?'

'They gave me some money and told me that there was more if I could assist them get 'old of any documents that had belonged to the dead man. I said that only Miss Grey would know where they were.'

Jones could scarce believe what he was hearing. This stupid, greedy man had taken a bribe to betray his country and then taken another to betray his fellow servant. Graves saw the revulsion in his face and grabbed his hand.

'I promise you, Mr Jones, I didn't know they would wreak revenge on poor Miss Grey. I was as shocked as anyone when I saw 'er dead. That's why I lied to Mr Nash and Mr Fielding. I feared that them that had killed 'er would kill me next if I told the truth. So I invented the tale of the man without a thumb.'

'You did what!' shouted Jones, wrenching his hand away. 'You mean that for days you have had us pursuing a man who never existed?'

'I meant no 'arm, Mr Jones. Truly I didn't. I jist thought it would stop 'em thinking I'd a hand in what 'appened. Believe me, I love my country. I want no papist as king! The news of this invasion is tearing me apart! I should never have aided the men that I did. My one consolation is that I've stopped them getting their 'ands on what they sought.'

'Getting their hands on what, Joseph? And which men are you talking about?'

Panic flared up in the old man's face. 'I daren't say, sir. Truly, I daren't. They'll torture me and kill me.'

'I think it likely that Mr Nash and Mr Fielding will kill you if you do not. Stay here while I go and fetch them. You can only make amends by telling us all you know, every single thing.'

Graves nodded his assent meekly and Jones rushed upstairs. His news was met with a mixture of astonishment and anger. 'Damn it,' said Fielding, 'We have been seeking someone who never existed whilst all the time we had the man who could tell us what happened here beneath our very noses. We must have been fools not to question him more thoroughly!' He and Nash immediately accompanied Jones back downstairs to the kitchen. However, when they entered the room there was no sign of the servant. 'The man's courage has obviously failed him and he has fled the house!' yelled Fielding in frustration. 'We must give chase!' He and Jones ran out into the street but they could see no sign of Graves in any direction. This news was relayed back to Beau Nash, who immediately left to give orders for the old man to be hunted down. The others remained in the house, hoping that Graves would swiftly be taken. Only when two hours had passed and it was clear that his capture was going to prove a longer affair did they reluctantly retire for the night.

The next morning Tom Jones rose very early because he was determined to join in the hunt for the missing man. Even though it was still only semi-light, he set off to wander Bath's streets and so he was one of the first to see the strange sight in front of Bath Abbey. The beautifully carved Jacob's ladder on the left-hand side of the façade of the church was supposed to contain only God's angels making their way between earth and Heaven, but now some of the lower rungs, normally golden bright, were streaked with dark reddish marks. The source of these was a dangling corpse that hung from the parapet that ran at the roof level of the abbey's side aisle on that side of the building. It was customary for the carving on the abbey to draw all eyes upwards, but it was all too apparent that this poor man had stared his last looking down. He had been lowered upside down from the roof with his feet facing the skies and his head the pavement below. His arms had been firmly tied behind his back and his legs had been bound tightly together and a gag had been placed in his mouth to prevent him summoning human assistance.

His murderers had left their victim with no recourse but to seek divine aid but it was obvious no guardian angel had come to his rescue. Once he had been firmly hung in position one of his killers had pulled the gag down onto his chin and sliced across his throat with a sharp blade, severing his vocal cords and making any cry for help impossible. Blood had splattered across a wide area, including onto the lower rungs of the nearby stone-carved ladder. His mouth had gaped open in screamless agony as blood from his split throat had poured down his bruised cheeks and into his eyes, before dropping onto the wall beneath him and onto a section of the flagged pavement of the abbey's courtyard. No one had heard the struggles of his final death throes and now the only movement was caused by the wind ruffling those hairs on his head that had not been reduced to a black sticky mess by his congealing blood.

News of the dangling corpse soon spread and it did not take long for a substantial crowd to gather and its members took a grim delight in the unexpected scene. A black-garbed cleric, looking bewildered and pale, tried in vain to make the spectators depart, saying that they should leave it to the authorities to attend to the matter. No one paid him any attention, though at first the nature of the tragedy made them unusually quiet except for that hum of noise that is so often associated with a gathering – the shuffle of feet, the coughing and blowing of noses, the occasional exchange of voices, the inevitable posturing and jostling for position. Those at the front fixed their gaze on the body as if their own lives depended upon it, while those who were unable to obtain such a close view because they were at the back stood on tiptoe and stretched out their necks as if somehow they could draw themselves nearer. A thin and sallow-faced youth who desired a closer inspection so exceeded his balance that he virtually tumbled on top of his squat neighbour, a man almost as broad as he was high. The fat man cursed the boy's stupidity, saying he deserved to be beaten and then strung up on the other stone ladder as a twin to the murdered man. This incident evoked some mirth and initiated a change in what until then had been a rather sombre attitude among the crowd.

Jones felt the back of his coat being tugged and, turning round, found himself gazing at what he could only surmise was a nymph drawn from the waters of the city. Tall and slender, the young girl was golden-skinned and golden-haired with a supple, lithe figure that her simple clothes did not mask. He gazed into her dark eyes and then recoiled slightly because only then did he realize that she was blind. Her hand again tugged at his coat. 'Will you tell me what you see?' she asked. 'I have heard a man hangs from Jacob's ladder.'

'Aye, miss,' he replied, 'but it is better that you cannot see him because he has been most cruelly murdered. He hangs upside down and his throat has been cut.'

As more people began to voice their feelings, the question that went repeatedly round was 'Who is he?' but none appeared to be able to answer that. Jones remained silent, surprised to discover that he alone knew who the man was. One bald-headed man, whose few remaining sparse locks clung to the back of his neck as if reluctant to lose their hold, suggested in a stentorian voice that the man was a warning sent by God to condemn the city's devotion to gambling and whoring, but this proclamation was met with hoots of derision.

'It is not the hand of God we see at work here,' shouted out Jones. 'It's the hands of men – and evil hands at that!' Most of those present murmured their assent and gazed in the direction of the speaker. They were at once struck by the fact that all his features bore the signs of having been in a fight of great severity. There scarce seemed an inch of his face that did not still bear the signs of having been recently cut or scratched or bruised. Only those closer could see that beneath the bruising and blackening he had all the features of a strikingly handsome man.

The bald man refused to be silenced by Jones's outburst and snapped back in response. 'Believe me, sir, God would not have permitted a good man to have suffered such a fate. The man hangs there as a sign of the fate that will befall all sinners.' He smiled grimly and, raising a cup that he held in his hand, drank from it as if relishing the prospect of such an event.

'Have you no humanity, sir, to savour such an ill deed?' declared Jones, refusing to be silenced. 'I am relatively new to this city but I know no man deserves such barbaric treatment and certainly not the old man who hangs there.'

'Do you not despise the pomp and vanities of this wicked world? Do you not wish to bruise the serpent's head?'

'Ignore his harangue,' said the man next to Jones. 'You will only encourage him and then he will go through his full range of godly discourses. He thinks he is an evangelist and that few can resist the power of his words. If you are not careful he will bombard us all with his tub-thumping nonsense!'

'I thought the fruits of faith were supposed to be brotherly love and Christian charity,' muttered Jones in reply.

What more might have been said was lost because all the crowd went silent at the sight of a man in a striking white hat making his way to the scene of the crime. 'What's happening?' whispered the blind girl.

'It's Beau Nash, the Master of Ceremonies,' explained Jones. 'He's talking to a cleric about what has happened. I suspect that he will get the constables to disperse the crowd so the dead man can be brought down.'

At that moment Nash spotted Jones in the crowd and beckoned him to join him. 'I need your help to get Graves down. He has suffered enough for his lies without letting him remain a public spectacle. I am sure that this is the handiwork of those Jacobite agents whose names he foolishly feared to tell us. Once you have helped cut him down, go and tell Lady Overbury and Mr Fielding that I must see them urgently.' Jones grimly gave his assent.

Two hours later everyone was gathered together in the drawing room in the house in Queen Square. It was Nash who spoke first. 'We must revisit all the events that have happened in this house in the light of Graves's deceitfulness. Agreed?' Nods indicated acceptance of this. 'Let me begin, and correct me if you disagree with anything I say. Miss Grey was acting as an agent for Lord Kearsley and began copying a document that contained the names of all those traitors who are prepared to join the rebellion against our lawful king. Unfortunately, she was discovered in the act of doing this and, as we read in her letter to Lord Kearsley, she accidentally killed the priest who was the main agent of the Jacobites in the resulting struggle. She hid the priest's body and the all-important documents. Whether she burnt the copy she had made or placed it with the original documents is not clear. She then wrote to Lord Kearsley, urging him to return here as soon as he could. As the days passed and Lady Overbury's arrival became imminent, she decided the corpse would have to be moved. For that purpose she used Joseph Graves, who was already blackmailing her over the priest's use of the house for secret meetings. Unfortunately he did not dispose of the body in the way that Miss Grey had envisaged. Instead, he carried the corpse to some of those traitors who had been involved in the meetings. Understandably they were frightened of discovery and so they determined to get their hands on the hidden documents.

He paused and the others nodded to show they all agreed with what he had so far said. 'Now I enter less sure territory,' he continued. 'There was an attempt by someone to get the information from Miss Grey. In that process she was killed. The fact that she held in her hand the button that was supposedly the pass sign between her and Lord Kearsley may well indicate how her murderer gained admittance.

'It is possible that Miss Grey told Joseph Graves to let in anyone who had a button with a fleur-de-lis on it and that he foolishly passed on this information to her enemies,' ventured Fielding and the others concurred.

'We can also surmise that Miss Grey did not reveal where the documents were because the next night there was another attempt to get them. Hence the fact that Mr Burnett was knocked unconscious. However, this second attempt coincided with the arrival of Lord Kearsley and as a result he was murdered.'

'All that you say makes sense, Mr Nash,' interrupted Lady Overbury, 'but what can it tell us about more recent events?'

'Simply this, your ladyship. Graves told Mr Jones that he had prevented the traitors obtaining the documents that would incriminate them. He has obviously hidden them somewhere and time for them is running out. The Young Pretender's army is now on its way south and our enemies want to convey to him the names of those who are prepared to join his cause. Already they grow bolder. Look at the way they have ruthlessly chosen to murder first their own assassin in the baths and now Joseph Graves on the west front of the abbey. They are making a public example of these men so as to let others know what will be their fate if they do not remain true to the Jacobite cause.

'I suspect there are other messages too in those actions,' added Fielding.

Lady Overbury looked puzzled. 'What do you mean?'

'Humphrey Watson was stabbed to death in the King's Bath. It was in that very place that James II's wife was supposedly made fertile and so gave birth to the child who is now known as the Old Pretender. Joseph Graves was strung up alongside Jacob's ladder or, perhaps I should call it a Jacobite ladder. They are deliberately bringing the name of this city into disrepute. Earlier today, Tom, you were speaking of joining the army. The best thing you can do for your country is to help us find the documents that will name these monsters and help us crush the traitors.'

Tom Jones stood up with all the immediacy and vigour of youth. 'Then let us search this house again! This very instant, sir.'

'What if Graves took the documents away from here?' answered Lady Overbury. 'That would explain why both our searches and those of our enemies have proved a waste of time! Perhaps he took them to his own home after Miss Grey's murder. He would have known that they had a value if sold to the right person.'

'I think Lady Overbury has got something here!' said Fielding in an excited voice.

'Then it is there that we must search and not here,' replied Nash. 'I suggest you stay here with Mr Burnett to protect you. Mr Jones and Mr Fielding can join me in going to Joseph Graves's house. It is not in an area of the city to which I can take a respectable woman.'

For once Lady Overbury did not demur. Even she accepted that she could not possibly go into the slum areas of Bath. 'I will pray for your success, gentlemen,' she said, 'and whilst you are gone I will question my maid to see if Graves said anything to her that might be useful.' While the men discussed precisely what they should do next, she rang the bell for her servant, but Darr did not appear. 'Damn it, where has she gone?' she muttered. She suppressed her irritation only because she saw that the men were about to depart. She knew how much hung on their expedition. 'May God go with you,' she exclaimed.

The route to Graves's house took the three men through an area of the city through which no visitor ever passed. Here there was none of the open grandeur of Queen Square. Instead a man was hard pressed to stretch out his arms without touching the houses on either side of the street and the ramshackle buildings bore every sign of their antiquity. Wood blackened with age, plaster smeared with unhealthy-looking mould, and mortar crumbling from years of damp and neglect. It was difficult to walk without stepping into the indescribable filth that covered most of the cobbled streets and at intervals mounds of half-decomposed debris almost entirely blocked the way. The air was filled with the stench from the unwashed masses who lived there and from a strange mix of slaughterhouses, breweries, tanneries, and other businesses. As they made their way through the streets some of the inhabitants looked at them with undisguised hostility. Others seemed indifferent, as if their mean lifestyle had robbed them of any human feeling bar an instinct for survival.

When they reached the house where Graves lived they discovered he only rented a small garret. It only took a small coin to persuade the skeletal-looking landlord to show them to this. The room matched its surroundings to perfection. It had nothing to commend it. Its walls were bare plaster begrimed with the filth of many years. Their only decoration was that provided by damp patches or by those sections where holes displayed what lay behind. The low-slung ceiling was cracked and almost as dirty and it was only possible for a man to stand up in the room's centre. The floor appeared to be little better than the alleyways through which they had walked. The only furniture in the room was a small worm-eaten table, an odd-looking chair that had been much repaired, an upturned ancient sailor's chest on top of a few garments, and a simple wooden bed, covered with an unattractive mix of dirty blankets. On the table were the remnants of the man's last meal and an empty flagon.

'At least it will not take us long to search the place,' commented Nash.

Fielding pointed to the upturned chest. 'I think the place has already been searched.' He picked it up and exposed the pathetic clothes that constituted Graves's few possessions. These he proceeded to look through. 'Nothing here,' he said, 'but there may have been. The chest could have contained the documents we seek.'

Nash struggled to keep his normal equanimity. 'Zounds! We are always one step behind!'

'Should we not ask the landlord who else has been up here?' queried Jones. 'We may yet get the lead we need.'

This they proceeded to do, but either the man knew nothing or he had been bribed or frightened into pretending that was the case. Frustrated and disillusioned the three men returned to the house in Queen Square. They were greeted by a very anxious-looking Lady Overbury. Before they could speak of their failure, she dropped her own bombshell. 'My maid has been abducted. Once you left I went upstairs to find out why she had not answered my summons. There was no trace of her. With the assistance of Mrs Fleeting and Mr Burnett, I have now had the whole house searched. All we have found is this.' She held out Sarah Darr's apron. It was streaked with blood. 'My God, gentlemen, why have they taken her and, if she is not dead already, what will they do to her?'

11

RESOLVING A MYSTERY

When Sophia Westbrook arrived in Gloucester from Stroud on the afternoon of 8 November it was immediately apparent that the city had not really recovered from the damage it had sustained in the English Civil War. She thought the place had little to recommend it other than its impressive Norman cathedral with its ancient grey stone tower. She hired a room for herself and Mrs Newton in the Bell Inn, mainly because the coach driver had told her that the mother of George Whitefield had once run it. Although the inn had seen better days it was still a hub of activity and boasted extensive facilities. These included a number of attached shops, one selling wine, and the others a variety of goods because they were hired for use by travelling merchants and pedlars. Sophia lost no time in booking places for her and her maid on a coach that would leave early the next day for London. She then ordered Mrs Newton to mingle among the many men who were loitering in the inn's courtyard in the hope of discovering where they should go to find the Methodists once they reached the capital. Lacking a male escort to protect her, Sophia was loath to risk making enquiries herself. To her sensitive eye too many of the inn's customers were unsavoury characters.

The task did not prove an easy one, but eventually Mrs Newton obtained the information her mistress wanted and so, four days later, Sophia found herself standing with her maid outside an old foundry in Windmill Street in London, quite near to the north-west corner of Finsbury Square. The foundry had been built very close to the open fields on the edge of the city and so was within an area that was a popular place to visit, especially in the summer months. Sophia could see that some of the nearby fields were laid out as pleasure grounds and so contained shrub-lined walks and tree-shaded promenades, though the winter weather meant they were not then in use. The Wesleyan Methodists had decided to use the foundry, which had become derelict, as a centre for their work. The largest building within it had been converted into a galleried preaching place, which held benches that were easily capable of holding over a thousand people. A notice informed any passer-by that there were daily services held at around six in the morning and six at night. As far as Sophia could tell one building was being used as a schoolroom while some others were obviously being used for accommodation and as a stable block for a coach and horses.

Sophia was slightly fearful what to do next despite her urgent desire to find Jenny Jones. The vitriolic diatribes that she had heard against the Methodists made her cautious of venturing among them. According to her vicar, they were presumptious and opinionated troublemakers out not only to break the peace and unity of the Church but also to disturb and divide the nation in such a way that the Jacobites could take over. He had constantly warned his congregation that the Methodists were full of wild religious fancies and dangerous enthusiastic nonsense. On the road to Stroud the old woman's son had presented her with a very different picture and more favourable report of their activities, but how reliable was his version? As she deliberated what should be her next step it became increasingly apparent to her that a crowd was collecting in the nearby fields, despite the cold weather. A simple enquiry to a passer-by brought the answer that the people were gathering to hear Charles Wesley preach. Curious to hear him, Sophia joined the crowd, despite a vociferous series of protests from Mrs Newton, who feared for their safety.

The two women soon found themselves surrounded by people of every description and class. Some appeared to come from a merchant or trading background, but the overwhelming majority of those present were ordinary working people of the kind who were never to be found within a church. While a few were already trembling over their sinfulness and bursting into tears on account of their damnation, most had obviously come to jeer and poke fun at the preacher. Mrs Newton told Sophia in no uncertain terms that many of these were thieves, prostitutes, or worse. Not surprisingly her mistress noted with some relief that there were also scattered among the crowd several gentlemen and a few ladies who appeared to come from a similar social order to her own. As she surveyed the scene, Sophia began to realize that there were at least a couple of thousand people in the fields. There was an almost instantaneous jeering among the more rowdy element when the preacher made his appearance and climbed onto a cart so that he could easily be seen. A man of only middling height, he was dressed in a plain coat and wig and, to Sophia's eyes, he looked surprisingly frail.

Charles Wesley lifted his hands up heavenwards and in a clear voice commenced with a prayer. He then opened his Bible and, choosing as his text 'Come unto me, all that are weary,' started to preach without the use of any notes: 'Look at mankind and you soon see that the whole head is sick and the whole heart faint. From the sole of the foot to the crown of the head there is no soundness in us, but wounds and bruises and putrefying sores. Our understanding is darkened, our will perverse, our affections set on earthly things. If you take away the spark of God from our soul, then there remains nothing but pure beast and devil. That is why there is not one person here who can earn their salvation. I know that from my own experience. I tried for years to lead a holy life and failed. Believe me when I say that your salvation can only come from the cleansing blood of Christ. I know some of you may feel that you are so sinful that God could never love you, but you are wrong. God's love is far greater than we deserve. Christ is the friend and saviour of all sinners.'

He preached in a similar vein for almost an hour and revealed a remarkable talent for expressing the most important truths with simplicity and energy. Shouts of 'Hallelujah!' began echoing round the crowd. Even the normally cynical Mrs Newton seemed affected. Those who were already Methodists began to sing as if the words and melody were engraved on their hearts and Sophia was deeply moved. She could not help but wonder if the clergy's opposition to Wesley stemmed from envy of his superior preaching talent. When he called on those who felt their heart awakened to come to the front a significant number did. 'Madam, this man is truly sent by God,' muttered Mrs Newton. I'll not believe anymore those that damn these Methodists as being a wicked people!'

The two women approached the preacher once the initial throng of people around him had thinned down. On closer inspection he proved to have a kind and attractive face – his eyes were soft and gentle, his arched nose well-shaped, and his mouth soft-lipped. There was a natural warmth to him that made them both feel instantly at ease in his company. Sophia introduced herself and her maid, who for once was unusually subdued in her manner, and then added, 'I confess, sir, that I did not think I would approve of this field preaching but you are a powerful preacher. I am surprised that you do not advertise yourself more.'

Charles Wesley shook his head. 'I do not like those preachers who promote themselves, Miss Westbrook. It looks to me like sounding their own trumpet. God may use me to strengthen the weak hands and feeble knees of others, but please do not place me on any pedestal. I judge myself to be a man in whom there is no strength. I am often weary and faint in mind and I do not always show the love to others that God desires or I would wish. If truth were told, I am continually tempted to leave off preaching and hide myself away. I should then be free of any temptation to take pride in what I do, and instead have leisure to attend to my own improvement.'

Both women were taken aback by the man's humility. They were used to clergy who were pompous and proud. 'No one is perfect, sir,' replied Sophia.

The preacher smiled back at her but there was no hint of flirtation in it. 'Once we have experienced God's saving grace we should strive for perfection because God's wonderful love for us demands no less.'

'I have heard say that in encouraging people to seek perfection you encourage religious extremism?'

'I should not judge any person by common report. I assure you that, whatever our failings, we are not fanatics. We are merely Christians who are trying to put our faith into practice. People are creatures of habit, Miss Westbrook, and so we encourage a daily routine of prayer and study of the scriptures and we expect people to feed and clothe the poor, visit the sick and imprisoned, and comfort the dying. We ask all to refrain from drunkenness and contentious argument and instead to toil day and night to bring the gospel message to all by word and deed. That is the method of living that our enemies deem enthusiastic madness and folly!'

All this was said with such conviction that Sophia could not help but admire hm. Nevertheless, she asked, 'Yet people also say that you are also secret Jacobites? Are you?'

Wesley laughed. 'Good gracious no!' he exclaimed. 'Both my brother and I have frequently made clear our loyalty to King George. It is a mere silly tale invented by those clergy who dislike us preaching in their parishes. They use it as an excuse to hire bands to drum out the sound of our preaching and mobs to attack us. We have had stones and dirt flung at us and clubs raised to strike us. Recently I even had a soldier put a sword to my breast and threaten to kill me. I have seen the homes of some of my friends literally pulled to the ground and our women semi-stripped and dragged through the streets with their petticoats pulled over their heads.'

'I do not know how you cope with such abuse, sir.'

'We cope because we know God is always with us in whatever we face. What we have felt and seen of God's love we tell with confidence and therefore our numbers continue to increase despite the persecution shown to us. Christianity flourishes under the cross. The key to everything in life is to trust in the Lord.'

'And is that what this nation must now do in the face of an invasion?' replied Sophia, deeply moved by his words.

'We must become more worthy. We cannot expect God to be on our side if the soldiers who fight for us remain as they are. Even a young lady like you will appreciate that their wanton blasphemy is a torture to any sober ear and evidence of their shameless wickedness. My brother, who is in the north of England, has been seeking to preach to our armies but he has been prevented.'

'I know that you must be a very busy man, especially in your brother's absence, but may I have a little of your time to tell you of a matter that is nothing compared the mighty issues with which you deal, but which means much to me?'

Wesley looked at her and sensing the anxiety behind her outward composure, replied quietly, 'It is a poor Christian who turns his back on someone who seeks assistance. Come inside the foundry and tell me what concerns you. These fields are no place to linger at this time of year. I already can see that you and Mrs Newton are beginning to shiver with the cold.'

To this suggestion Sophia willingly agreed and soon she and her maid were drinking a cup of tea as she told the preacher all about her situation and about her desire to discover the truth about Tom Jones's parentage. Charles Wesley listened attentively, only occasionally stopping her to clarify a point. To her surprise he expressed no judgement against her having run away from her father's command to marry a man she did not love, and she could not help saying, 'I feared, sir, that you might not choose to help one who has disobeyed God's command to honour one's parents.'

'That is not a reason for parents to command love where there is none and expect unquestioning obedience,' he replied. 'I know that from my own family's experience. My father forced my sister Hetty to marry a man who was most unsuited to her and her husband has wrecked her life. He rails against all religion and he has so frequently abused her that I have had to offer her refuge here to protect her from his drunken behaviour.'

'I am very sorry to hear that, sir.'

The look in his eyes acknowledged her sympathy, and he smiled before adding, 'But you may not be sorry to hear that the person who nurses my sister is Jenny Jones and she is almost certainly the person you seek for I know she comes from Bath.'

This news was far better than Sophia had dared hope for in her wildest dreams and she leapt up in excitement. 'Please may I see her immediately?' she pleaded.

'Wait here a moment. Let me go to my sister's room and see Jenny first. I'll explain the situation to her and, if she is willing to see you, then I will tend my sister for a time so that she can come here and speak to you.'

Sophia thanked him profusely. Time seemed to stand still as Sophia and her maid waited for the outcome. Then there came the sound of steps and the door opened to reveal a slender woman dressed in the simplest of clothes. Her narrow frame made her look younger than her years but her manner was quite agitated and she nervously clasped and unclasped her thin-wristed hands together. She had blue eyes, a small nose, high cheekbones, and a wide-lipped mouth, and, although her face was heavily lined and her brown hair streaked with grey, she had retained enough beauty in her features to show that she must once have been a very attractive woman.

It was Sophia who spoke first. 'Are you Jenny Jones?' she asked, scarce daring to hope that it really was the woman that she travelled so many miles to find.

'Yes, I am,' the woman replied, in a voice that slightly trembled. 'But I have no reason to be proud of the fact because for years I was like a Pharisee, who sees the sins of others but not his own.' Seeing Sophia knew not how to respond to this, she continued, 'It was only five years ago that God was pleased to convince me of my sinfulness. I heard Mr Whitefield preach and he gave me the knowledge I was sinking into Hell. That was in the March and I suffered much until I heard Mr Charles Wesley. It was through him that I saw my Saviour bleeding on the cross, dying for all our sins. I trembled so much that those around me had to hold me up and some said that I had gone mad. However, it was the hard work of the Lord letting me know that my sins were forgiven and offering me his peace. Since that day, I have been full of joy and lost in wonder at what God has done for me and I trust I shall not rest helping others until I die and enter the glory that He has prepared for me.'

For the first time, Sophia understood why some of the clergy viewed Methodism with such suspicion. There was such passion in Jenny Jones's voice that it made her feel uncomfortable. Mastering her nervousness, she replied, 'I am pleased that you have found such a strong faith and you feel your sins to be forgiven and I am sorry that I have come to remind you of the past when, by your own admission, you were a sinful woman. But, as Mr Wesley has doubtless told you, I desire to know more about the illegitimate child to whom you gave birth all those years ago.'

'I have committed many sins in my life, Miss Westbrook, but illicit love is not one of them. I want you to know from the outset that I am not and never was Tom Jones's mother.'

This announcement took Sophia completely by surprise and rendered her momentarily speechless. It was left to Mrs Newton to break the silence. 'Then you'd better answer who was his mother, as well as who was his father, and explain why you allowed people to think that poor Tom was your's and the local schoolmaster's.'

Jenny Jones struggled visibly with conflicting emotions before summoning the courage to respond. 'I know that concealing the truth has caused much pain to me and to others and there has not been a day pass without me regretting that. However, you should know that Mr Wesley has persuaded me that the time has come for me to tell that which I have kept hidden for over twenty years. To continue hiding what really happened all those years ago is no longer necessary because the person to whom I pledged my silence is now dead.'

'It would indeed be a Christian act to reveal the truth, Miss Jones,' interjected Sophia.

'I may have been bad in many ways in my youth but I loved Miss Woodforde very much. No lady could have been kinder than she was to me. It made serving her a joy rather than a duty. Such was the interest that she showed in me that, when she saw how ashamed I was that I could not read or write, she paid for me to have lessons with the schoolmaster, Mr Partridge. He too was very kind to me. I think he would have liked me for his wife but I was young and flighty and saw not his worth as a husband. One of my bitterest regrets is that I paid him back ill for all that he did for me.' She paused and her misery found expression in the tears that formed in her eyes.

'Your silence over who was Tom's father caused his dismissal.'

'Unfortunately it did. I thought his innocence would mean that my silence would not harm him, but its impact was the reverse. I have prayed often for God to forgive me for the pain that I caused him.'

'If it is any consolation, he is well, calls himself Peartree, and is now the landlord of a successful inn.'

'I am pleased to hear it and I will thank God for the mercy that he has shown.'

'Why did you permit people to believe that you were Tom's mother and stay silent about his true parentage?'

Jenny Jones looked at her with a mixture of pain and defiance. 'The reason was simple. I had promised Miss Bridget I would say nothing and I kept my word.'

The truth behind what had happened all those years before suddenly struck Sophia and she asked anxiously, 'Was your silence to hide the fact that Miss Bridget Woodforde was Tom's mother?'

'Yes, but I do not wish you to condemn her. She suffered much for that sin.'

Just how remarkable a young woman Sophia was became apparent in her reply. 'I believe that when a crowd wanted to stone a woman to death for committing adultery, Jesus said that only those without sin could cast a stone. None was able to therefore act against her. I am not sinless and I will not even try to judge Miss Woodforde until you tell us what happened.'

'For those kind words may you one day join the immortal choir in their hallelujahs, Miss Westbrook!' replied Jenny Jones. Her face reflected a variety of emotions but relief and gratitude dominated. She knew that most women would be far quicker to judge and condemn her former mistress, but for the moment she enjoyed the pleasure of meeting someone whose mind was more open to forgiveness. It made telling her story so much easier. The rather cold façade that she had built up over the years to protect both herself and Bridget Woodforde for the first time seemed no longer necessary. She relaxed to the extent that Sophia caught a glimpse of the young girl who had sacrificed herself for her mistress all those years ago.

'Believe me, Miss Westbrook, my mistress was a woman who would have made a wonderful wife to any man, but it was her misfortune not to be blessed with beauty. The men who courted her – and for a time there were many – made plain that they were more interested in her wealth than in her. She wisely refused to enter into a loveless marriage and so took the decision to remain a spinster, though society then judged her a failure. The one person who did not condemn her was her brother, Thomas Woodforde. He loved her for her many virtues and, in return, she threw herself into supporting the many charitable ventures in which he engaged.'

'I have heard much from Tom about her many kindnesses to people.'

'It was her kindness to one in particular that caused her downfall. The squire took an interest in a young lad whom he judged very talented. The youth had hopes of one day becoming a great writer and Miss Woodforde encouraged this. The bond between them grew and she spent many enjoyable hours in his company. On her part the interest turned to love. I know not all the details, but one day, consumed by passion, she offered herself to him and they made love. It was a sinful act and one they both immediately regretted. On his part there was no real love. How could there be? He was still a mere boy of sixteen and she was more than twice his age. Once he had satisfied his lust for the first time, he was embarrassed at what had happened and sought to avoid her. For her part she felt she had seduced an innocent and was deeply ashamed. What made the matter even worse was when she discovered that she was with child. How could she face her brother with such evidence of her wicked sinfulness? In her frightened state she confided in me.'

'And what did you advise her to do?'

'I told her that she must hide what had happened if she did not wish to ruin four lives.'

'I can see that her reputation would have been ruined, but who were the other three?'

'Her brother would have become a laughing-stock; her lover would have had his career ruined; her child would have to live in the knowledge of the shameful behaviour that had led to his or her birth. Miss Woodforde cared not for her own reputation because she felt that her actions deserved whatever opprobrium society chose to cast at her, but she wept bitter tears at the havoc her actions might generate for the others. For that reason, I suggested that she did not tell the youth that their brief intimacy had led to her being with child and that she should disguise her motherhood from her brother. I vowed that, once she had given birth, I would hide the child in such a way that her brother would discover it. Knowing his kindness, I was sure he could be prevailed upon to care for the babe, even though its parentage was unknown.'

'And she obviously agreed to your plan.'

'Yes, though not without some soul-searching, and at first my plan appeared to work beautifully. I hid the baby in the squire's bed so he would discover it on his return from a trip to London and, as I had thought, he ensured that it was well looked after. He even suggested that his sister should help care for it. Unfortunately I had not counted on two things. The first was that suspicion would fall on me as being the mother. When that happened, how could I deny it? I knew if I accepted the blame, then it would guarantee my mistress's guilty secret would never be uncovered, and so I said that I was Tom's mother. It cost me dear because, of course, I was then dismissed and sent away.'

''Tis amazing what we maids will do for our mistresses,' muttered Mrs Newton.

'And I suppose the other thing that went wrong was Mr Partridge being named as the father,' added Sophia.

'That is true, but the other thing to which I was referring was the doctor's betrayal.'

'The doctor?'

'Miss Woodforde did not have an easy time in the latter stages of being with child. We had to call in a doctor and swear him to secrecy. His name was Burnett and he confided what had happened to his brother, who was a captain in the army. This brother then blackmailed poor Miss Woodforde because he wanted her money. He told her that he would inform the world what had happened unless she married him.'

'That explains why she so surprised everyone by her marriage and why it was such an unhappy one!' exclaimed Sophia.

'Yes. She paid dear for her sinfulness. The only thing she refused to surrender was Tom. Captain Burnett was keen to have the child removed, especially when he had a son of his own, but she resisted that. She regarded Tom as her true son because at least there had been some love in the act that gave him birth. There was no love on either side when her other son, John, was conceived. Only the satisfaction of her husband's desire for an heir.'

'So what happened to the young man who never knew that he was the true father of Tom Jones?'

Jenny Jones opened her mouth as if to reply and then suddenly changed her mind. A flicker of uncertainty flashed across her face. Sophia and her maid held their breath, unsure of why she had become silent. After all that they had been through, was she still going to deny them knowledge of Tom's true father? Jenny Jones paced up and down before them, her face pale, her hands so clenched that the knuckles on her fingers shone white. Finally, she turned and, looking direct into Sophia's face, said, 'I have decided this matter is too sensitive to be shared with anyone but you. I must therefore ask that you send away your maid so we may speak in private.' She turned in Mrs Newton's direction and added, 'I have nothing against you, but there is no need for you to know. The fewer who are told the better because the more people who know the more the story will sooner or later pass to those who will make mischief out of it. They can do no harm now to the mother, but Tom's father is alive and well. If news of his youthful indiscretion became public I am sure that it would prove a source of great embarrassment.'

Sophia could see that her maid was bristling at the implication that she could not hold her tongue, but also knew enough of Mrs Newton's character to know that Jenny Jones was right. Though her maid was essentially a very good woman, she had a pretty free tongue when it came to gossip. As a consequence it did not take long for Sophia to agree to do as she was bid and to ask Mrs Newton to join Mr Wesley so that she and Jenny Jones could be left alone for at least ten minutes. Needless to say, this did not happen without her maid making her hurt feelings known. Even once she had left the room, the sound of her continued protest could be heard going down the corridor. Jenny Jones remained silent for a few more moments and then suddenly confessed, 'Tom's real father went on to become a very popular playwright in London. I believe that he now writes novels. His name is Henry Fielding.'

There was a deep intake of breath from Sophia at this unexpected revelation. Fielding was well known to her because of his long-standing friendship with the Woodforde family. She and her father had met him on a significant number of occasions. She had come to like him for his warm-hearted, generous, and good-humoured nature. She admired the fact that he was always sympathetic to the problems of others because of what he had suffered in his own life. She had particularly appreciated his interest in Tom and the way he had championed his cause when he had unwittingly offended the squire. Knowing how lonely and dispirited Fielding had been over the death of his beloved wife, she was confident that the writer did not know that he had a son in Tom. If she revealed what Jenny Jones had told her, what impact would that have not only on Fielding but also on Tom? And how would the information of Tom's true parentage affect Thomas Woodforde and her father? Would the squire be repelled by his sister's sinful behaviour and deception, or would he rejoice in discovering that Tom was his nephew? Would her father's attitude to Tom change if he knew that he was a Woodforde, or would he still insist on her marrying John Burnett?

'I tell you this so that you may inform Mr Fielding,' continued Jenny Jones. 'There is no need for others to be told, not even Tom. He has lived all these years without knowing who his father was.'

Such was the turmoil in Sophia's mind that later she could not recall what she said to Jenny Jones before the woman returned to her nursing duties. Such was her dazed state that Charles Wesley took pity on her when he rejoined her. He sat alongside her and gently took her hand in his. 'Listen to me, Miss Westbrook, why don't you and Mrs Newton stay here till you decide what next to do? You are a stranger in this city and London is not a safe place for two unprotected women. We have a spare room and I can arrange for your belongings to be brought here from the inn where you stayed last night. I can assure you that you will be most welcome.'

'I thank you, sir,' replied Sophia, desperately trying to pull herself together. 'You are most kind and I would like to take up your offer. If truth be told, I have not felt safe since we left Bath and I am uncertain what next to do. I now know the truth about a man's parentage but not whether I should reveal what I know to him and those whom it affects most. Before I came here it all seemed straightforward. I thought if I could find out who was Tom's father it might help reconcile my father to him. Now I am less certain because of the impact the knowledge may have on others. Jenny Jones has made it quite clear that I should only inform Tom's father of the truth.'

'Why don't you sleep on the matter before taking any decision. Another day will not matter to a secret that has lasted over twenty years.'

'Has Jenny Jones told you what she told me?'

'Yes, she has. Not because I asked, but because she felt she wanted me to absolve her from what she did all those years ago.'

'And have you?'

'It is not for me to absolve anyone. That rests with God. But I believe He has long forgiven her and I have told her that. What she did she did out of love, even if it was mistaken.'

'And what would you advise me to do?'

'To pray to God for his guidance.'

'But you must have an opinion that you can share with me before I do so.'

Charles Wesley smiled at her persistence. 'Very well. I think that truth is more important than falsehood and that a man has a right to know who is his father. Equally a father has a right to know that he has a son. Jenny has kept the secret too long to know what now is right. If I were in your position, I would inform Mr Jones, Mr Fielding and Squire Woodforde what you know. Let them determine how they should respond to the information. Whether you should tell your father is far more questionable. From what you have told me, he may not be so polite in keeping the matter to himself. I would suggest it is up to the three men most intimately affected to decide whether anyone else should be told. There is no reason for anyone else to know if they would prefer the world to be kept in ignorance.'

His words resonated in her heart and gave her a sense of direction that she found most comforting. 'I cannot thank you enough, Mr Wesley.'

'Give your thanks to God, not me. I believe it is He who has protected you on your journey and it is He who has directed you here. Now, if you will forgive me, I have other matters to which I must attend. I will tell Mrs Newton what is happening and direct her to return to you. One of the women here will direct you to where you will be staying.'

She held on to his arm to prevent his immediate departure. 'Please can you do one thing more for me?' He nodded. 'Can you persuade Mrs Newton not to spend her time trying to get me to tell her what I now know?'

He laughed. 'There are certain things even a minister of God might not be able to achieve! But I will do what I can.'

12

THE TRAITOR REVEALED

Lady Overbury looked out of the window at the grey, rain-soaked sky and the weather matched her sombre mood. She had only recently arrived back in London and the ten long days since the terrible events of 12 November had been among the worst of her life. She had tried to divert herself by participating in some of the pleasures offered by Bath, but this had done little to help. To her mounting consternation Beau Nash and Henry Fielding had been unable to uncover a single clue that might point to who had killed Joseph Graves, even though they had discovered how his body had been carried onto the aisle roof. His murderers had hired an upstairs room in one of the houses that backed onto the abbey and from there had clambered onto its roof and thence onto the aisle roof. Unfortunately none could be found who could describe the person who had hired the rooms because payment had been made to the landlord's daughter, the blind girl whom Jones had encountered. Fielding and Nash had drawn an equal blank when it came to finding what had happened to either Sarah Darr or Sophia Westbrook. It was as if both women had simply disappeared from the face of the earth.

Throughout her remaining time in Bath, Lady Overbury had taken up residence in a large house in the Orange Grove run by a Mrs Hodkinson because Fielding had finally persuaded her that it was unsafe to remain in Queen Square. Her new residence was known for its finely proportioned rooms, comfortable down beds and excellent food, but entering it had seemed an acknowledgement of defeat. Moreover, she had found it far noisier than the house in Queen Square because a seemingly endless murmur of voices had percolated through to her rooms, interrupted only by the occasional sound of the creaking and crashing of trunks and the trampling of porters, or by bursts of music played on instruments that were not always in tune, or by the more harmonious peal of the abbey bells. This had not provided her with the silence and repose for which she longed. Nor had it helped her frame of mind that the house's other residents had been obsessed with speculating about the danger posed by the advancing Jacobite army, especially when reports came through that Carlisle had fallen to the rebels on 15 November without a shot having been fired against them.

At first, whenever the weather had permitted, she had taken to getting away from the unhelpful gossip by going out for a walk unattended, a practice that was regarded as socially acceptable in Bath though very unusual elsewhere. Experience had soon taught her to avoid the busier areas of the city, especially Stall Street. It bustled too much with people arriving and departing and there was nothing but noise and tumult. The grinding and rumbling of carts and carriages, the yelling of porters and servants, the squealing and squawking of pedlars, and the sound of snarling dogs and weary horses had merely served to give her a headache. She had much preferred strolling along the elm-lined gravel walks of the Orange Grove. The elevated platform on its western side provided good views across the neighbouring countryside, although the river looked dirty and the surrounding fields and hills carried the unattractive features of the onset of winter. The rather bleak vista matched her mood far more than looking at the delights of the many shops that surrounded the Orange Grove, though they were undeniably full of the most varied and elegant of goods. Somehow purchasing the latest perfumes or fashionable clothes had seemed inappropriate against the backdrop of events she had faced. What did fan or feather matter if tragedy could strike so unexpectedly and frequently? Even all the famous culinary delights of Mr Gill's pastry shop could not tempt her to indulge herself.

Lady Overbury had sought solace in music and fortunately there had been plenty of that available in Bath. She had taken to attending the concert breakfasts and on a couple of afternoons she had sat entranced in Bath Abbey listening to the playing of its talented organist, Thomas Chilcott. She had also gone to two of the concerts that he had organized in Wiltshire's Consort Room and particularly enjoyed a programme of Handel's music. One aria from *Theodora* called 'Angels ever bright and fair' had moved her to tears. Knowing her love of theatre, Fielding had tried to encourage her to also attend performances of Shakespeare's

Othello and *Romeo and Juliet* by a company who described themselves as 'the best actors in the world', but she had declined, saying she had seen enough real tragedy without watching imaginary ones.

Instead, for a time, she had tried to extend her walks and take some pleasure in exploring the area around the city. She had hired a carriage to take her to the village of Kelston and followed the lower road towards Bristol, enjoying the changing vistas provided by the wind-swept hills and valleys all around her. She had no doubt that the ride would have been more beautiful in the summer months with all the flowers and foliage at their height, but even in November the scenery had a stark attraction that made her for a time forget what had happened in Queen Square. The highlight of her travels had been a trip on a rare bright sunny day to Lansdown. The ascent was a difficult one, but, once the height had been reached, she had enjoyed the bracing air and open views. In one direction she had been able to see the city of Bristol and, beyond that, the Bristol Channel and the mountains of Wales. In the other direction she had looked over the rolling countryside of Gloucestershire and Wiltshire and beyond.

It had taken all Beau Nash's skills to persuade her one Tuesday evening to attend a ball at Mr Harrison's Assembly Rooms, but her acceptance had proved a mistake. It had begun after six o'clock and followed the formula that Nash had devised many years before. He selected the most important gentleman and lady present to dance a minuet and, once this was completed, he led the woman back to her seat and brought back another to dance with the man. For the next two hours each gentleman present in turn danced with two ladies. Nash had jokingly made it a Bath rule that no gentleman or lady should take it ill that another danced before him or her, but Lady Overbury was amazed at the impassivity of countenance of those who danced. There was no sign of any cheerful face or of any enjoyment in the music. The gentlemen in their tricornes and silks and the ladies in ostrich plumes and hoop skirts seemed more concerned to display their finery than to dance and both sexes appeared petrified of making a misstep.

Sitting at the side of the room throughout the succession of dances, Lady Overbury had become increasingly bored by the whole process. She knew it simply pandered to the social snobbery of so many of her class, and all around her she had been conscious of a constant stream of salacious gossip and matchmaking. Nash had told her that he thought scandal was the mark of a foolish head and a malicious heart and he had made it a Bath rule that those who spread scandal should be shunned. The evening convinced her it was a rule honoured more by the breach than the observance. When the minuets finally ended, country dances began, but they were scarcely less formal. The only difference was that the order was determined entirely by the rank of the ladies. It was not until the clock struck eleven that Nash ordered the music to stop by lifting his finger.

Lady Overbury had vowed never to repeat the experience and she had refused to try the Friday balls at Thayer's Assembly Rooms. Instead, some of her time in the evenings had been spent with Henry Fielding's sister, who had also taken temporary lodgings in the city. The two women had talked a little about Sarah Fielding's upbringing in Salisbury under the care of her maternal grandmother, Lady Sarah Gould, and the time she had spent in London and Bath with her brother during his wife's illness. Miss Fielding was unusually well educated and knowledgable on the subject of classical poetry, which she seemed to be able to quote effortlessly. She had described how she had been permitted to assist her brother in his literary endeavours and how in return he had helped her write her own novel, *The Adventures of David Simple*, which had been published the previous May. Lady Overbury had tried to divert herself by reading it, but its theme of a naïve hero dealing with the double-dealing duplicity of a malign world was unappealing. Moreover, she found the novel lacked character development and a plot of any note, even though it shared much of the wit and irony found in Henry Fielding's novels.

Lady Overbury had hoped that returning to London might help her to forget all that happened but so far that had proved a mistake. Now, looking at the clock on the mantelpiece in her parlour, she saw that it was almost time for the Reverend Charles Wesley to arrive and curiosity began to dispel some of her gloom. The London broadsheets were daily full of vitriolic attacks against the Methodists and, when he had requested to see her, she would have refused to see him had not one of her friends, the Countess of Huntingdon, urged her to do so. She had presented a far more positive picture of Charles and of his brother John Wesley than the one given in the popular broadsheets. According to her, the brothers had spent the early years of their lives in rural Lincolnshire where their father was a rector. John had won a scholarship to Charterhouse and Charles, who was four years younger, to Westminster. Both men had then gone to university in Oxford, been ordained, and become missionaries in the newly created American colony of Georgia. On their return they had determined to create a religious revival in the Church of England with some of their former Oxford friends who had also become clergymen, including George Whitefield and Benjamin Ingham. The countess felt strongly that all the anti-Methodist hysteria stemmed from misunderstanding and mischief.

Although she had agreed to meet Charles Wesley, Lady Overbury remained unsure about whether that was a wise choice. Having been denied access to the pulpits of his fellow clergy, Charles Wesley was choosing to preach in the open air. This was hardly what any respectable clergyman would do and some of the broadsheets were certain that his meetings were acting as a cover for Jacobite traitors to meet together. Her greeting was therefore a cautious one when he entered the room. 'I have heard much about you, sir,' she said, 'but sadly most of it has not been very flattering.'

'I am aware that the common press say all manner of things about me that are not true, your ladyship,' he replied with a quiet dignity, politely inclining his head towards her. 'However, the only opinion that matters in judging what we say and do is that of God and so my conscience is clear. You will forgive me if I prefer to obey His commands rather than seek the favour of men.'

'But is not this preaching in the open air a vile thing to do?'

'I think you will find that Jesus set us a precedent in this matter. Did he not preach most of the time in the open air?'

Lady Overbury had the intelligence to acknowledge this argument had validity and, as someone who frequently resented the strictures imposed on her by what society deemed appropriate or inappropriate, began to warm to the man. 'I had not thought of the matter in that light, sir.'

'I will be honest with you, Lady Overbury. Neither my brother nor I like preaching outside but we do so for two simple reasons.'

'And what are they?'

'The first and most important is that we are convinced it is what God wants us to do. He is using our preaching to reach the hearts of many who otherwise would know nothing of the gospel message. We are able to speak to thousands who would never set foot across the threshold of a church. The second is that my fellow clergy have left us no alternative by denying us access to their pulpits. They are more concerned about protecting their authority within their parishes than communicating the faith.'

Lady Overbury felt her initial suspicion dissipate. The Countess of

Huntingdon had told her that Charles's friends referred to him as a man made for friendship and she could now see why that was. He had an affable manner and she had no doubt that he was highly intelligent, warmly empathetic, and naturally good-humoured. She was astute enough to see why his intensely religious approach would have led some to label him a dangerous enthusiast. The open way in which he expressed the depth of his faith would make those who preferred their Christian commitment to be nominal uncomfortable – and she knew quite a few clergy who were in that category. 'It has won you nothing but condemnation from the Church,' she said but in a tone that was far more considerate.

'I hope that the Church will reconsider its position when it sees the fruit of our work,' he observed. 'Until that happens, your ladyship, I invite you to come and see the holy lives lived by many of those who have been awakened by our preaching and to judge for yourself whether the current condemnation is justified.'

Lady Overbury was surprised to hear herself say, 'I would like very much to see your work at first hand.' What even more astonished her was that she knew she meant it. There was no doubt that this preacher had both authority and charm.

'I commend your openness, Lady Overbury, and we can arrange a visit at a future date, but for the moment I have more pressing business with you.'

'And what might that be?'

'I come to bring you back a friend. She is in my carriage that waits outside your door, having been in my care these past eleven days. Had she not been the victim of a protracted fever I would have sought to bring her to you earlier.'

Delight spread across Lady Overbury's face. 'Is it my maid?' she asked. 'Have you found Sarah Darr?'

'No, madam. I said that I brought you a friend not a servant.' He moved to the window and gave a signal. Lady Overbury crossed over to where he stood and, to her delight, saw Sophia Westbrook stepping out of the carriage with the assistance of a woman whom she assumed was Mrs Newton, her maid. Such was the relief she felt at this sight that she was rendered speechless. A few minutes later Sophia was ushered into the room and she flung herself into Lady Overbury's arms. Only then did the older woman find her voice again and it shook with emotion. She expressed all the fears that had so dominated her thinking since Sophia's disappearance and her intense joy that these had proved unfounded. It was only as she spoke that she took in how pale and drawn the young woman was. This was living evidence of the illness that had so recently laid her young friend so low.

Sophia chose not to dwell on her experiences but outlined as briefly as she could the events of her escape and how she had found Jenny Jones and discovered the true parentage of Tom Jones. She confided all that she knew about the affair between Squire Woodforde's unfortunate sister and the young Henry Fielding. Then she recounted all the help and support given to her by Charles Wesley and other Methodists at the old foundry, especially after she had fallen ill. 'I think,' she concluded, 'that my sickness stemmed from that first night of our flight. We travelled for too many hours in the cold and then we were soaked. I am fortunate that I fell into such kind hands here in London or else I might have died.'

Lady Overbury turned to Charles Wesley, who had stood patiently aside while the two women had been speaking to each other. She said very softly, 'I cannot thank you enough, sir, for all that you have done.'

'It is no more than anyone with a Christian heart would have done,' he replied modestly. 'But you can do what I cannot, Lady Overbury.'

'In what way?'

'You can help reconcile a father to his daughter and you can help Miss Westbrook explain to Squire Woodforde and Mr Fielding the surprising news of their relationship to Mr Jones. They may not find it easy to accept what Jenny Jones has said, but I can assure you that she is now telling the real truth about what happened all those years ago. I will confess that I was not sure that Miss Westbrook was wise in her desire to tell you first. There are too many women who love to gossip. However, now that I have met you and seen the way you love her, I admit I was wrong. She will benefit from your wise assistance.'

Lady Overbury acknowledged his praise with a smile and slight inclination of her head. 'Sir, I will do all I can to speedily bring matters to a happy conclusion by arranging to return with Miss Westbrook to Bath as soon as we can board an appropriate coach. In return I ask one thing of you.' She paused and he saw that she still had a troubled mind, despite the happy reunion. 'Please pray that I may also one day discover what has happened to my lost maid and see her captors brought to justice. Her abduction weighs heavily upon me.'

'Her abduction?' queried Sophia, looking puzzled.

Lady Overbury swore them both to secrecy and proceeded to explain all the events that had happened in Bath and how they had culminated in the death of Joseph Graves and the disappearance of Sarah Darr. Sophia could not help herself dwelling on Tom Jones's brave role so it was left to Wesley to bring a more perceptive mind to the startling account. He asked her to provide him with a description of her missing maid and this she provided with admirable clarity. He immediately looked very worried. 'I have met someone called Sarah Darr and she was of the age and appearance you describe. If it is the same woman then I fear you may have been most grievously deceived. How long was this maid in your employ?'

'I only acquired her as my maid shortly before I travelled to Bath. My previous maid resigned unexpectedly and I was in a state as to how to quickly replace her with someone dependable. I was enormously relieved when Lady Rudd said she knew a girl who was very reliable and sent me Darr. But what do you know of her?'

'In the summer of 1743 my brother John asked me to travel throughout the south-west preaching and that included going to Cornwall. Some of the clergy made out that I was a Jacobite agent and raised mobs against me in Bodmin, Redruth and St Ives. The longer I stayed in the county the greater the attacks became. My enemies raged and roared like lions, but I persevered because thousands of tinners, who had never before heard the gospel, were coming to hear me. At Gwennap near two thousand hungry souls devoured the word of reconciliation and gave God their hearts.' He said this without a hint of pride or any attempt to make them admire his bravery. 'When the time came for me to go back north, I vowed to return and it was on that second visit in July of last year that I first heard about Sarah Darr and the tragic circumstances surrounding her birth.'

Wesley took a few moments to compose his thoughts before continuing his story. 'I found the whole county was alarmed because of the increasing fear of a Jacobite invasion. As a consequence mobs were hurling bricks and stones through the windows of any deemed to be Methodist. One stone almost killed a sleeping child in St Ives and, when the mother complained to the authorities, they refused to act, saying they were not prepared to extend justice to traitors. It was because the words Methodist and Jacobite had become synonymous that Sarah Darr came to hear me in early August when I was at Penryn. People had been pouring in all day from Falmouth and the surrounding area and I exhorted them not only to give their hearts to the Lord but also to condemn anyone who sought to bring conflict to this country and to pledge their loyalty to King George. She had not been expecting to hear such loyalty from me and it greatly displeased her.'

'But why should such a young woman support the Jacobites?' interrupted Lady Overbury.

'That became clear when she demanded that Thomas Meriton, who was my companion on the tour, bring her to see me in private. She entered the room where I was staying in a highly agitated state. Her face was flushed and she shouted at me with venom in her voice, "I came to hear you because I thought you were here to rally the people in support of their true king and instead you call upon them to renew their loyalty to the usurper who wrongly sits on the throne!" Hoping to calm her down, I suggested that she should explain to me why she was so bitterly opposed to King George. In reply she told me the sad history of her father, Henry Darr, who had been a well-respected Cornish innkeeper in St Columb Major. Like many others thirty years ago, he could not understand why the government in London chose to offer the crown to a minor German prince from Hanover, who could not even speak English, in preference to the son of James II.

'Henry Darr was persuaded by a colonel called Maclean to support the Jacobite rebellion in the south-west in 1715. Unfortunately Maclean was in fact a government agent and he secured the arrest of the two key Cornish Jacobite leaders, Sir Richard Vyvyan of Trelowarren and John Anstis, the MP for Launceston. A man called James Paynter, who came from a wealthy family in St Buryan, urged all Cornishmen to raise the standard of rebellion immediately before more were arrested on the information provided by Maclean. Henry Darr was one of the very few who responded. He got up with Paynter in the market square at St Columb Major and proclaimed James Francis Edward Stuart as rightful monarch.'

'A brave act but a very misguided one in the circumstances,' commented Lady Overbury.

'I agree. The two men were immediately forced to go into hiding. Eventually they fled to London where they were hidden from arrest by their fellow Jacobites. Unfortunately for them James Paynter had taken with him a servant who wrote love letters to the sweetheart he had left behind. These letters were intercepted and handed over to the authorities, who thus discovered where Paynter and Darr were staying. Both men were sent to Newgate to be tried for high treason. Henry Darr never got a trial. He died within the prison's grim walls and his grief-stricken wife soon followed him to the grave, leaving the newly-born Sarah an orphan. That is why she is a professed Jacobite who wishes to see the triumph of Bonnie Prince Charlie. Her heart is filled with hatred for those who destroyed her parents.' He looked at both women, who had listened to his story with mounting interest, and added, 'I therefore strongly suspect that it is too much of a coincidence to think that all the wicked events that happened in Queen Square happened without any assistance from her. Although I did all I could to persuade Miss Darr that she should replace the anger in her heart with the peace that only God can provide, it was to no avail. She left me still bitter and tormented.'

Sophia did not know what to make of Charles Wesley's unexpected revelations about Sarah Darr's links with the Jacobites, but it did not take long for Lady Overbury's astute brain to begin re-examining the events in Bath in the light of this new information. Wesley refrained from speaking further because he saw that she was deep in thought. He could almost sense her mind going around various possibilities. Sophia also kept silence though the impatience of youth made the wait seem interminable. Finally Lady Overbury began to speak. 'I fear, sir, that you are right and Sarah Darr has been acting all along as a Jacobite agent. It makes sense of so much of what has confused me ever since these terrible events began. I can only surmise that somehow the Jacobites gained access to the contents of Miss Grey's letter to Lord Kearsley. Determined to get their hands on the incriminating evidence they probably bribed my maid to resign so that I would require assistance and then used Lady Rudd to persuade me to hire Sarah Darr.'

'A clever ploy!' muttered Wesley.

Lady Overbury swallowed hard and a hint of her internal anger flashed across her face. 'Yes, and, once she was in the house in Queen Square, she acted swiftly. I have long puzzled why I heard the noise of Miss Grey's murder that first night because my bedroom was so far removed from hers. Now I suspect that the noise that woke me was made by Darr so that she could deceive me into believing that the murder had just taken place and at a time when she was asleep in bed. In reality I think she had murdered the unfortunate housekeeper long before then. Miss Grey did not meet her death because she opened the house in Queen Square to a stranger or because anyone had broken in; she died because she accepted the fleur-de-lis button shown to her by Darr and arranged to meet her in her room after I had gone to bed.'

'But why did she not hand over the documents to Darr if she thought Lord Kearsley had sent her?' queried Sophia.

'Presumably because something must have made the housekeeper suspicious and made her refuse to hand over the documents,' replied Lady Overbury. 'And her refusal led to her murder.'

'Hatred breeds a wickedness that destroys anyone who stands in its path!' said Wesley, shaking his head at the thought of how much Sarah Darr had permitted herself to be consumed by unholy passions. His face creased with sorrow at her folly and its tragic outcome.

'But surely,' intervened Sophia, 'murdering her meant she had destroyed the one person who knew where the documents were!'

Lady Overbury acknowledged the correctness of this with a slight inclination of her head. 'And that is why it must have been Darr who was searching the house at night in an attempt to find them. I cannot be certain but I suspect it was she who knocked out poor Mr Burnett and shot Lord Kearsley.'

'His arrival would have almost certainly compromised her deception,' agreed Wesley.

'I also suspect that it was Darr whom Tom Jones pursued upstairs,' continued Lady Overbury. 'She locked the door to prevent him catching her and then, while he went to fetch Mr Nash and Mr Fielding, she made her escape. We were looking for an intruder and could not find one because there never was one!'

'But surely she had nothing to do with what happened to my poor Tom on Guy Fawkes' Night?' questioned Sophia.

Wesley was touched by her naivety and replied gently, 'From what Lady Overbury told us earlier, Mr Jones was acting as a good watchdog and I suspect that restricted Sarah Darr's ability to search for the missing documents. I would therefore not be surprised if she was the person who determined on his permanent removal. Whether she, or one of her fellow Jacobite traitors, hired Humphrey Watson to do the deed we shall probably never know.' He saw Sophia recoil at the idea that any woman could be so callous as to condemn a man to be burnt to death, but Lady Overbury nodded her agreement. 'From what you have told me about events in the King's Bath,' he continued, 'it is possible that the hired assassin was murdered by her. She was not with you at the time the man was actually stabbed and his removal ensured that he could not betray her.'

Lady Overbury flinched at the thought of such a possibility, but saw the sense in what he said. 'I hate to say it but you may be right, Mr Wesley. She certainly got us both away from the scene of the crime with amazing speed. However, that is not to say she wielded the knife. There is another possibility. We know that there are other Jacobites in Bath because of the way in which Joseph Graves was murdered and one of them could have killed Humphrey Watson on her orders.'

Wesley shrugged. 'Either way she was probably responsible for his murder and also for Graves's capture and subsequent death. She probably overheard the conversation between him and Jones and then acted to prevent the old man speaking further to Mr Nash and Mr Fielding. How she persuaded Graves to accompany her we will never know unless we can capture this wicked woman.'

'And capture her we must because she alone probably knows what happened to the documents after they were taken from Graves's room!' exclaimed Lady Overbury in reply. 'I will immediately write to Sir Robert Benson so that he can alert the appropriate authorities in London and I will personally go and inform Beau Nash. I was going to return to Bath in order to help Sophia but now I have a second reason for going.'

The preacher grimly nodded his agreement. 'The Highlanders continue to move southwards and there is no doubt their aim is to seize control of London. Should Sarah Darr still be in Bath, the nation will be deeply in your debt, Lady Overbury, if you can help Mr Nash and Mr Fielding find her and extract from her who is and who is not a potential Jacobite supporter.'

'I will have my servants prepare my things for the return journey and book seats for me and Miss Westbrook on the first available coach back to Bath. Believe me, sir, when I say that we will do all we can to bring Sarah Darr to justice for what she has done.'

'Amen to that!' added Sophia, grasping Lady Overbury's hands in hers. 'My blood boils when I think how she tried to destroy Tom!'

'May God go with you both!' said Charles Wesley.

13

THE BEGGAR'S OPERA

It was fortuitous that Beau Nash always made it his business to greet new coach arrivals because that meant no sooner had Lady Overbury taken up residence again at Mrs Hodgkinson's in the Orange Grove on the late afternoon of 25 November, than he arrived to greet her and she was able to inform him of Sarah Darr's treachery. He was immensely grateful for this new information but he was forced to confess that, as no trace of her missing maid had yet been found, it made no immediate difference to resolving where the vitally important documents were. What, he assured Lady Overbury, it would do was reinvigorate the search for her former maid, because that had largely been abandoned. Such was Nash's agitation and desire to act on what she had revealed that he only gave the other passengers who had arrived that day a cursory greeting. It was therefore easy for Sophia Westbrook to pass herself off under an assumed name, especially as she had muffled herself up in order to hide her appearance.

Lady Overbury requested that Nash should tell Fielding and Jones her news about Sarah Darr as soon as he could and she asked him to also pass on to them that she had acquired some information that was of importance to Squire Woodforde and his friend, Mr Westbrook. For that reason she would be glad if her friends would delay coming to see her at her lodgings until they could bring the two men with them, preferably the next day. Nash agreed to do as she asked and so Fielding and Jones were amazed to hear Lady Overbury's news from the Master of Ceremonies later that evening. Like him, they were much annoyed that they had not suspected Sarah Darr at any stage in the proceedings. Jones was all for going to see Lady Overbury immediately because he was desperate to know what she might have found out about Sophia Westbrook, but Fielding told him that it was too late and that they should wait until they had done as she had requested and notified the others. He had no doubt that Lady Overbury would have her reasons why she wanted all four men to be present for whatever she had to say.

That very night Jones communicated the request for a meeting to Thomas Woodforde, who was staying in the city, while Fielding made arrangements for a messenger to ride first thing the next morning to inform George Westbrook at his home. They thought that waiting for Westbrook might cause a considerable delay in them seeing Lady Overbury, but in the event the distraught father responded to the news by recklessly galloping to Bath as fast as he could. He arrived mid-afternoon and he and the others at once made their way to Mrs Hodgkinson's house in the Orange Grove, each showing varying degrees of anxiety and puzzlement as to what news Lady Overbury might be going to reveal. Sophia Westbrook and her maid had taken up separate rooms from Lady Overbury and so they were hidden from their sight. Of the four men Jones and Westbrook were the most agitated. Jones's manner displayed all the hope and fear of a lover who knows not what has happened to the person he adores, whilst Westbrook was obviously in a foul mood. This was partly because he had spent the whole journey to Bath wondering what ruin his daughter might have brought on his family's good name and partly because he hated being in the presence of Tom Jones, whom he blamed as the cause of his daughter's flight.

Lady Overbury greeted them all warmly and invited them to each take a seat on one of the mahogany chairs that graced her main reception room. Fielding, Woodforde, and Jones did as they were bid but Westbrook was in too much of a turmoil to sit down and instead chose to stand by the fireplace so that he was as far away from Jones as possible. Lady Overbury immediately tried to set all four men's minds at rest.

'I think it important that you should all know from the outset that Miss Westbrook and her maid are safe,' she said reassuringly, 'and that, when they left here, they took refuge with a clergyman.' She turned to look specifically at Westbrook and added, 'So you need not fear, sir, that your daughter has in any way compromised herself or you.'

'I'll have my daughter back and she'll marry whomever I choose for her, whatever any damned clergyman has to say about the matter!' Westbrook immediately stormed back, hiding his relief at his daughter's safety with an outward defiance. 'And I can tell you now,' he added, pointing at Jones, 'it will not be to this pauper!'

Lady Overbury glared at him and only just managed to refrain from telling him that he was a pompous and ill-mannered ass. 'I suggest that you sit down and calm yourself, sir. Mr Jones is not the man you think him. I know his true parentage and I think when you hear to which family he belongs, you may not be so opposed to the match.'

'I'll be the judge of that, damn the insolent bastard!'

'Mr Westbrook, I'll not have such language in my presence,' she responded indignantly. 'I must have your word you will properly hear me out, or you must leave now. If you cannot be civil you will never know where your daughter is!'

Thomas Woodforde rose and crossed the room to his friend, putting his hand gently but firmly on his arm. 'Come now, George, be sensible. You forget your manners. Come, sit down with us. Will you not hear what Lady Overbury has to say like a gentleman and without interrupting her?'

Westbrook reluctantly nodded his acceptance and did as the squire bid but his brow remained thunderous.

'Good. Now I can begin my tale in full,' said Lady Overbury. She smiled and looked directly at Tom Jones, whose attention had been focused entirely on her since he had entered the room. 'Whilst I was in London I received information about how Jenny Jones had recently confessed the truth of what really happened all those years ago and that her confession revealed you had an entirely different parentage from the one commonly believed.' She paused to look at the impact of her words on the others. Fielding looked surprised, Woodforde appeared shocked, and Westbrook's expression was one of utter disbelief.

'Then she was not my mother?' The muscles in Jones's neck tightened in anticipation as he tried to keep the extent of his emotion out of his voice.

'If it was not Jenny Jones, it was some other strumpet!' interjected Westbrook.

'No, sir!' shouted back Lady Overbury and her cheeks flushed red with annoyance. 'I can assure you that Mr Jones's mother was a good and kind lady and one much loved by all who knew her.' She paused to find the right words. 'But a woman who, in a moment of weakness, surrendered her virtue to a young man.'

'Then she cannot have been a woman of any moral substance,' said Woodforde with a slight sneer.

'I think you will disagree when I tell you it was your sister, Miss Bridget.'

The squire recoiled as if he had been hit in the face. 'How dare you insult her memory by such an allegation!'

'It is not an allegation, sir. Trust me, it is the truth. Your sister became with child and sought to hide the fact. She took Jenny Jones into her confidence, little knowing the trouble that would cause for her servant. She had no desire to see what she had done cause you pain and no desire to let her child grow up unloved. The solution was to have the son to whom she secretly gave birth placed in your bed. You know the rest. She encouraged your natural kindness and you adopted the child. She thus got to see her son grow up and she was able to ensure that you provided him with the best possible education. Unfortunately she paid a very heavy price for her action. The doctor who came in secret to deliver the child threatened to betray her unless she married his brother, who was a destitute soldier.'

Woodforde's heart told him that Lady Overbury was speaking the truth and he suddenly looked both vulnerable and miserable. 'So that's why she married Captain Burnett! It was the one act in her life that I never understood. How my sister must have suffered!' Tears began to form in his eyes. He swiveled round to face Tom Jones and said emotionally, 'I loved you when I thought you were no one. I have even more cause to love you now that I know you are my nephew.' Not caring what the others might think, the two men rose and embraced with tears in their eyes. Then Woodforde turned to Westbrook. 'George, this boy is as much part of my family as John Burnett and I can assure you that he will inherit half my estate because I will split it between him and his half-brother. Unlike John, he loves your daughter. Do you still therefore wish to refuse him as a prospective son-in-law?'

'Can we be certain that this Jenny Jones is telling the truth? I doubt it,' replied Westbrook taciturnly. 'And even if she is, what kind of father would permit your sister to face what she faced in marrying that dreadful soldier? Why did he not do the honourable thing and marry her himself? It is certain that this lad's blood will have been tainted by having a most inappropriate father.'

Lady Overbury controlled herself with great difficulty, resentful of Westbrook's constantly negative attitude. Her mouth twitched with irritation. 'Tom's father did not know that Miss Bridget was with child. She never told him.'

'You expect me to believe that?' he snapped back.

'There are reasons that I am not yet at liberty to say.' She turned to Henry Fielding. 'Before I go any further in this matter I will require your advice.'

He paled and with a slight huskiness in his voice murmured, 'You know that I will help in whatever way that I can, Lady Overbury.'

'Then please accompany me into the next room. I would speak to you in private.'

All Fielding's normal lightness of manner disappeared. He looked very troubled, but with his customary unfailing charm he followed her out of the room meekly, leaving the other three men bewildered at what might happen next.

'I think I know what you are going to say, Lady Overbury,' Fielding said drily as soon as he and Lady Overbury were alone together. 'I am Tom's father.'

She nodded, but without a hint of disapproval in her face. 'Poor Miss Bridget loved you enough not only to seduce you but also to hide the fact. I think she did so not just because she felt deeply ashamed of having had an affair with a boy so young but because she did not desire her folly to wreck your career.' She paused and looked at him and, after a moment's hesitation, said, 'Do you want the others to know?' Seeing his obvious discomfort and doubt, she then added, 'Or do you want to keep it a secret that you are Tom's father?'

Fielding considered for a moment how to reply and realized his emotions were too confused to permit a rational response. With typical honesty he replied, 'I do not know what I want, Lady Overbury. This all comes as a great surprise to me.' For the first time his voice cracked and he lost control. She saw him visibly pull himself together and then he said carefully, 'I want Tom to marry Sophia and to know that I am his father and proud to be so, but equally I do not want the story of what has happened to sully Miss Bridget's memory or make Squire Woodforde a laughing stock.' He ran his hands across his agitated face. 'And I have no idea what Mr Westbrook might say or do if he hears I am Tom's father. The man is far too unpredictable to hazard a guess.' He hesitated and then added, 'What would you advise me to do?'

'It is unfair to pass the responsibility for what you should do onto me,' she protested. He knew that she was right and inwardly cursed his weakness. She saw the misery in his face and her heart went out to him. Almost instinctively she continued, 'But I will give you an answer out of the friendship we have long had.' He smiled through his pain and his eyes conveyed his gratitude. She reached out and took one of his hands in hers. 'I have given the matter some thought since I first heard the account of Jenny Jones. I think Tom needs to know who his father is and the truth provides the best chance he has of gaining Mr Westbrook's assent to him marrying Sophia. However, I can see no reason why the world need know. Let the squire formally adopt Tom as a member of his family. That will cause no surprise. His love for the lad is widely known. Let him and Mr Westbrook agree Tom's marriage to Sophia. That will cause no comment. It is known that Mr Burnett has no desire to marry her. Let you and your son see as much of each other as you desire. That will evoke no suspicions. He and you have forged a friendship that will permit you to continue meeting without the world having to know your true relationship.'

'And what of John Burnett? Should he be told?'

'No,' she responded coldly, pursing her lips. 'I do not trust him. I believe he might threaten to tell the world if it suited him.'

'As ever, Lady Overbury, I bow to your wisdom and common sense.' The tenseness in his shoulders remained and there was a fine sweat across his brow but it was evident from the firm way in which he said this that he had regained mastery of himself. 'Let us return to the others and let me speak of what happened all those years ago. Your part is done.'

The outcome when the others heard what Fielding had to say about his youthful indiscretion was better than Lady Overbury had dared hope. For a start Westbrook surprised everyone by his willingness to accept what had happened without even the hint of a sarcastic or prudish comment, while Woodforde placed no blame for his sister's condition on the writer. Rather he pitied both of them for engaging in such a momentary madness and the truth enabled him to understand her reluctance to let society know what had happened. In an odd sort of way he was grateful to know that the blood that ran through Tom's veins came from such good stock. Jones shared his uncle's relief. He had long held Fielding in high regard and he could have wished to discover no better father. Once the initial emotions of all present had settled, there was unanimous agreement that no one else should be told, not even John Burnett. 'He will just have to accept that I have formally adopted Tom as a member of the family so that he can marry Sophia,' commented Woodforde, 'and while I have no doubt that he will resent it, he will not think it strange. It is no secret that I have long loved Tom.'

It was at this point that Lady Overbury left the room and then shortly returned with Sophia, having first told her all that had transpired. Any possible awkwardness between her and her father was averted by the young woman immediately throwing herself into his arms and begging his forgiveness. This Westbrook duly gave and it was he who then, to everyone's surprise, graciously led his daughter over to Jones. He placed one of Sophia's hands in that of the young man. 'It was far too easy to hide my daughter's disappearance from the man I thought she should wed because he showed no interest in seeing her. I will not seek to give her any more to such a man. Your feelings for her have always been far stronger and, now that I know that you have a father that I can respect, it puts your love in a different light, especially as your uncle is the best friend that I have and your mother was a woman whom I deeply admired and whose folly I can bring myself to forgive. Take my daughter's hand in marriage and take care of her. She may be errant and headstrong but her actions have shown me how much she clearly loves you and I will not seek to give her any more to a man who does not deserve a woman of her worth.'

There was much to rejoice in that afternoon as tales were exchanged and more was said about what Sophia and her maid had done in the time that they had been away, including the assistance provided by Charles Wesley and the mistaken prejudice against his followers. The conversation flowed freely between them all for over an hour until Fielding, his face alight with joy, ventured to suggest that they celebrate their combined happiness with a visit to see a performance of *The Beggar's Opera* that was scheduled to commence at six o'clock and for which he had a reserved box.

'What a splendid idea!' exclaimed Sophia, rising to her feet and giving him a dazzling smile.

'I must warn you before you become too excited, that the production is not taking place in a proper theatre,' responded Fielding. 'The small playroom built by George Trim was closed when its site was chosen for the new Royal Mineral Water Hospital. The travelling company putting on *The Beggar's Opera* is therefore performing at the Globe Inn near the Westgate. It is not the best of locations but I can assure you that those who go are well entertained and at half the price of what they would pay to see a play in London.'

'It is not appropriate for the ladies to go there,' interrupted Westbrook, his face showing his irritation at the turn in the conversation. 'I do not know what I deplore more – the scandalous behaviour of the actors and actresses and those who gather round such playhouses, or the lewdness and impiety of the plays themselves. The players who perform in the Globe are profligate wretches and, in my opinion, there is not a performance that does not corrupt the onlooker. I am with the famous Mr Law in thinking that those who take to the stage are the vilest vermine that hell ever vomited forth.'

'I think you overstate your case, sir,' muttered Fielding, trying not to show his amazement at Westbrook's puritanical stance. 'I wrote plays myself until the Licensing Act swept away my ability to offer topical satires and I do not judge myself to be the kind of person that you describe!'

'Then you are a rare exception, sir. And you must, from your own experience, know that those who perform on stage are the scum and stain of humanity. They set out to debauch our minds and morals.'

Fielding shook his head. 'There are works, such as those by Shakespeare, that enlighten the human soul, Mr Westbrook, and, as far as less moral works are concerned, it seems to me that there is nothing wrong in making people forget their sorrows and anxieties by indulging for a time in amusing scenes or foolish fantasies.'

Westbrook's face reddened and it was obvious to all the others that he was not going to back down. 'Fine words,' he said, swallowing convulsively, 'but everyone knows that *The Beggar's Opera* is designed to simply seduce the audience into liking rakes and bawds. And it is common knowledge that half the whores in this city hang about wherever plays of this sort are being performed, knowing they can get ready customers from those who have had their consciences corrupted! Pickpockets and other thieves also make the Globe their haunt.'

Fielding saw that the man was far too pig-headed to listen to the voice of reason and confined himself to saying, 'It seems to me that this particular opera encourages us to believe that it is better to enjoy life for a while and die on the gallows than have no fun and die in the gutter. I am not sure that is an entirely false premise.'

'Honesty and modesty are jewels in their own right, sir,' uttered Westbrook pompously.

'That may be so, but it is only to be expected that some people will choose a life of crime rather than exist in hopeless poverty or seize moments of pleasure in a world that often denies happiness.'

Lady Overbury sensed that the discussion was leading to needless antagonism and feared that, if it were permitted to continue unchecked, it might cause Westbrook to reconsider whether Fielding was a suitable father-in-law for his daughter. She therefore looked at the writer and intervened in a typically decisive manner. 'As you know, Sir Henry, I love a good play, but I will support Mr Westbrook on this particular production. He is quite right. From all that I have heard *The Beggar's Opera* is not a salubrious work and the venue does not suit me. I would therefore prefer to remain within my lodgings tonight, especially if Sophia might be permitted to stay here with me for a few days. I would welcome her reading to me on an evening.' She looked beseechingly in the direction of Sophia's father. 'I have grown to value your daughter's company and I would prefer not to be in Bath unaccompanied during my short time here. I know that you have just been reunited but surely, Mr Westbrook, there is no need for Sophia to immediately return home. It would do her good to spend a little more time with Mr Jones after all that has happened and I am happy to act as chaperon.'

Sophia looked anxiously in her father's direction. Being permitted to stay near her lover was far more important than any visit to a playhouse. Westbrook smiled triumphantly, feeling vindicated by Lady Overbury's support. 'You are a woman of integrity, madam. I know my daughter is in safe hands in company such as yours. For that reason I am content for her and her maid to remain with you until you return to London. You can help her prepare sensibly for her forthcoming marriage.'

'Thank you, sir. I am much obliged for your confidence in me.'

On this happy note Westbrook and Woodforde shortly afterwards took their leave so that the latter could find appropriate lodgings for the night before returning home the next day. No sooner had they gone then the mood of those who remained visibly lightened. The unpredictable and often irrational behaviour of Westbrook had been a little trying even if none had chosen to refer to it.

'And what would you have me read this evening, Lady Overbury?' asked Sophia.

'Nothing tonight, my dear.'

'But I thought you wished for that?'

'I do, but it is not necessary tonight. This evening I am content to stay here and read by myself. I suggest that you and Mr Jones go with Mr Fielding and see the opera at the Globe together.' She laughed at the surprise shown by her young ward to this declaration. 'The opera may not be salubrious but it is fun and you will enjoy it. Whatever your father says, I do not think it will destroy your morals. Treat it for what it is – a bit of foolish nonsense. Just don't tell him I let you go and see it!'

Sophia needed little encouragement. The thought of spending an evening with Tom was happiness enough and the exciting prospect of doing so at the Globe was like the icing on a cake. 'Who wrote this opera, Mr Fielding?' she asked, unafraid of showing her ignorance.

'A man now dead called John Gay who came from Devon. I met him once or twice. He made his name from a combination of using his wit and acquiring the right connections. Alexander Pope, Jonathan Swift, and others promoted his talents as both a poet and a dramatist. Gay made a habit of frequenting those places that polite society would not dream of visiting and so was well placed to portray the lives of those who dwell in London's shady taverns and houses of ill fame. He discovered that there may be little honour among thieves but there is plenty of humour. *The Beggar's Opera* is full of it.'

'I was one of many who saw the original production when it opened in the Lincoln's Inn Fields Theatre in 1728,' added Lady Overbury. 'A run of more than a dozen nights was considered a success. It ran for sixty-two consecutive performances, longer than any other production had ever achieved. It made its theatre manager, John Rich, so wealthy that he was able to build the Theatre Royal in Covent Garden. Since then it has been regularly revived. I am sure that you will find it as fresh and witty as if Gay's pen had just written it today.'

'Then why not come too?' enquired Sophia artlessly.

Lady Overbury laughed. 'Because I said to your father that I would not go and I will keep my word. Besides, it will be good for the three of you to spend some time together without having me with you.'

Sophia flung her arms around her and whispered into her ear, 'I wish that I could have you as my newly discovered mother!'

'Don't be foolish! Whatever next!' responded Lady Overbury, seeking to hide the tears that sprang to her eyes because she had indeed come to look on Sophia almost as a daughter.

It was not long afterwards that Henry Fielding, Tom Jones and Sophia Westbrook made their way to the Globe. The inn was built round four sides of a courtyard and its wide, double-tiered timbered balconies provided an excellent vantage point for the performances that were enacted below in the summer months. However, it was impossible to use the yard in the cold, dark months of winter, and so the owners of the inn had created an alternative indoor venue for winter productions by making alterations to a very large, rectangular hall within the main building. A stage area had been built along one of the short sides and three entrances had been made to this from a room that backed onto the hall and which served to hold the actors and actresses when they were not on stage. It was to this hall that Fielding led the two young lovers.

The three of them then made their way through the packed playhouse to one of two small raised areas which had been created to either side of the performance area and which offered more space to the onlooker than was possible in the tightly packed seating that directly faced the stage.

Sophia found it all very exciting and relished the buzz of anticipation that filled the hall, even though the lighted tallow candles and sheer number of people in the audience made for a rather oppressive atmosphere. Many in the assembled throng had been there for over an hour in order to ensure a good seat and so their entry did not go unnoticed because they were among the last to arrive. Their departure had been slightly delayed because of Sophia's insistence on first changing into a special peach-coloured dress for the occasion. The result had taken Jones's breath away and her appearance at the inn when she removed her cloak was sufficiently striking to cause a considerable stir among the theatre audience. Sophia could not help but blush at the comments of the more rowdy members of the audience, though she took their remarks as a compliment.

Hardly had they sat down when a small band struck up the overture. Both Fielding and Jones had been to other productions and so brought a slightly more jaundiced eye to the opera that followed, but Sophia was immediately entranced by its witty dialogue and by its constant flow of tuneful songs. The main plot, such as it was, concerned how a wicked fence called Peachum was seeking to have a highwayman called Macheath caught and hanged for having secretly married his daughter Polly. As the plot progressed Sophia had to admit that her father's criticisms had not been entirely unfounded because there was no attempt to disguise either Macheath's criminal pursuits or his immorality when it came to seducing women. She found herself blushing when she heard the highwayman sing 'Would you have a young virgin?' and felt Tom's left hand envelop hers. Equally, she could not prevent herself thinking of her own position when Polly Peachum defended her love of Macheath by singing the song 'Can love be controlled by advice?'

The audience and its reactions were as surprising to Sophia as the performance. There were people from all walks of life present and the social mix seemed to encourage a boisterous atmosphere in which the audience participated almost as much as the performers in what was happening. Here was no silent, reverent audience hanging on the words of actors and actresses, but a voluble mass who commented freely on the appearance and actions of those on stage and off it. Some clearly gave most of their attention to the drama being played in front of them, but others were happy to indulge in flirtations with their neighbours and in gossip about whatever took their fancy. Others delighted in shouting out what they took to be witticisms directed against the performers or other members of the audience. Each song tended to be met with a round of clapping and yelling and a demand for an encore.

Both Fielding and Jones took as much pleasure in seeing Sophia enjoying herself as in watching the performance until towards the end of Act II when Macheath was arrested and locked up in Newgate Prison. Then their eyes were drawn entirely to an actress who entered upon the stage for the first time in the opera, playing the part of Lucy Lockit, the daughter of the corrupt gaoler. She was dressed in a simple but very effective green dress that emphasized her naturally fine figure. Her extraordinarily pretty face and dark hair had won over half the audience before she even opened her mouth. Here was an actress with real stage presence. All eyes were drawn to her as she began scolding Macheath for having agreed to marry her and then broken his promise. When she began to sing her pure voice held the entire audience captivated.

Sophia suddenly became aware that Tom was completely absorbed in staring at the actress. Before she could take any offence at her lover's fickle behaviour, she heard him mutter, 'My God, I know this woman.' He turned to Fielding and she heard him whisper, 'Her hair is dyed a different colour and her manner and dress is entirely different, but I'm sure that the actress playing Lucy Lockit is Sarah Darr!'

Fielding was instantly oblivious to the action of the opera. He stared at the actress and then replied as quietly as he could, 'Because of her make-up and changed hair I might not have noticed had you not said so, but, you are right, it is her. But what on earth is she doing on stage here?'

'I have no idea. What shall we do?' responded Jones anxiously, acutely aware that he and Fielding were as much visible to the audience as any of the performers.

'As soon as the opera is over I will accompany Sophia back to Lady Overbury's lodgings. It would not be seemly for you to take her unaccompanied by a chaperon. You must get backstage as quickly as you can. Make sure that this clever deceiver does not disappear again. If necessary, restrain her by force until I can return. I'll see if I can send a message alerting Beau Nash so that he will join us.' Fielding looked at the actress as she continued to dominate the stage. 'It is vital we find out more about the most unusually talented Miss Darr.'

Jones readily assented, although Sophia whispered her concern that he might be yet again placing his life in danger. While everyone else in the audience was caught up watching Lucy Lockit help Macheath escape and then try to poison Polly Peachum, Fielding and Jones pondered what had led Lady Overbury's former maid, if she wanted to evade capture, becoming an actress. It was hardly a sensible thing for her to be appearing on a stage in the city. Had she no concern that she would be spotted and identified? Surely she was not so stupid as to think that a spot of greasepaint and a change of hair colour would prevent people recognizing her? Their thoughts were interrupted only when the audience yelled for an encore as the opera came to a dramatic end with a reprieved Macheath publically proclaiming his marriage to Polly Peachum yet singing of his continued feelings and desires for all women, black, brown, and fair. Fielding at once got up to leave, taking Sophia gently but firmly with him.

Jones tried to make his way backstage. His progress was not swift because many of the audience had poured onto the stage area. However, his mounting panic that he might find Darr already gone proved groundless. As he slipped through the door that led from the stage to the room behind he saw her sitting on a bench. She appeared to be engrossed in talking to some of her fellow performers and so she did not see him enter. Looking at her he could see no trace of the woman who had served Lady Overbury. Here was a woman who was outgoing, a strong personality with the world at her feet. She appeared to be in sparkling form and whatever she was saying was causing much mirth. Hoping that she would not look in his direction he moved as quickly and silently as he could towards the room's other exit and hid behind a rack that contained costumes.

From there he watched her without being visible. His mind whirled with questions. What had led such a talented actress to take on the subservient role of maid to Lady Overbury? If what Charles Wesley had said was true, her motivation stemmed entirely from hatred of the government that had destroyed her father. But what links could this woman have developed with the Jacobites? She had been but an infant when the 1715 rebellion had taken place. She had gone to Wesley in the hope that he was a Jacobite supporter and to show her support for Bonnie Prince Charlie. This in itself argued that she had at that time no strong connections of her own. So who had subsequently recruited her and persuaded her not only to become a maid but also to murder first the unfortunate housekeeper Miss Grey and then Lord Kearsley? More importantly, did she now possess the incriminating documents following the killing of Joseph Graves? And why was she still in Bath and performing in such a public place?

His reflections were interrupted when the actor who had played Macheath moved away from the group towards the room's exit. Effectively this meant that he had to cross behind the costume rack, moving out of Darr's sight but straight into the area where Jones was hiding. Jones decided his best course of action lay in barring Macheath's path. There was just a chance that he could extract information from him that might shed light on what Darr was doing. Knowing that few are immune to flattery, he immediately opened a conversation with the actor by saying, 'I cannot praise your performance tonight enough, sir. It was superb!'

These words had the desired effect because the actor did not walk past Jones. Instead he stopped and smiled. 'Thank you, sir. I thought it went well tonight and the audience was certainly a very receptive one.'

Jones gave the man one of his engaging smiles. 'Have you worked long with this company?'

'A couple of years.'

'You must all know each other very well.'

The man who had played Macheath nodded. 'Aye, though we have a few new people who have just recently joined.'

'The actress who played Lucy Lockit being one, I surmise, because I have not seen her before.'

'Yes, and we were very fortunate to get her. None of us know why but Sally – her predecessor in the role – disappeared a few nights ago.' His mouth relaxed into a smirk and he winked at Jones. 'Gone after some man or other I suspect.'

Jones thought it more likely that the unfortunate Sally had met the same fate as others who had crossed Sarah Darr's path, but he made no reference to this. 'So who is the new actress who plays Lucy Lockit so well and from whence did she come?'

'Her name's Kitty Pike and fortuitously for us she heard of Sally's desertion. She had only just arrived in Bath and was looking for new work, having performed for some months in London. Take my word for it, she's far better an actress than Sally ever was. You were lucky to see her perform because we move on tomorrow.'

'Where is your next engagement? I enjoyed myself so much tonight that I think I might like to follow and see you perform again.'

The actor laughed. 'I think you will change your mind when I tell you that our next two engagements are in Coventry and Warwick.'

'You are right – that's far too far for me,' replied Tom, trying to hide his amazement. 'I would have assumed you would have a normal touring pattern that involved less travel.'

'We do, but it has been cancelled. The whole company has been specially commissioned to perform at the homes of two lords.'

'They must be paying your manager a pretty penny for him to abandon your normal tour.'

The actor shrugged his shoulders. 'I suppose so. I don't know the details. It all happened very recently. If you had asked me two days ago, I'd have told you we were going to Oxford.' He stopped to yawn. 'I must move on to my bed. We have an early start tomorrow because we have been told we must travel with all speed.'

Jones did not try to stop him lest he arouse his suspicion. Instead he began reflecting again. If Sarah Darr had joined the company it must be so she could travel with it to Coventry and Warwick. But why did she want to go to those places? And why had she chosen this particular means? It was hardly the quickest of travelling methods, however fast the company moved. These reflections were broken by the sound of the other actors and actresses also leaving for their rooms. Kitty Pike, alias Sarah Darr, was among them. Jones moved into the shadows as she passed and she appeared too engrossed in discussions with her fellow players to notice him. He heard her say to a companion that her room in the inn was a comfortable one and this led him to cease worrying that he might lose her. He determined to go out into the inn's yard and await Fielding's return, confident that his astute friend would know what to do next.

'Shall I get you a drink, sir?' Jones was startled by this unexpected request. It came from a young lad. He had a wide face dominated by a short but strong nose and freckled cheeks. His thin-lipped mouth and small black eyes did little to enhance his appearance, but he appeared honest enough. The fact that he wore an apron indicated he must work at the inn. 'There's plenty of space inside, sir, but, if you prefer to stay out here in the cold night air, I can get you a whisky to warm you up.'

'Aye. Fetch me a drink while I am waiting for my friend and I'll pay you well for it.'

The youth disappeared and very rapidly returned with a well-filled glass. Jones gratefully took it and handed him a few coins. Then he drank the whisky, welcoming its warmth in his throat. Within minutes an overpowering sleepiness flowed over him and he felt increasingly dizzy. It was as if all his vitality was seeping out of his system. His vision became blurred and, before he could summon assistance, he collapsed unconscious onto the ground.

'Help me get him to a room before others get involved,' said Sarah Darr, emerging from the shadows. 'If anyone asks, we'll say he's had a bit too much to drink.' Gone was the sparkling and witty actress and in her stead stood a cold, calculating woman, whose eyes gleamed with a murderous fanaticism. The youth nodded. It was clear from his manner that he was very scared of her. He placed his hands under Jones's armpits whilst she took hold of his feet. Together they lifted up the unconscious man and carried him first through a side door and into a corridor and then into a bedroom. They lifted him into a chair and a grim-faced Darr proceeded to strap him securely to it by means of a strong rope. Once this was done she placed a gag in his mouth. She turned to the youth. 'Go and find John and tell him what has happened and that we must leave Bath at once. While you are gone I will wake this stupid clown and find out what he knows before killing him.'

14

THE IDENTITY OF THE ACCOMPLICE

Had the youth waited just a few minutes longer his path would have crossed that of Henry Fielding in the inn yard. As it was, neither saw the other. Fielding had been looking for Jones with mounting concern. 'Where on earth has the young lad gone?' he muttered to himself. He did not know whether to be cross or fearful. Had Jones tried to confront Sarah Darr on his own and been perhaps injured or had he followed her to some other place? It was with some relief that Fielding saw the figure of Beau Nash emerging out of the night because he knew that the Master of Ceremonies had the authority to act in ways that were not open to anyone else.

Even as the two men were voicing their anxiety at his disappearance, Jones was being rudely awoken from his induced slumber by his captor, who was waving a phial of smelling salts below his nose and slapping his face vigorously. As the drugged man's vision slowly came into focus he saw Darr's blue eyes staring harshly at him. There was no hint of the attractiveness with which she had endowed the role of Lucy Lockit, or of the subservience that had marked Lady Overbury's maid. Instead malice seemed to seep out from the very pores of her skin. 'You don't know when to leave things alone, do you, Mr Jones?' she snarled viciously, giving him a final hard slap that rocked his head backwards. 'I would have thought your experience on Guy Fawkes' Night would have warned you to stay clear of matters that don't concern you. Why have you sought me out?'

She removed the gag and desperately Jones tried to clear his befuddled brain but he found himself unable to think of any story that might deceive her. She lashed out at him again, hitting him so hard that his head felt as if a hammer had hit it. Blood trickled out of his mouth. He glared at her but started to answer her question. 'I followed you because the truth has come out. We know about your early life and what happened to your father. We know that you wish success for the Jacobites who invade our nation. We know that it was your hand that lay behind the deaths of Agnes Grey and the others.'

'How do you know this?' she asked. Not a flicker of emotion crossed her face as he proceeded to tell her of how Lady Overbury and Sophia had returned to Bath with the news, having uncovered her past history in London. Once he had finished, she said almost nonchalantly, 'It does not matter. When the true king has taken up his rightful place on the throne I will not only be pardoned for all that I have done but also richly rewarded.'

'That time will never happen,' he replied. 'England will not support the Jacobite cause, whatever you may think.'

'That is where you are wrong. The Hanoverians have not won any great loyalty among the people of this country. Why should they? They are Germans and it is obvious to all that they have used England as a pawn to promote the interests of Hanover. Have you not heard the latest news? The Jacobite army has already moved into England and Carlisle has surrendered without a battle having to be fought. As we speak, Bonnie Prince Charlie is leading his army towards London. It is only fear of the consequences should there be another Jacobite failure and not love for the Hanoverians that now stands between him and success. In my hands I have the means of removing that fear. It is a document signed by many pledging their loyalty. Once it is in his hands it will be read out as a proclamation and others will then flock to his cause. Support for the usurper George II will crumble and London will welcome the prince with open arms.'

'Then why are you still here in Bath?'

Her eyes narrowed. 'A good question and, as your life will soon be over, one I am prepared to answer. We lack at the moment just a couple of key signatures, but this was to be remedied at two secret meetings, one in Warwick and the other in Coventry. A performance by this touring company at each place was to have provided the necessary cover for those meetings to take place without the authorities becoming suspicious.' She paused and smiled. Jones could see the fanaticism in her eyes. 'After that,' she continued, 'a trusted rider was to take the completed list of signatures to the prince at whatever place his

Highlanders had reached.'

Jones's mind reeled with the enormity of what he was being told. All he could hope was that he might keep her talking until Fielding managed to find them. He surmised that it was highly unlikely that he had been carried any long distance from where he had been drugged. 'Was it not foolish to appear in public when people were looking for you?' he enquired.

'An unfortunate necessity. I had to replace an actress and prove my worth – that required me to perform here tonight. I knew that Lady Overbury had returned to London and so I thought I would get away with it. It was just unfortunate that you chose to see the play this evening. I doubt if anyone else would have identified me.'

'But how did you know I was here and had seen you?'

'Foolish man! Did you really think that if you could see me on stage I could not see you in the audience? You and that interfering novel writer. I was certain that you had both recognized me and I therefore expected one or other of you would attempt to follow me. I saw you hiding in the shadows and speaking to the actor who played Macheath.' She pulled out a blade that had been hidden within her costume. 'It would have been better for you had Mr Fielding acted as the spy, leaving you to escort home the young lady who accompanied you. As it is, it is you who will now suffer the consequences of your pathetic pursuit of me.'

Tom refused to be cowed. 'Whatever you do to me, your plan is in ruins,' he responded defiantly. 'My removal will not prevent Sir Henry putting an end to this company touring northwards.'

Her face visibly darkened with irritation. 'Yes, my cover here is lost and that is very annoying, but I will use it to good effect.' She smiled at him in such a way that his flesh crept. 'I know a way of ensuring that Mr Nash and Mr Fielding will follow me southwards while John travels northwards to obtain the final signatures even though there will now be no play to provide cover for the meetings.'

'How do you know they will seek out only you?'

She held up the blade before his eyes, letting him see its fine edge. 'Because your death will blind them to all else, Mr Jones. Their desire to avenge you will make them lose sight of everything but finding me.' She thrust the gag back in his mouth. 'We don't want to make this too noisy an event, do we?' The knife in her right hand began to move slowly towards his throat. 'Don't worry. Close your eyes and I'll make it quick.' This was said without there being a hint of mercy in her voice. Jones knew she was enjoying playing with him like a cat tormenting the mouse that it is about to destroy. 'You see I quite liked you,' she continued. She moved the knife away from him and her left hand gently caressed the side of his face. 'Indeed, had things been different I might have had some fun extracting you from the arms of that weak Westbrook woman.' For a moment her hand moved over his chest and came to rest on his groin. Denied speech, all Jones could do was glare his defiance. She laughed and, as she pulled her left hand away, she once again brought the knife in her right hand towards him. 'Trust me, it will be easier if you close your eyes. I'll even let you say your final prayers, which is far more than I did for the others.'

Jones had no desire for his last image on earth to be her vicious face and so shut his eyes as she suggested. However, his last thoughts were not a prayer for himself but one for Sophia. How would she cope with the news of his murder? She had endured so much for him and now he was to be taken from her forever. He prayed that God might comfort the woman he loved more than any other in the world. It was as if Sarah Darr could read his mind. 'Thinking of her, my dear?' she teased. 'So am I. When the true king reigns I will beg him a favour.' She paused and leant closer towards him. 'That he ensures both Lady Overbury and Miss Westbrook suffer for their interference. I am sure that my former mistress will benefit from swinging on the gallows and, as for Sophia, a spell in prison will soon remove her good looks and her good nature, don't you think?'

Tom felt the sharp edge of the blade touch his neck, but then a shot rang out and he heard Sarah Darr give a deep groan. He opened his eyes and saw that she was clutching her side with her left hand and blood was flowing out freely between her fingers. She looked at him and a bitter smile twisted her lips. She lifted the knife in her right hand but then suddenly slumped forward, almost landing on top of him. Jones looked up and saw Henry Fielding in the doorway. It was he who had shot her and who now moved rapidly across the room. He dragged the injured woman off her intended victim and then pulled the gag out of Jones's mouth and began untying him.

'That was far too close for comfort,' he muttered. 'A minute later and I would have been too late.' He fought back his emotions but Jones sensed the anguish in his heart at such a horrendous thought. He heard his father whisper, 'I do not think I could have coped with the loss of the son I had just gained.'

'This day I have learned to twice owe you my life, sir,' Tom replied with equal emotion. 'Once for giving me birth and once for preventing my murder. I'll never forget that.' His own voice cracked with the intensity of what he felt. Never had life seemed so valuable. He struggled to his feet from the chair, still feeling slightly unsteady because of whatever drug he had been given. 'How did you find me?'

'Beau Nash used his authority to extract from the landlord that the actress who played Lucy was called Kitty Pike and that she had a room at the inn. We found that she was not there but there were two other women in it – actresses with whom she shared the accommodation. They claimed to know nothing of her or your whereabouts. Mr Nash left to see if he could pick up your trail because he assumed that Sarah Darr had fled and that you had followed her. Fortunately I chose to make some further enquiries before leaving and spoke to the actor who played Macheath. He said that he had seen you and that, seeing you were a handsome chap, he thought it possible that Kitty might have taken a shine to you. At first he would offer no suggestion as to where the two of you might be, saying that it was none of his business to get anyone in trouble. However, hearing that Kitty was not all that she seemed, he directed me to try this room – apparently it is a place set aside for assignations that require a degree of privacy. I think Mr Nash will have something to say to the innkeeper about that!'

A heart-rending groan stopped further discussion between the two men. They looked at Sarah Darr lying on the floor. Her face was contorted with the pain from the terrible wound in her side. Despite all that she had done, the two men felt pity for her. Her skin had lost all its vitality and taken on a sheen that betokened her imminent death. They lifted the seriously injured woman onto the nearby bed in order to try and make her more comfortable. 'Let me die in peace,' she whispered through gritted teeth as she sought to suppress any further groan. 'I do not want your pity.'

Tom, despite her murderous intent on his life, gently wiped the drops of pain-induced sweat from her brow. 'Shall we get you a priest?' he asked.

'A priest?' Even in her pain she seemed to find this amusing. 'No. God knows how much I have suffered and I care not whether he pardons me or not. I have lived my whole life in Hell. Why should death bring me anything different?'

'Are you not repentant?'

She shook her head feebly. 'I would do again what I have done.'

An increasing delirium meant that she then began wavering in and out of consciousness. The bleeding seemed to subside but her laboured breathing became increasingly hoarse and there was a sort of rattling in her throat. Just when they thought the end had come, she suddenly struggled to raise herself up and she looked at Jones with frightened eyes, her lips flecked with blood where she had bitten them to prevent screaming out in pain. 'I am finished,' she murmured, 'but John will ensure that the victory remains ours.' Her head once again fell back on the pillow and she lost consciousness. The remaining hint of colour in her once rosy cheeks seemed to drain away. She heaved a deep final sigh and her mouth dropped open. Fielding passed his hand lightly across her face, closing the lids across her sightless eyes.

'Who is this John to whom she referred?'

'It might be the youth who helped drug me or it could be another of her accomplices. Whoever it is, we have to find him.'

The two men agreed that it made sense for Jones to fetch the night watch and to find Beau Nash and inform him of the latest developments. While he was away, Fielding stayed beside Darr's body in the hope that the youth who had assisted her might return. This proved pointless because the news that the actress had been shot and killed soon spread. As a consequence none but the curious made any appearance at the room. Once Nash arrived enquiries were set in motion but no trace could be found of the youth and no one appeared to know who he was. Nash therefore turned his attention on interrogating the manager of the touring company, but this too drew a blank. The manager was adamant that he knew nothing of any Jacobite plots. He had merely accepted the offer of a special payment for performances in Coventry and Warwick. As for Kitty Pike – or Sarah Darr as he now discovered was her real name – all he knew was that she had turned up at the very time he needed a replacement actress. Of her previous history he claimed ignorance. All Nash could do was order him not to move his company northwards and threaten to have him tried for treason if he disobeyed.

After two days of fruitless enquiries, Nash called a meeting at his house on the morning of the 29 November. Lady Overbury was given permission to also attend, but Sophia Westbrook was not, much to her annoyance. The account of Tom's near murder had made her most desirous that he should not place himself in any further danger and she feared that, in her absence, he might commit himself to some action or other demanded by the older men. As Jones was about to knock on Nash's door, it opened suddenly and a man in black appeared at the entrance and hurriedly brushed past Lady Overbury and Henry

Fielding. From the bag that he carried in his hand they surmised that he was an apothecary.

'Get out, sir! Damn it! I'll have none of your hypocritical quackery here!' bellowed a voice from within that they recognized as belonging to Nash.

'You cannot judge my skills, sir, because you insist on ignoring what advice I give and refusing to take what medicine I prescribe,' complained the doctor from his place behind Fielding. 'Why won't you follow my prescriptions?'

'Egad, sir, if I had followed your last prescription, I should have broken my neck for, in my disgust at your nonsense, I flung it out of an upstairs window,' came Nash's prompt response. 'Get out!'

A bottle hit the door and smashed into many pieces, some of which struck Jones. The doctor muttered that he preferred to treat ailments than deal with insanity and then departed. Jones, brushing off splinters of glass from his coat, knocked at the semi-open door. 'Have I not told you to leave?' Nash roared.

'I beg pardon, Mr Nash, but I think you mistake me for your doctor, who has truly gone.'

A slightly dishevelled Nash appeared and his anger turned almost immediately into embarrassment. 'My apologies, but all this business has made me unwell. I do not like being so frustrated at every turn by these traitors in our midst. Early this morning I called that buffoon to ease my thumping head but the man only arrived a few minutes ago. He tried to excuse his late arrival by saying that he was called up at all hours, sometimes to set a broken arm, leg, or the like. I told him it sounded to me as if it was merely by accident that he got up at all! Then he wanted to purge and potion me to extinction and I would have none of it. Come in, come in.'

They duly followed Nash into what was a very fine room richly furnished. He beckoned them to sit down and proceeded to get down to the business of their meeting as if nothing had happened prior to their arrival. 'I have sent messages to the government warning them that a most dangerous set of documents is probably heading in the direction of the Jacobite army. I have no doubt that they will send out men to try and intercept whoever is carrying them. However, I am not confident that they will succeed. They have no leads except that we believe secret Jacobite meetings were scheduled to occur in Warwick and Coventry.'

'But surely those meetings will not happen now because of what has happened here in Bath?' queried Fielding.

'I agree and that is why I think our best chance of success is if we can identify who this "John" is and so follow him in order to prevent his treachery. I am not convinced it was the youth who helped poison Mr Jones. Such important documents would not be given to so callow a youth. We must all think about all that has happened since that fateful day when Miss Grey was murdered. It is just possible that by sharing our memories a clue to the identity of Sarah Darr's accomplice may emerge.' He hesitated and then looked in Lady Overbury's direction. 'I suggest that you speak first, your ladyship, if you are happy to do so.'

She nodded her acquiescence. 'I am content to be the first though as yet I have no answers, despite going over and over what has happened in my mind. The only thing I am certain about is that Sarah Darr was a most ruthless woman. She murdered the housekeeper Agnes Grey when she refused to hand over the documents she sought. She then began searching the house in Queen Square and not only attacked John Burnett but also murdered Lord Kearsley. After that she ordered the viciously cruel attept on Tom's life on Guy Fawkes' Night and, when the assassin failed, she either murdered him or had him murdered in the King's Bath. When she discovered that Joseph Graves had the documents she sought she ensured his murder. Had Sir Henry not shot her, she would have slit Tom's throat without the slightest remorse. All this shows that we were dealing with a woman completely consumed by wickedness but it gets us no closer to identifying the man whom she called "John".'

'Unless the two Johns are the same John,' interrupted Fielding.

The others in the room all looked bewildered and it was Nash who voiced their confusion. 'What on earth do you mean?'

'Could John Burnett be the man we seek?' asked Fielding.

There was a deathly silence as the others absorbed this new possibility. 'I think it strange that Sarah Darr got away with doing so much in the house in Queen Square,' commented Lady Overbury. 'If she had an ally in John Burnett, then it would make more sense. It would certainly have made Lord Kearsley's murder easier. Indeed, maybe it was Burnett who killed him. I seem to recall, Mr Nash, that you were suspicious at the time as to whether the blow to Burnett's head was a genuine attack.'

'Yes, but I wrongly attributed the blow to being a put-up job by Tom. At the time I gave no thought to the possibility that Sarah Darr might have inflicted it to disguise the fact that Burnett was her accomplice.'

'And possibly more than just an accomplice,' said Fielding. 'Although I said nothing at the time it has always seemed strange to me that

Burnett was so reluctant to marry Miss Westbrook. She has everything a man could want in terms of beauty, character and wealth, yet a selfish and greedy man like Burnett had to be more or less forced into accepting that he should marry her. Could it be that was because he loved Sarah Darr?'

'But we have no sign that she loved him,' interposed Nash.

'A woman like Sarah Darr would be perfectly capable of wrapping a man like Burnett round her finger if she chose, whether she liked him or not,' replied Lady Overbury rather acidly.

'Whatever their relationship, Burnett's involvement would make sense of what happened on Guy Fawkes' Night,' resumed Fielding. 'The nature of the attempt on Tom's life always struck me as odd. Why try to burn someone alive when a simple knife thrust would suffice? Now I think I have the answer. It was Burnett who made the arrangements for Tom's murder. He hated Tom because he had become so obviously the favourite of his uncle. From his perception, how dare the bastard take precedence over the person who was the squire's true heir? He therefore deliberately devised as cruel a death as possible for the man he loathed.'

Jones shuddered at the memory of that terrible night and, although so far he had said nothing, he now felt compelled to add, 'Since we were children I can vouch for the fact that John always had a love for the dramatic. Though it pains me to say it, I can see him taking pleasure in not only hiring a man to burn me alive but hiring men to string up Graves onto the west front of the abbey. He and Darr doubtless overpowered the poor old man. Darr then saw to his removal from the house, leaving Burnett to hand us her bloodstained apron and to mislead us into thinking that she had been abducted.'

'So where is Burnett now?' asked Nash.

'The strange thing is that none of us has bothered to ask that question before,' muttered Fielding.

Lady Overbury nodded. 'For my part I never liked the man and was happy to see the back of him when I moved out of the house in Queen Square and no longer required his services.'

'And Fielding and I let him go after the search into Darr's disappearance proved a failure,' added Nash. 'If he was her accomplice, he may well have contributed, of course, to that unsuccessful enterprise.'

'As for me,' said Jones, 'I avoided any mention of the man because I knew he was the cause of Sophia's flight.'

'So where is he now?' said Fielding, echoing Nash's earlier question.

'The obvious person to ask is Squire Woodforde,' rejoined Jones. 'I'll ride out to him at once.'

'Do so,' urged Nash. 'We may all be grasping at straws and unnecessarily maligning the man, but I think we urgently need to question John Burnett. When can you get back to us?'

'If I ride quickly I can just get back here before it gets too dark this evening.'

Nash looked pleased. 'Then let us say that we will resume our meeting here at five o'clock in anticipation of your arrival around then.'

The meeting at five o'clock proved a tense affair because Jones did not make an appearance and Sophia, who had insisted on joining them, became increasingly agitated. The others tried to reassure her whilst all the time looking at the ticking clock and wondering whether he was safe or not. Too many people had died for them not to be concerned. It was not until six that they heard a knocking at the Master of Ceremonies's door. To their relief it was Tom who was admitted into the room shortly afterwards by Nash's manservant. He looked exhausted but he was obviously unharmed. Sophia abandoned all the norms of polite society and flung herself into his arms. Once he had disentangled himself, a rather red-faced Tom began telling them what he had discovered.

'When I arrived at Squire Woodforde's I was told that John had been there the day before, looking agitated and deeply distressed. My uncle, being the kind man that he is, tried to get him to talk about what was upsetting him. He wondered whether news of my betrothal to Sophia had somehow reached him, but, when he raised that subject, John replied that he had not the slightest interest in whomever Sophia chose to marry because she meant nothing to him. He then went on to curse my existence, saying that I had cost him the one person he had ever truly loved. John then stormed off and for the rest of the day no one saw him. Yesterday evening he reappeared and announced that he would require the best horse in the stables because he had a long journey to make. Squire Woodforde willingly agreed to let him select the horse of his choice but then sought clarification as to where he was going. John refused to answer, saying he was not a child and saw no reason why he should have to recount his plans to anyone. He left early this morning as soon as it was light.'

'In what direction?' asked Fielding.

'According to the stable hand, he took the road northwards, travelling very light with only a small bag in his possession.' Jones looked at the faces around him and saw in their eyes the same belief that he now held about John Burnett being Sarah Darr's accomplice. 'He carries with him the documents that endanger the crown.'

'Unfortunately I am not sure that we have time to alert the authorities to stop him,' groaned Nash.

'I thought you might say that,' replied Jones. 'That is why I am so late. I have already been around all the saddlers in the city and acquired the best horse I could hire – a fine black stallion standing seventeen hands high, well capable of bearing my weight and a creature of tested stamina and endurance. It is saddled and ready for me to depart as soon as it is light again. John may have a twenty-four-hour start but I vow that I will do all in my power to catch and stop him.'

No father or future wife could have been prouder than Henry Fielding and Sophia Westbrook were at that moment and their emotion kept them initially silent. Lady Overbury too found herself too choked to speak. It was left to Beau Nash to growl their approval. 'A hearty Amen to that, young man,' he said.

15

THE RIDE NORTH

The next morning Jones was dressed and ready to depart the minute it became light. Once he was out of the confines of the city he spurred on his horse and set off at a steady but not over-demanding gallop. The slight breeze made the wintry leafless branches of the trees on either side of the road appear to dance as he rode past them. A few frightened birds flew out of their resting places at the sound of his horse's hoofs and he took this as a good omen. If successful, was he not going to strike an even greater fear into the hearts of his country's enemies? He felt elated as the beautiful creature that he rode got fully into its stride and the keen, sharp air whistled past his face, because not only did he sense the power of the beast beneath him but also the youthful vigour of his own body. It was almost as if he could feel his blood coursing through his veins in the cold morning air.

At first the territory through which he passed was not unknown to him because he had travelled that section of the Fosse Way near Bath on a number of occasions. He travelled up the steep Foss Lane, passing woodland that had long since lost its last leaf to emerge on a hilltop with sweeping views. He then rode along what was little more than a narrow switchback country lane for about twelve miles. All around him pockets of arable land lay empty, the harvest no more than a distant memory, but there were still herds of sheep to be seen grazing in the fields even at that early hour. He saw little sign of any other life except an occasional frightened rabbit rushing into its burrow at his approach, or a wild bird flying overhead, silhouetted against the grey sky. This did not matter because the scenery was varied enough to maintain his interest as he moved through valleys and across hillsides that bore all the signs of the wintry season, occasionally crossing a bridge or passing through a hamlet or village. He enjoyed in particular the sight of swirling smoke rising from a distant cottage or farmstead, and the winter sun flashing through a break in the clouds to shine upon the steeple of a church, making its stone momentarily sparkle.

However, as time passed his initial exhilaration was replaced by mounting weariness, not least because the appalling state of the road required constant vigilance. There were deep and semi-frozen ruts everywhere and the uneven surface caused his horse to stumble on a number of occasions and once to almost fall onto its knees, even though he was as vigilant as he could be in directing its path to avoid the worst sections. In the end Tom judged it safer to loosen the reins in order to let his horse judge the best route, relying on the creature's superior natural instinct. This proved a better solution, though the pace at which they travelled then diminished. Aware that no man could be on the alert for hour after hour, he took to dismounting and walking for a mile or so alongside the horse. This relieved him whilst also giving his horse a welcome break from the burden of carrying him. What kept Tom going was the significance of his mission, even though he had some qualms about its potential outcome. At one crossroads he saw a gibbet from which dangled the tattered remnants of a felon, the rags-wrapped bones rattling loudly in the breeze. If he was successful he knew many a Jacobite would face a similar fate.

By the time daylight began to fade he estimated that he must have travelled over thirty-five miles. Fortunately the sky had become increasingly cloudless as the day had gone on and so, as night began to close in, the moon cast its light over the roadway. Without such assistance Jones would have soon lost the ability to keep to the track. He therefore stroked the sweat-soaked neck of his horse and permitted it to slacken its pace yet more. The beast responded by pressing on as best its failing energy would permit. It came as a relief to Jones when he suddenly became aware he had reached the outskirts of the market town of Cirencester. He rode up to the front of the Golden Cross Inn and dismounted. Almost immediately an ostler came out to attend to his needs, having heard the clatter of hoofs on the cobbles. The man's snow-white hair and heavily lined face bespoke a person of advanced years but he was obviously very familiar with the needs of horses and he moved speedily to address the exhausted animal's requirements. He chose not to take offence at Jones's attempt to lecture him on what was required after such a long day of riding. Instead he simply made reassuring sounds and led the horse away to the stables.

Jones entered the inn and, as he crossed the threshold, he welcomed not only the sight of the wooden settles and the fire burning in the hearth, but also the smell that came from the bubbling pot that hung above the flames. To his surprise he saw that there were only a couple of other guests in the place and they were playing cards in a far corner of the heavily panelled room. They appeared an unlikely pair. One was an elderly fat man, ugly of demeanour, unshaven and unkempt. His heavily tanned visage and large muscular hands pointed to him being a local farm worker. The other was a wiry, thin young man with a long nose and pale cheeks and eyes that were heavily bagged. His face bore signs of an intelligence that his older companion lacked. Despite the warmth of the room, the young man was wrapped in a faded cloak that entirely hid his attire so it was impossible to judge his social standing, but Jones surmised that he must be a fellow traveller because the cloak bore the same journey stains that his own clothes carried. Both men looked up at his entry but neither greeted him.

Behind the bar of the inn stood a tall man, with an almost soldierly bearing, dressed in unfashionable but serviceable garb. Jones rightly assumed that this was the landlord and he took heart from the fact that he appeared an honest fellow. He had a broad brow, a fine nose, kind eyes, and a warm smile. Conscious of the late hour of his arrival and that his face and clothes were caked with dust and grime, Jones immediately handed over enough coins to show that he was a person worthy of attention. 'I would like a comfortable chamber with your best bed and your softest sheets. My ride has made me most weary and I want a good night's rest because I face an equally long journey tomorrow. See that a good, hearty meal is prepared for me and a bottle of your best wine to accompany it. Please also ensure that I have ample hot water sent up to my room so I can clean myself up.' He paused and looked sternly at the innkeeper. 'I warn you: do not try to palm me off with a hard bed, or some stale, musty leftovers, or a flagon of piss.'

'I can assure you, sir, that your every need will be met,' replied the landlord, pleased at his unexpected good fortune in acquiring a wealthy visitor at such an unexpected hour. He looked Jones up and down with a discerning eye, and held out his hand in hearty welcome. 'My daughter will show you to the best room that we have and get you all that you require, whilst down here my wife will prepare you a feast. You can smell that there is a good broth on the hob and, though the hour is late, I am sure that she can rustle up one of her good meat pies from the larder. As for drink, I will go down into my cellar and lay my hands on a fine bottle of Burgundy if that will suit?'

Jones nodded his assent and he had scarcely time to remove his outer coat when the innkeeper's daughter made her appearance. She was dressed in a plain blue gown that was neither fashionable nor becoming but she still looked surprisingly pretty. Her hair was a mass of golden curls, her eyes a cornflower blue, and her lips an open invitation to be kissed. As Jones followed her shapely form upstairs he realized just how stiff his limbs were from the saddle, but, exhausted though he was, he could not help flirting with such an attractive girl.

'How comes it that one so beautiful has not yet found a husband?' he said, with a twinkle in his eye. 'Is there no handsome man who has caught your fancy?'

'If I waited for a man to catch my fancy, I would never marry, sir. The men round here are far too dull.'

'And what if I should stay here? Might I then attract your heart?' he replied, treating her to one of those smiles that he knew the opposite sex usually found irresistible.

She smiled back at him but then gave an unexpected response. 'I grant you, sir, that you are very pleasing to the eye, and I suspect that you have a wit that would lighten the weary hours that I have to work, but I am sure you are not the man for me.'

He looked at her curiously. 'And what makes you so sure of that?'

'I am my father's only child and I must marry someone who has the business head to run this place when it passes to me. I see in your face a desire for adventure that means you would never think of settling down here and helping me entertain our customers.'

'How about entertaining this customer?' he joked.

The smile on her lips faded away and the skin on her face flushed a deeper pink. 'If it is bawdy entertainment you seek, sir, then I think you must find another hostelry. This is an honest house and I am no whore.'

Jones also coloured and said ruefully, 'Forgive me. I only jested. I can assure you that my heart is already given to another. I see that you are as virtuous as you are pretty and I admire you all the more for it.'

Two hours later there was a knock at Jones's door and the landlord entered to ask if he wanted anything else.

'No, sir, I have been well fed and the wine was excellent.'

'Very good, then, with your permission, I shall just clear away the remnants.' As he proceeded to do so, the landlord sensed his visitor was in the mood for conversation and, in order to satisfy his curiosity, observed, 'It is obvious that you have travelled very far today, sir. My ostler says that your horse was so exhausted that it was close to collapse. If I may be bold, what brings you here and so urgently? I judge from your speech that you are not from these parts.'

'It is not fitting that I should entirely tell you my purpose, sir,' replied Jones. 'May it content you to know that I am on a mission that may help end the thread posed by these damned Jacobites.'

'I confess, sir, I come of Roundhead stock and it is nothing to me whether we have a German or a Scot upon the throne. I would rather we were ruled by Parliament than by any monarch. However, I have no time for any who dare choose to invade this land, and, were I a young man, I daresay that I would be foolish enough to volunteer to join King George's Army rather than see foreigners seize English soil. If you are headed to join the royal troops – as I surmise may be your intention – then I salute your courage and I will drink to your success. Fill up your glass!' He poured more wine into Jones's cup. 'Here's a toast for you! Damnation to all perfidious princes and may there be a speedy end to the insurrection!'

Jones thought it prudent to take the toast with good humour. 'I think, landlord, that now the bottle is empty and I am filled, 'tis time that I spend as much of the night in repose as I can. I must have an early start. See that I am awoken just before dawn.'

'Very well, sir. You will not know such comfort as this for many a day to come.'

The next morning, which was the first day of December, Jones awoke and, after some brief ablutions, went outside to look to his horse. He was pleased to discover that the skilled attentions of the ostler and a night of rest had performed wonders. The animal looked as fresh as it had when he had first mounted it the previous day. He returned inside and ordered a breakfast that was almost as hearty as his meal the night before. It was as he sat eating this that the landlord handed him a parcel and bid him open it. 'I have decided that it is not right that a young handsome lad like you should face the enemy bare-chested,' he said, 'This was my grandfather's in the Civil War and I have no son to pass it on to. May it offer you some degree of protection in battle.' Opening what he had been given Jones discovered an ancient cuirass made from layers of hardened leather. 'I know it will not stop the ball from a musket nor even a sword if driven with strength,' went on the landlord, 'but, if you wear this beneath your coat, it will protect you against any glancing blow. I am told it saved my grandfather from serious injury on more than one occasion.'

Jones was highly dubious about the efficacy of what he was being offered. Buff coats and the like had long gone out of fashion. However, he was too moved by the landlord's kindness to reject it. After a moment's thought he decided it might provide him with an extra layer should the weather turn colder. He therefore thanked his host profusely and agreed to put it on before he renewed his arduous journey. It was a decision that he was not to regret because he had not travelled far out of Cirencester when the clatter of a horse's hoofs made him realize that he was being followed. What was at first a distant blur soon resolved itself into a horseman, body bent low. As the rider drew nearer, Jones saw that it was the thin man who had been in the inn the previous night. Unsure of what to do, he pulled up his horse and awaited him, using the time to draw out his pistol and uncock it. He had heard too many tales of highwaymen and of corpses left by the roadside to judge the rider anything other than a potential threat.

Seeing the weapon, the thin man slowed his approach as he drew near and in a reassuring tone asked, 'Have I the honour of addressing Mr Tom Jones?'

'You have the advantage of me, sir. I am Tom Jones, but I do not know who you are or how you come to know my name.'

'My name is Oliver Fairfax and Mr Fielding has sent me to join you in your endeavour.'

Jones knew at once this was a lie but gave no indication of his feelings, judging it was important to discover more about the man first. 'Then why did you not reveal yourself to me last night when we were both at the inn?' he replied.

Even as he spoke, the man moved his horse alongside with such surprising swiftness that Jones had no opportunity to defend himself before a sword sliced itself across his chest. Had not the cuirass absorbed its cutting power he would have been instantly disabled. Almost instinctively Jones pulled back his horse and fired his pistol. At such close range there was no opportunity for him to miss. His opponent instantly tumbled from his horse, a look of surprise across his face. Having recovered from the shock of the attack, Tom cautiously dismounted and approached the apparently lifeless body. There was no movement and blood was oozing out of a gaping hole in the man's chest. His potential assassin was wearing the same cloak that had obscured his dress the previous evening, but now it no longer hid the broadcloth coat, the cambric shirt and the satin breeches that indicated here was no common footpad but a man of substance. A brief search revealed a plentiful supply of money in his pockets. Jones surmised that Burnett had left the man behind to kill anyone attempting to follow him. He dragged the body of the failed assassin into the midst of some bushes where he hoped it would lie undiscovered for at least a few days. Then he slapped the man's horse on its rear so that it headed off in the opposite direction to the one he was taking.

Jones then resumed his journey, conscious that Warwick was almost forty miles away. Fortunately the straight line of the Fosse Way took him through Bourton-on–the-Water, Stow on the Wold, and Moreton on the Marsh without demanding anything in the way of difficult terrain. It was a tedious journey with the road seeming to stretch ahead forever into the shadowy horizon. He made no stop other than to occasionally water and rest his horse. The hearty breakfast that he had eaten stood him in good stead and it was not until he reached the Halford Bridge Inn in the afternoon that he briefly delayed to eat a light meal. He then travelled the remaining ten miles in ever darkening conditions, grateful once again that a cloudless sky provided welcome moonlight. It was not until the early evening that he finally arrived at his destination. Fifty years before a fire had destroyed much of Warwick and so he discovered most of the houses in the town were surprisingly uniform, having been built to rigid specifications that dictated all buildings should be two or three storeys high and created either of brick or stone with roofs of tile or slate.

He sought accommodation in the Warwick Arms, which was not far removed from the town's ancient castle. The landlord happened to be in the yard when Jones arrived. He was obviously a man who enjoyed the comforts of life because his red face and nose bore all the signs of heavy drinking and his belly was excessively large. However, there was nothing dull about his mind. He quickly observed the quality of Tom's horse, even though it was obviously exhausted, and he recognized that its rider had an air that distinguished him from the vulgar. He gave Jones a welcome in a voice that was ingratiating but not unpleasant and, ushering him inside, invited him to dine in his company whilst his wife prepared their best room for him. Jones willingly accepted, hoping that their conversation might provide him with some information as to whether Burnett was still in the town or whether he had already moved on further northwards.

The food was good and the wine even better but in the course of the meal it became apparent that the landlord preferred entertaining to working. He expected his wife to undertake all that was required in running the establishment. This she did, but not with good grace, and the landlord's conversation with Jones was therefore interspersed with bouts of wrangling with her. The fact that she carried an ugly bruise on her right cheek was testimony that their quarrels were not always confined to words. Jones could see that in her youth she had been a very attractive woman but years of servitude had taken their toll. Her hair was lank, her skin sallow, her eyes cold, her mouth bitter. He hoped that the young girl with whom he had flirted the previous evening found a better life partner for herself than this woman, though he had to admit that the landlord had a ready wit and was a fund of amusing anecdotes.

Almost inevitably, their conversation turned eventually to the threat posed by the invading Jacobite army. 'I am afraid that the news is not good, sir,' confided the landlord. The Highlanders have taken Carlisle, Penrith, Lancaster and Preston without facing much opposition. According to the latest reports that have reached here they now threaten to take Manchester. Indeed, for all we know, that city may have already fallen as we speak. There is talk that Derby may be next. Understandably there is mounting panic about what will happen here if, as is almost inevitable, they begin moving southwards towards London. All I can say is God be praised that General Ligonier has set out with the forces assembled at Coventry. I hear he has over two thousand men.'

'That is far fewer than the Highlanders,' remarked Jones.

'Aye, but I am sure they are better disciplined and that matters much in any battle. Moreover, they fight for liberty and God as well as their country. I won't tolerate any in here who think we should be transferring our loyalty.'

'Would you then serve your King if given the opportunity?' enquired Jones.

'Aye, that I would.'

Jones leaned forward. 'Then help me. The reason that I am in Warwick is that I am pursuing a traitor who is taking important information to the enemy. If I can prevent him, it may throw the Jacobite forces into disarray. Unfortunately the only lead that I have is that a meeting of traitors was to take place here under cover of a touring group of players performing *The Beggar's Opera*.'

'Aye, there was to have been a performance of that here in the morning and another in Coventry in the evening, but they have been cancelled. The players have not turned up.'

'That is because they have been prevented by those loyal to King George. The traitor of whom I speak is called John Burnett but he may well be travelling under an assumed name.'

'Describe him to me.'

'He is not a fine man to look at. He has a pale face that is badly pock-marked and lank black hair and he has a habit of screwing up his eyes and pursing his lips. His nose is hawk-like and his chin pointed. He is of my age but acts much older.'

The landlord swallowed convulsively. 'A man of that description came here on horseback at lunchtime and ate a hearty meal. He then asked for directions to Kenilworth Castle.'

'Did he say why he was going there?'

'No, but I did not bother to ask him.' The landlord paused and then added as justification, 'He was not a man that I took to.'

'Where is this castle and who resides within it?'

'The castle dates back to the Normans and lies midway between here and Coventry but it is largely ruined thanks to Cromwell's actions after the Civil War. It was almost like a royal palace in Tudor times when it was the home of the Earls of Leicester, but Cromwell destroyed one wall of its great tower, various parts of the outer bailey, and all its battlements, and he drained away the lake that for centuries had surrounded and protected it. Only the gatehouse was permitted to survive intact and that was in order that a Parliamentarian colonel could make it his home. When the monarchy was restored the castle passed to Sir Edward Hyde, the Earl of Clarendon. The family still own it but they live elsewhere and the place is now just a farm.'

'And do you know anything of the Clarendon family's political views?'

'The current earl is a Tory but his son, Henry Hyde, Viscount Cornbury, got himself into trouble about twelve years ago by trying to sponsor a French invasion in support of the Old Pretender. Since then he has seemingly mended his ways and he is now the Member of Parliament for Oxford.'

'So, it is possible that the man I seek is secretly meeting the viscount at Kenilworth with a view to persuading him to rejoin the Jacobites?' The landlord nodded his assent and Jones rose to his feet with excitement. 'Then I must also ask you for directions to Kenilworth and you must wake me very early so that I can get there in time to prevent the meeting having the success that our country's enemies desire.'

The landlord agreed and, as a consequence, Jones found himself once more rising whilst it was still dark so that he could ride out at the first glimmer of morning. On this occasion, he drove his horse as fast as it could go because the landlord had told him the castle was a mere four miles away. Even on a bleak morning in early December the sight of the ruined castle rising above the bare trees took his breath away when he reached it. He had not envisaged anything on its scale. Its red sandstone walls dominated the skyline, the massive ruins testifying to the castle's former splendour. Jones imagined it as it must have been in its prime – the sweep of its outward walls ornamented with banners, the majesty of its outer bailey with its succession of commanding towers, the beauty of its extensive inner court with its striking mix of medieval and renaissance buildings, and, over it all, the dominating presence of its central Norman citadel with its huge corner turrets. As he drew nearer he saw that what had once been the castle's surrounding lake was now little more than a swamp covered with the decaying remnants of rushes. There was no trace at all of the knot gardens that had once entertained the most noble in the land. Even more sadly the countryside around, once richly wooded and full of deer and every species of game, was deforested.

Jones rode past the three-storeyed red sandstone gatehouse that had been converted into a residence. It was built of red sandstone ashlar, rectangular in plan with octagonal turrets at each angle and a battlemented parapet. He suspected that inside there was now little evidence of the building's original purpose. The landlord had directed him to go to the nearby village, and travel down its High Street to the medieval church of St Nicholas and from there had given him instructions how to find the workshop of a man called John Littleton, who took horn from the local tanneries in order to make combs. He had told Jones that Littleton was utterly loyal to the government and a man who could be relied upon in an emergency because he was both brave and level-headed.

When Jones pulled up outside the workshop he found that, despite the early hour, there was already a man working. He was tall and rather angular in appearance. Despite the urgency of his mission, Jones could not help but admire the man's skill. Using tongs the comb-maker had just extracted some horn from a brick kiln and was hitting it with a pruning knife in order to assess by the sound whether the heat had sufficiently softened it. Judging it had, he drove his knife into the thickest section and proceeded to cleverly bring it down in a spiral. He took a piece of what he had sliced and began flattening it by reheating it. Jones knew that this was just the beginning of what was an arduous process because the flattened horn would then have to be marked and cut to shape and ground smooth and, finally, polished to bring out its natural lustre. Dismounting from his horse, Tom spoke to him. 'It looks hard work, sir, and I am sorry to interrupt you, but I am hoping you are John Littleton. The landlord at the Warwick Arms gave me your name as an honest man who would help me.'

The comb-maker put down his tools and looked up at his visitor. He had an intelligent, ruddy-skinned face and there was both humour and shrewdness in his striking blue eyes. His nose was slightly crooked as a result of some physical altercation earlier in his life and his brown hair was beginning to be flecked with grey, though Jones judged him to be only in his early forties. Physically he was obviously strong, his frame well built and muscular. 'Aye, I'm John Littleton,' he said in a voice that was gruff but which did not lack grace. Jones quickly explained his purpose, ending his account with a description of Burnett. Littleton stared at him throughout as if assessing whether he was being told the truth. Not a muscle moved in his face. There was a brief silence after Jones's account had finished and then the comb-maker thrust out his right hand and grasped that of his visitor in an iron-like grip. 'I am no lover of traitors and I am happy to shake the hand of a man who would assist in the downfall of those who destroy the peace of the realm.' He smiled and the genuine honest worth of the man shone through. 'As to the person you seek, I saw a man of that description arrive here yesterday though I have no idea where he may have spent the night. What I can vouch for is the fact that he has already departed. He rode past my workshop on a white horse less than fifteen minutes ago, taking the road to Coventry.'

Jones's jaw tightened with frustration. 'Then I must follow him at once before I lose his trail. Pray show me the road that he took.'

'That's the direction he took,' said Littleton, pointing down the street. 'Given what you have told me, sir, I pray that you may not fail to catch him.'

Jones wasted not a moment. Shouting his thanks, he at once remounted his horse, dug his spurs into its sides, and set off at a gallop down the road. His eyes watered as the cold wind cut into them but he hardly noticed the discomfort, such was his determination to catch up with Burnett. For some half an hour he travelled without any slackening of his pace and then his heart leapt with excitement at the sight of a rider on a white horse ahead of him in the distance. He raised himself in his stirrups to see if he could detect any shortcut that might increase his chances of catching up with his enemy, but, judging the terrain too dangerous, decided that he would have to stick to the road. He could only hope that his horse would prove the faster animal. He dug his spurs into its sides. The poor animal reared with pain but then broke into a gallop, scattering a shower of small stones as it went. The gap between him and the rider ahead gradually narrowed until the sound of his approach made Burnett turn around. Even at a distance Tom could see the shock on his face as he saw who was pursuing him.

Now began a desperate race as the horses responded to the demands of their masters and for what seemed an eternity the gap between the two riders failed to narrow. It was Burnett's horse that eventually tired first. He heard its breathing becoming increasingly laboured as it struggled to maintain the pace he desired and he sensed it would not be long before it would collapse under him. He therefore reined it in and swung it around to face his pursuer. He drew out his pistol, uncocked it, and, once he judged his pursuer was in range, pulled the trigger. However, the flintlock mechanism failed to ignite in the damp air. Cursing, he cast the useless weapon aside, and swung his horse back round to resume his flight. The beast did its best to respond but then stumbled, throwing him heavily to the ground. Jones reined in his horse and swiftly dismounted, but even as he did so he saw Burnett stagger to his feet.

'You will not leave this place with what you carry,' shouted Jones, 'Hand over whatever documents you have in your possession in the name of King George!'

Burnett wiped blood from where his mouth had been cut by his fall and his lip curled up in a sneer as he drew his sword. 'That German usurper has no right to my allegiance nor that of any true Englishman. 'Tis I who serve the rightful king and, in his name, I demand that you let me continue my journey or you will face the consequences.'

'A direct fight is not your usual method, John. I seem to recall that you prefer to seek to injure people without forewarning them, or else employ others to do your dirty work. Why should you now risk your life for a pretender?'

Burnett's voice cracked with intense passion as he replied, 'For the sake of her whom I loved.'

'You refer to Sarah Darr? Can't you see that she was no more than a murdering, treacherous whore?'

Burnett's face distorted with rage. 'She was worth ten of your stupid, whimpering, ludicrously innocent Sophia!'

'So was it her who recruited you to assist the Jacobite cause?'

'No. That was a decision that I made long ago of my own volition, but I knew not what to do to show my loyalty. By stature and temperament I am not cut out to be a soldier. I was unaware that Sarah was an agent of the Jacobites when I first entered the house in Queen Square. I knew nothing of her family or youth, nothing of her desire for vengeance. The first intimations came the night that Lord Kearsley returned. I heard him enter the house and challenged him. He managed to surprise me and knock me unconscious. By the time that I awoke Sarah had killed him.' He stopped for a moment. His loss was still too raw for him to think of her without pain. 'She told me of her reasons for hating the government and how she had been selected to infiltrate the house. From that moment all I wanted to do was assist her. We worked first as partners and then as lovers.'

'Her way of paying for your services, perhaps?' goaded Jones.

The taunt roused all Burnett's suppressed anger and he hurled himself at the man whom he had hated since childhood. Fortunately Jones had already drawn his own sword and, although caught offguard, he parried the immediate thrust with ease. Nevertheless, such was his half-brother's fury that he soon found that he could only just manage to keep his enraged adversary at bay by every moment changing his position, even though he had the advantage of height and weight. Neither man was a skilled swordsman and what ensued was no contest fought to fencing rules, but a frenzy of cutting, thrusting and slashing. It was Burnett who eventually drew first blood because the point of his sword struck Jones in the chest, but the blow lacked power and so did not penetrate the cuirass that still lay beneath his coat. Realizing that Jones was wearing some form of protection over his chest, Burnett sought to disable him and immediately followed up the blow with a second vicious thrust that entered the inside of Jones's sword arm and made its exit at the outside of the elbow. Jones sprang backwards, dislodging the hostile blade from his arm. Such was the flow of adrenaline that he was able to wield his weapon with the same dexterity as before, though the wound began bleeding freely and the sight of this led Burnett to be less cautious. Jones parried a flurry of blows that grew ever more reckless and then, when exhaustion finally caused Burnett to draw breath, he shifted his position and suddenly thrust his sword directly at his opponent's face. Taken completely by surprise, Burnett had no time to block the blade. It entered his right eye, penetrating his brain and killing him outright.

For a moment Jones looked at the corpse at his feet, almost expecting Burnett to get up again. Then, as he realized the fight was indeed over, he sank to his knees, his chest heaving. He knew that he had been very fortunate and that, had he not been wearing the cuirass, he might well have been killed. Despite all that Burnett had done, Jones felt only pity for his half-brother. From childhood his nature had been such that none had found him lovable, not even their mother or their uncle. He had been forced to endure seeing an illegitimate foundling receive the affection that was denied him. No wonder he had grown up full of hatred. No wonder that, when the opportunity had arisen to have Jones removed on Guy Fawkes' Night, he had wished that to happen in the cruellest way possible. Jones thought it likely that Burnett had first taken up the Jacobite cause not because of any deep-seated political or religious views, but because the Jacobites had offered him what he desperately sought: acceptance and recognition. Almost certainly Sarah Darr had manipulated him. When Burnett had finally unlocked his heart, he had given it to a woman more cold and calculating than himself.

Staggering to his feet again Jones looked around to see what had happened to the horses and was greatly relieved to see that both of them had not moved too far away, despite the noise of the fight. He moved slowly towards each of them in turn, making reassuring sounds until he could grasp their reins. He quickly secured both horses to the low-slung branch of a nearby tree. By now he was conscious that he had lost a lot of blood. The slight wound to his chest was only seeping a little, but his arm was still bleeding quite freely. He moved back to Burnett's corpse and, opening his coat, pulled out the man's shirt so he could rip off some material with which to temporarily bind his injury and so reduce the blood flow. Then he searched the dead man to see if he was carrying any papers on him. There was nothing. Jones moved over to Burnett's horse and opened the bag that was strapped behind the saddle. Within it was a letter and other documents. Suddenly he felt very light-headed and it dawned on him that, unless he received treatment for his wounds, he would never get the names of the traitors into the hands of the government. But where was he to go for such help?

16

THE COUNCIL MEETING

Three hours later Tom Jones was feeling far better because not only had his wounds been properly dressed but also he had been well fed by John Littleton, to whose house he had returned. The comb-maker had listened to his account of what had happened and been more than generous in tending to his needs. Jones now felt sufficiently recovered to examine the documents that he had won. They comprised a number of sheets on which were the signatures of those who supported the restoration of the House of Stuart. Trying not to overly damage its seal, Jones gently prised open the accompanying letter, which was addressed to Lord George Murray, the main commander of Bonnie Prince Charlie's army. Its contents revealed the peril in which the nation truly stood and, unsure what to do, Jones summoned Littleton and read him what it said:

My dear Lord George

I regret that as yet I do not stand by your side, but the time is not far removed when I will. I hope that you will take comfort from the accompanying list of names and signatures. Each person on it is now pledged to bring men and weapons in support of the prince. There are others who will also join. It has been a difficult task to win over people to support our side openly, not because they desire to keep the German usurper, but because they fear that this attempt to restore the true king will end like those before it in failure. Too many families have suffered for their past loyalty to enter into another venture without there being a strong indicator of likely success. All that is required is that your Highlanders should now continue to outmanoeuvre the government forces until they have crossed the

River Trent. To have reached so far without any assistance is the proof that the English Jacobites require to convince them to rise in force. Men will be stationed so that the news of the crossing can be quickly communicated to all. Within days the prince will find his army doubled or trebled. I am certain the City will fall without even a fight.

Please convey to his royal highness my deepest love and my undying loyalty,

Henry Hyde

'This is not good news,' said Littleton. 'Even though Lord Murray will now not receive this information, it is likely that the Highlanders will press on towards London. Why should they turn back when they have got so far? As soon as the army crosses the Trent the English traitors will then rally to their cause.'

'I agree. At all costs we must stop the Highlanders from moving south of Derby!'

'But that will require an army,' observed Littleton, in a voice that could not hide his despair.

'Not necessarily,' replied Jones. 'What if I take Burnett's place and take the message to Lord Murray that the English Jacobites have decided not to risk supporting the prince? Surely the impact would devastate their morale and there is just a chance that they might decide to go back to their homes.'

Doubt still flickered in Littleton's eyes. 'But will Lord Murray believe you?'

'He will if we rewrite this letter from Henry Hyde. It is not beyond the wit of man to forge a letter and reapply the seal so it does not look as if it has been tampered with. I did my utmost to cause minimum damage when opening it and I think I have the skills to undertake copying Hyde's handwriting.' He looked questioningly at the comb-maker. 'Have you the skills to mend and reapply the seal?'

Littleton cautiously nodded his assent. However, it was obvious that he remained unconvinced about the plan. He pursed his lips and then commented, 'Even if we do this, you are injured and Derby is still a considerable distance. Can you reach Lord Murray in the time required?'

'I have no choice but to try!' responded Jones, his eyes alight with determination. 'Tell me the best route that I may take because if I leave after we have forged the letter there will not be much daylight time left for the first stage of the journey. At best I will only be able to ride for maybe two hours.'

'You can try and get as far as Nuneaton. That would leave you with almost forty miles to cover to reach Derby by tomorrow evening. No easy task for a fit man and a fresh horse let alone someone who has lost as much blood as you riding a horse that has already covered so many miles.' Littleton paused and then said, 'Let me go in your stead.'

Jones was deeply moved by the man's offer, but he shook his head. 'No, it has to be me who pretends to be Burnett. If they question me, I know enough about him to answer appropriately. You would not.' He smiled grimly. 'However, while I go to Derby, you could ride to Warwick on Burnett's horse and hand the documents containing the traitors' names to the appropriate authorities. I suspect pressure can be brought to make some of these men reconsider their position – especially if the Highlanders cease their advance southwards.'

'That I will do,' replied Littleton, grasping Jones's hand.

Immediately the two men set about their purpose and within an hour they had completed the forgery. Jones then set off for Nuneaton, wishing the comb-maker all the best for his journey to Warwick. The terrain through which he passed was not too difficult for the injured man but the weather was appalling. Heavy icy rain that had threatened earlier in the day began to fall almost as soon as he set off. By the time that he reached Nuneaton he was soaked through and almost frozen with the cold. Fortunately the inn where he chose to stay had a roaring fire, good food, and a comfortable bed. Nevertheless, it took him all his determination to get up early the next morning in order to start riding as dawn was breaking. His whole body ached and the wound in his arm throbbed with pain.

For the first ten miles or so the weather stayed dry but then it began to rain, first intermittently and then incessantly. He did his best to pace his horse so only at intervals did they make good speed. Though he found this frustrating he knew he had no choice in the matter. He dared not risk his horse collapsing with exhaustion. Despite its remarkable stamina, the beast was clearly reaching the end of its capacity to sustain such relentless travelling. About three o'clock in the afternoon the rain ceased and the clouds began rolling back. This was fortunate because it meant that moonlight helped illuminate the final stages of his journey. It was entirely dark by the time that he reached the outskirts of Derby and saw the light of the newly set up Jacobite camp-fires.

Jones stopped when a sentry challenged him and, not without some difficulty after so many hours in the saddle, dismounted. He at once requested that he should be taken before Lord Murray. The Highlander did not seek to argue with him. Jones's haggard face and the bloody evidence that he was injured offered proof enough to him that this was a genuine messenger with an important communication. Instead he nodded to Jones and, pulling a canister out of a leather bag that was attached to his belt, offered him a drink. Jones willingly accepted and a welcome warmth spread from his throat and embraced his body.

As the sentry led Jones through the camp the stars in the ink-black sky shone down on a scene that could have been taken from Milton's description of the damned. The shadowy figures of exhausted men seemed to clutter the ground everywhere like drunken men after a night of carousing. As far as he could tell most wore a large and filthy plaid patterned with green and yellow and scarlet and blue. This hung over their shoulders and was fastened below the neck with either a small fork or knife. A belt gathered the material around their waists in such a way as to form a kind of petticoat that reached halfway down their thighs. Each man appeared armed with both a short dirk and a fiercesome basket-hilted and double-edged broadsword that was over a yard long. Many wore bonnets strangely adorned with a sprig of plant. Jones was later to learn that this marked to which clan they belonged and was seen as a charm against bad luck. What surprised him most was that many were without shoes or wore footwear that was next to nothing.

As he passed one of the camp-fires, he peered at those lying nearest and, through the flickering light of the flames, caught glimpses of their weary and grime-lined faces. Their obvious exhaustion bore witness to the weeks of marching, as did the state of their muddy clothes. Some slept with their swords in their hands as if ready at an instant to fight the foe that had as yet eluded them. Others looked almost child-like in their innocent slumbers, as if their mothers had tucked them to bed for the night. The few who were awake made no effort to speak to him lest they disturb their comrades. Occasionally a Highlander would stir and turn his body to seek greater comfort but for a place so packed with humanity it was eerily quiet. The only sounds he could hear was that of snoring and the gentle crackling sound made by the fires that kept the soldiers from freezing.

The man who escorted Jones led him to a man in his mid-forties who was attired in more civilized clothes. He wore trews of skin-tight tartan and over his shirt a tartan waistcoat and jacket. Over this was a plaid that fell from a silver brooch on the left shoulder. This marked him out as one of the chiefs. The two men exchanged a few words and the chief then told Jones that he should follow him. He took him to a house within which Lord Murray had taken lodgings and indicated that he should stay outside until he had spoken with the commander. A few minutes passed and then Jones was bidden to enter. He was taken into the drawing room where sat the commander who had secured the Jacobite victory at Prestonpans and so created the conditions necessary for the invasion of England.

Though still in the prime of his life, Murray looked older than his fifty or so years because of the dark circles under his eyes and his furrowed brow. The candlelight emphasized how much he had aged by picking out all the lines that had etched themselves into his features. In happier days he had been a man whose company men sought but the burden of the past months had made him increasingly morose. Jones thought that beneath his wig his face was somewhat too long and his mouth too broad for him ever to have been judged handsome, but there was still an indisputable air of authority about him and this was magnified by his military manner. His every gesture showed he was used to being in command.

'Welcome, young man,' he said in a voice that was deep and rich if heavy with a Scottish accent. 'I gather that you come from Henry Hyde.'

Jones bowed nervously, his body aching with tension and his heart pounding. 'Yes, my lord. I have a letter from him.'

'Good. I was expecting him to send me information.' Murray eyed Jones up and down with a precision that was unnerving. His eye took in the messenger's very pale and strained face, his bandaged arm and blood-marked clothes, and the many signs that he had travelled long and hard. 'But,' he added candidly, 'I had expected a fitter man to bring it.'

Jones dug his nails into his palms in an attempt to avoid showing that his hands were trembling. He knew this was not a man whom it would be easy to dupe. 'There were those who tried to prevent me, my lord. My path has not been an easy one.'

'That I can see. Give me what you have brought and then sit down before you fall down.'

For the first time Jones appreciated that beneath the military air was a kind and considerate man. He obeyed gladly because all the blood that he had lost was making him feel faint.

'What is your name?'

'John Burnett,' replied Tom, without a hint of hesitation in his voice.

Murray turned to the chief who had brought him. 'Get Mr Burnett something strong to drink and something hot to eat. He looks very much in need of it.' To Jones's consternation he then began examining the letter that he had been given in order to check that the seal was unbroken. Jones held his breath. Would he detect that it had been resealed? The general looked up, obviously unhappy. For a moment Jones feared he was lost. 'You should be more careful, Mr Burnett. I know that the conditions under which you have travelled have been atrocious but you have allowed this letter to get wet by not enclosing it within a protective cloth.'

'My apologies, my lord.'

Murray took out a knife and broke the seal. As he read the contents of the letter his face went white and the muscles at the side of his mouth twitched. He angrily turned to Jones. 'Do you know what this says?'

'Yes, my lord, and I wish at this moment that I was not an Englishman. Those who voiced their loyalty have turned coward. I know you have borne much to bring the prince this far south but the English Jacobites are refusing to take up arms because of the size of the three Hanoverian armies that have been gathered to destroy you.'

These words did nothing to dispel Murray's anger. 'Damn them all for the craven liars that they are! They promise their support and yet, despite all that we have achieved, they now turn their back on us! May they rot in hell!' The general crushed the offending letter in his hand. 'We will continue to march on London and, when we are victorious without them, I'll see they get what they deserve for such base deception!'

'There is a reason for their cowardice, my lord,' interrupted Jones, facing him squarely, 'though it is not one that would make me abandon my promised service to the true king.'

'And what is this reason?'

For a moment Jones found himself unable to answer. All now rested on whether he could make Lord Murray believe his cause was lost and the immensity of the moment rendered him speechless.

'I asked for the reason, sir, and I am not used to being kept waiting!'

'My apologies, sir,' replied Jones, finding his voice, 'but I dread having to give you the news that I bring. It is not just the scale of the forces gathered against us, it is where those armies are. As we speak, two of the government armies are almost upon you – not only that of Cumberland, whom you have so far avoided, but the much larger army from London. I believe Wade's army is also no longer at Newcastle but rapidly moving south. The intention is to surround and destroy you as soon as you cross the Trent. The English Jacobites know this and fear your cause is already lost. It was to prevent me telling you about the perilous nearness of the enemy forces that I was pursued by a government agent called Jones.' He paused for effect. 'Fortunately I was able to dispatch him, though not before I sustained the injuries that you can see.'

All the energy drained from Murray's countenance at this devastating information. When he spoke, it was with a voice that had temporarily lost its authority. 'There are times, sir, when ignorance is better than knowledge. Your news is the worst I have received since I first started serving the House of Stuart over thirty years ago. My father called me a fool for joining in the rebellions in 1715 and 1719 but I ignored him and paid the price for my loyalty through years of exile. I have again followed my conscience against the wishes of friends and family but, until your news, I had believed victory was this time within our grasp.' The pain in his eyes was clearly visible. 'You have robbed me of any chance of sleep this night, Mr Burnett, because now I must think what I should advise the prince to do. Do we march on to almost certain death in order to retain our reputation, or do we return to Scotland with our tail between our legs in the hope that we can live to fight another day?'

He turned to leave the room and then, remembering his manners, looked back at Jones. 'I have already given orders for you to be fed. Go and take proper refreshment and rest. I will need you beside me first thing tomorrow morning, whatever I decide.'

'Thank you, my lord. I am only sorry that I cannot be the bearer of better news.'

That night it was not only the general who did not sleep. Tom Jones slept but fitfully. He knew that he had sown the right seeds but whether they would bear the fruit he hoped was still uncertain. It was therefore with much anxiety that he accompanied a Highlander back to Lord Murray's quarters early on the morning of 5 December. As on the previous evening, he had to wait to be taken into the commander's presence. When he did enter the audience room the atmosphere was distinctly cold. Though desperate to know the outcome of his deception, he stood silently for what seemed an eternity, judging correctly that he should let Lord Murray speak first.

When the veteran soldier did speak it was in a voice that commanded his respect because it gave no hint of the internal agonies that Murray had suffered throughout the intervening hours since he had first met Jones. 'With deep regret I have decided that the news that you brought gives me no alternative but to argue for a rapid retreat. I therefore wish you to come with me to where His Royal Highness is lodged in Exeter House in Full Street. I need you because His Royal Highness does not understand military matters as I do. Make no mistake about it, Mr Burnett, it will not be easy to persuade him to agree.'

Trying not to show his jubilation, Jones said as calmly and firmly as he could, 'I will tell His Royal Highness, my lord, what I have told you, though it pains me to have to cause him such grief. I begin to wish now that I had not survived the attacks of our enemies. I would then not have to participate in such unhappy discussions.'

'Do not say that, Mr Burnett. Your information may have prevented our slaughter. Come, follow me.'

Jones did as he was bid and soon found himself approaching the building in which Bonnie Prince Charlie had slept the night. Just before they reached its main entrance the door opened and out came a number of military gentlemen and Highland chiefs. In their midst was a strikingly tall and handsome young man who bore himself with a natural grace. He wore no wig but permitted his hair to fall in long ringlets on his neck and this set off his oval face with its well-formed features. His light blue eyes flashed with good humour yet also conveyed a dignity that was attractively charismatic. Without anyone having to inform him Jones knew instinctively this was Bonnie Prince Charlie. Such an easy and graceful manner could only stem from someone born into the highest rank. Though his enemies denounced him as a pretender, this was indeed a prince in whom the blood of one of the most ancient of royal families flowed.

After a brief exchange of courtesies Lord Murray gave vent to his anxiety, his face tight with apprehension. 'Your Highness, I must ask that we review our situation in the light of information that I have received. It is now certain that the English Jacobites will not rally to our aid.'

The prince was obviously unimpressed. 'What do you mean, sir? They may not yet have chosen to join us, but I am confident that ultimately they will. We have gone too far with this enterprise to do anything but march on.'

'I have reliable information newly arrived that the forces of our enemies are already awaiting to destroy us as soon as we cross the Trent.'

'What does it matter how many armies block our path, when God is on our side?'

'We need more than God's blessing,' replied Lord Murray. 'We require men to face the armies gathered against us. Faith is not enough, sire. Where is the support with which we were supposed to be met? Where is the Earl of Barrymore, or the Duke of Beaufort? Where is Sir John Hynde Cotton, or Sir Watkins Williams Wynn? None has come to our side. You have sent messages to them and no reply has come back. We have been marching southwards since we left Edinburgh on 30 October and scarce a man has joined us. I received a letter last night from Henry Hyde that informs me none ever will.'

'Then curse Hyde for his cowardice!' snapped back the prince. 'I am no ordinary man who will turn from his duty simply because there are weaker men around me. Why should I fear the forces of the German who has usurped what rightfully belongs to my father? Is it not obvious that God is on our side? Look at the progress we have made. We cannot turn back – that would be to ruin our cause. All we need is one victory here in England like that of Prestonpans and I am sure that the people will come flocking to our side. And if we remain true, God will grant us that victory.'

'With respect, Your Highness, right does not in itself determine who wins. Military strength and firm discipline and experienced leadership matter more. And we lack all three! A victory is the very thing we cannot now deliver. Our men are tired in body and, what is worse, tired in heart. Why else did I ensure at Macclesfield that we avoided battle with the forces of Cumberland when our scouts brought news that our enemy was at Lichfield?'

'And maybe that was a mistake. If our own men are beginning to lose confidence, it is because they need another victory to raise their spirits. Victories cannot be won if we are forever avoiding the enemy.'

Murray replied with the patience of a man addressing a wilful child. 'We avoid the enemy because he greatly outnumbers us. I am not prepared to lead my men into a situation in which they will be massacred.'

'If we retreat, their morale will collapse and then where will we be?' countered the prince.

'I know that it is difficult to maintain morale while retreating, sire. For that reason we will not tell the men immediately. They do not know this country or understand maps. We can pretend that we are still going to London until the time comes when we can afford to tell them the truth because we are nearer home and can make a rapid final push, even if they are then dispirited.'

'Dispirited! They will be furious with rage at having been so betrayed and deceived! I know my Highlanders would rather die in battle than live in ignominious shame. In the time we have been here in Derby I have heard them sharpening their dirks and swords. They may be very tired, but I have no doubt that their hearts still yearn for glory not humiliation. Why should they not remain confident of victory? We may not, as yet, have acquired English military support, but has not almost every town received us with the ringing of bells and with celebratory bonfires to mark the public rejoicing at my presence?'

'Bells and bonfires do not win battles. I am sorry, Your Highness, but I must request that we hold a council meeting. We have scarce two thousand men who are truly fit to face a proper army. The rest may have courage but they lack skill and training. It is not sufficient to rely on their bravery.'

'Their lack of military training did not prevent them winning at Prestonpans.'

'On that occasion the enemy underestimated us and therefore made fatal mistakes. Cumberland and Wade are men of far greater skill and they have better disciplined troops under their command. They will not make foolish errors.'

Although still unconvinced the prince sensed that he would have to bow to Lord Murray's wish for a military council. 'Very well, Lord George, we will hold a council but I am sure the others will agree with me on the matter, whatever your reservations. Make no mistake about it, any retreat will be judged by our enemies to amount to an acceptance of defeat.'

'If that is the council's judgement, then I will abide by it, sire,' responded the commander, delighted to have won the case for a meeting. He knew that his best chance of success lay in a public debate. Left to private discussion, too many of the other leaders would permit their love of the prince to sway their better judgement.

Within an hour the dark, handsome ancient oak wainscotting of the first-floor drawing room could scarcely be seen for the crush of people gathered there. Jones stood behind Lord Murray, who had demanded he attend. It was the prince who opened the proceedings and he left no one in any doubt about his wishes. 'My friends, I am grateful for the loyalty that you have shown and now that loyalty faces its toughest test. The day has come when we should decide to begin our final march on London.'

Before anyone could agree Lord Murray voiced his opposition. 'My lord, as you know, I do not think that it is prudent to march further. The French have provided no troops and there has been no English rising in our favour. Only a tiny handful of Englishmen have joined us. I know there are many in this land who would prefer the House of Stuart to the House of Hanover but they recall what happened in the North of England thirty years ago when those loyal to your father were either butchered or ruthlessly punished by loss of land. Before raising a sword they are waiting to see the outcome of a battle between us and King George's troops. Yet the truth is that we cannot face the Hanoverian forces without their aid.'

He beckoned to Jones to come forward and then waved the forged letter that had so deceived him before their eyes. 'Here is the letter that this brave man brought last night. It comes from Henry Hyde and so its contents can be trusted. It says that the English loyal to the House of Stuart have regretfully decided not to join us because they have seen the strength of the forces that are gathering against us. It says that Wade has an army of ten thousand and the Duke of Cumberland one of eight thousand, whilst a third army has been raised in London using regiments that have been brought across from Holland.' Murray paused and then, turning to Jones, he said, 'Tell them, Mr Burnett, what you told me last night.'

The eyes of all looked at the frail and battered figure that stood before them as Jones repeated the lies with which he had deceived Murray.

'Each day advances the power of our enemy!' resumed the general. 'We must return to Scotland and resume the invasion only when we have French support. The odds against us are too high.'

'I agree. A march on London at this juncture would simply mean walking into certain defeat against such large enemy forces,' said a distinguished looking man, whom Jones later discovered was Lord Elco. 'Do you not agree, Lord Ogilvy?'

'Aye, I do. Even if, against all the odds, we won the battle against one army, we would be seriously weakened and unable to face a second, let alone a third. Not a man here would ever see Scotland again! I only supported our march on London because I thought the English Jacobites would flock to the prince's standard. Instead this man brings evidence of the reverse. Any idea of crossing the Trent is now sheer madness.'

These first two responses opened the floodgates. A storm of protest at marching further south poured forth. Only when the clamour had begun to die down did Murray resume, saying in his ponderous but powerful manner, 'No man wishes more than I for the restoration of the true king and no man dares do more than I, but I have no doubt that marching to London will shatter all prospects of success. We are hopelessly outnumbered. Even if by our sheer determination and courage, we defeated one army, we would not have the men left to face the other two. I am confident that we can withdraw to Carlisle without loss and, once there, we will be able to hear whether the French are going to send us an army. If anyone has better advice, please provide it.'

Only one man spoke out – Jones later heard this was Lord Perth. He argued in favour of moving off towards Wales in the hope of raising support there. This argument understandably won no support. It was the prince who once again took the floor. Fuming with anger, his voice resounded across the chamber as he launched into an attack on the cowardice of his followers. 'Had I listened to the pessimistic voice of others, I would never have gone to Scotland,' he roared. 'I would never have raised my standard in Glenfinnan nor fought my enemies at Prestonpans. There were many who said to march on Edinburgh was foolishness yet, when I did, the city welcomed me with open arms. Why should I listen now? After Edinburgh was ours I wanted us to immediately march on London but you demanded I wait. And what has been the outcome? You merely gave our enemies time to raise the armies that you now fear! How dare any of you gainsay my judgement on the matter. Do you believe for one instant that my loyal Highlanders will share your opinion? Have I not daily walked with them all the way here and am I now to turn their sacrifice to naught? If necessary I will stand alone against the Duke of Cumberland and with my own sword settle this war once and for all!'

For the first time Jones knew why the prince had been so successful. Here indeed was a man worth following! Had he been a Jacobite, he knew that he would have followed him to London whatever anyone else advised. However, the prince's words had no impact on Murray. He replied coolly, 'You know I am no courtier who flatters and fawns and for that reason Your Highness may judge me too blunt and overbearing, but may I remind you that I alone have the military experience to judge these matters. London is not Edinburgh and if, having heard my judgment, the majority declare in favour of return, then you will have to accept their decision.'

'Then their decision must be taken only after they have had time to reflect on what I have said,' responded the prince. 'I dismiss this council. Let it reassemble this evening.' It was a trump card that only he could play and he stalked out before anyone could protest.

One by one the others present left till only Murray and Jones remained. Murray was clearly agitated. 'The prince hopes to divide and rule. He will spend this afternoon looking for support for his wish to continue marching on London. Mr Burnett, you must accompany me and help me convince the chiefs that we have no option but to retreat.' Jones once again did as he was bid, praying that Murray would win the day despite the prince's charismatic leadership.

After an afternoon of intensive discussion the council gathered again. Once more Murray urged a retreat, but the Duke of Perth, who had been won over by the prince's arguments, openly disagreed. He argued instead for an immediate attack on whatever English army was nearest, saying that a Jacobite victory would cause the other two armies to melt away. The prince agreed with the duke's assessment of the situation and added that, far from making their position safer, retreat would risk complete destruction for them all. The government forces would relentlessly pursue and harry them. Jones looked around the room. It seemed to him that the supporters of Lord Murray's position were beginning to waver. Was all his work going to be undone by the sheer bravado of the prince?

It was at this critical juncture news was brought that fresh information had arrived and into the room came John Littleton. As he swept past Jones he gave him the slightest of winks. He bowed low before the assembled gathering.

'Who are you, sir?' demanded Bonnie Prince Charlie.

'My name is Dudley Bradstreet, Your Highness, and I fear that I bring very bad news. The enemy army that was raised in London has advanced more quickly than we thought possible. It is already poised to await your attempt to cross the Trent. It numbers some nine thousand men and our spies report that it is under the command of either Lieutenant General Hawley or Lieutenant General Ligonier. By tomorrow it will be joined by the forces of Cumberland, bringing the total number of the enemy facing you to at least seventeen thousand.'

The news acted like a shockwave throughout the assembled men. Murray spoke first. 'Gentlemen, we now know we have no choice. We cannot pick off one of the enemy's armies in the hope of deterring the other two. That moment is lost. Against odds of over four to one, we must retreat!' A swell of assent filled the room. A voice was even heard to say, 'We have given the prince so much rope that he now threatens to hang us all by his wishes.' In vain Bonnie Prince Charlie made one last plea, shouting out, 'Gentlemen, you ruin, abandon and betray me if you do not march on.' One by one the majority of those present expressed their support for Lord Murray's solution.

While this was happening, Littleton moved over to stand by Jones. At an opportune moment he whispered, 'I thought your story might need some corroboration and so decided to follow you. Do not worry, my wife has taken the documents to Warwick and she knows to whom they should be delivered.'

'But how did you persuade them that you were a genuine messenger?'

Littleton smiled and opened the palm of his hand. In it was a fleur-de-lis button. 'I found this at the bottom of the bag that contained the documents. 'I've no idea why Burnett was carrying it but the French symbol was all I needed to carry me through the lines of the Highlanders and bring me to one of their chieftains.'

Prince Charles accepted his defeat with as much dignity as he could muster while remaining defiant. 'I accept your decision and I will do what you want, but I think you have forced me into making a ruinous step,' he announced. 'Rather than go back I would wish to be twenty feet underground. We are only a few days' march from London. What do I offer my followers now? Ignominious retreat! I, who have always been the optimist, am now thrust into the deepest pessimism. I fear my brave Highlanders will pay the price of your cowardice! We have frightened the German usurper and he and his ministers will wreak a terrible vengeance on all of Scotland.' He paused as emotion overwhelmed him and then concluded in a voice that echoed around the room. 'Gentlemen, this is the last council I will ever hold and, in future, I will hold no obligation to any man except my father. You are dismissed.'

The prince's sombre words shook many present. One of the few who had supported him urged him to ignore the meeting's decision. 'My lord, I suggest you walk out of this room and set off for London on your own. Whatever Lord Murray says, the clan leaders will not desert you and, if they see you determined to proceed, they will follow.' An Irishman called O'Sullivan supported this. 'It is not too late, sire. What men may say when together can be changed when they are presented with the case individually. Have each leader speak to you alone and I believe each will reverse his decision. It was a mistake to ever let Lord

Murray speak to them all. I for one will draw my sword and die for you rather than run away.'

The prince took no comfort from their words. 'No, I have given my acceptance of the council's decision and I will not go back on it. We will retreat. But mark me, though I willingly walked with my Highlanders every step of the way here, I will not walk back with them. Let Lord Murray maintain morale now. I will ride separately to show I am not party to this unbearable betrayal.' He looked at O'Sullivan and there was immense sadness in his eyes. 'We who were seen as invincible will now show to the world our vulnerability and there is not a member of the council who will not live to regret this day.'

Jones was deeply moved. 'I must hope that I have done the right thing,' he said to himself, 'because truly this man deserved to be a King.'

AFTERWORD

Their goal achieved, Tom Jones and John Littleton returned to their respective homes, but neither sought any reward for their actions. Both men had been too deeply moved by the courage of Bonnie Prince Charlie to seek any profit from their part in his destruction. Their use of pseudonyms meant that it was easy for their role in what had happened to be hidden. Littleton was content to resume his work in Kenilworth and his family continued to run the comb-making business there for over a century. Tom Jones returned to Bath and, once he had recovered from his injuries, he married Sophia Westbrook to the great rejoicing of Lady Overbury and Squire Woodforde. Even Mr Westbrook took pleasure in his daughter's marriage and in the grandchildren that soon resulted from it.

Henry Fielding hated hiding the fact that he was Jones's father and therefore decided to immortalize the name of the son he loved by making him the hero of his next novel. *Tom Jones* was published in 1749 to great acclaim. It did not betray the true secret behind Jones's birth. Nor did it contain anything about Lady Overbury, or Sarah Darr and the murders in Queen Square, or all that followed from those tragic events. Fielding did not wish to jeopardize anyone's safety. He knew there were still Jacobites around who would have taken revenge for what had happened. Those who did feature in his invented tale had their names changed. Thus Sophia Westbrook became Sophia Western and Squire Woodforde became Squire Allworthy, whilst Burnett was transformed into a character called Blifal.

There was no happy ending for the Highlanders. The prince was right. The decision to retreat proved a disaster. It ended in the bloody and ruthless slaughter of his army on the field of Culloden on 16 April 1746. Such were the atrocities committed during and after the battle that the Hanoverian Duke of Cumberland earned himself the title of 'Butcher'. Following this the order went out that the Scottish glens should also pay for their treason. Homes were burnt and lands confiscated, men were shot or hanged, women were raped, and thousands of cattle were driven south so that many more would starve. For five months the prince hid in the Highlands, protected by the loyalty of the people who still loved him. Though he eventually escaped to the Continent, he never recovered from what had happened and became an alcoholic. He died in 1788 leaving behind him no heir. Lord Murray also escaped but the prince always refused to see him, blaming him for the decision that had cost him the throne and so many their lives.